"十三五"国家重点出版规划项目

杜甫诗歌英译
Fu Tu's Poems in Chinese and English
With Annotations

赵彦春 译·注
Translated and Annotated by Yanchun Chao

上海大学出版社
·上海·

图书在版编目(CIP)数据

杜甫诗歌英译/赵彦春译、注.—上海:上海大学出版社,2020.11(2021.3重印)
ISBN 978-7-5671-4065-3

Ⅰ.①杜… Ⅱ.①赵… Ⅲ.①杜诗-诗集-英文 Ⅳ.①I222.742

中国版本图书馆 CIP 数据核字(2020)第 227819 号

策　划　许家骏
责任编辑　王悦生
助理编辑　陆仕超
封面设计　王兆琪
技术编辑　金　鑫　钱宇坤

杜甫诗歌英译

赵彦春　译·注

上海大学出版社出版发行
(上海市上大路 99 号　邮政编码 200444)
(http://www.shupress.cn　发行热线 021-66135112)
出版人　戴骏豪

＊

南京展望文化发展有限公司排版
江苏凤凰数码印务有限公司印刷　各地新华书店经销
开本 710mm×1000mm　1/16　印张 21.25　字数 348 千字
2020 年 12 月第 1 版　2021 年 3 月第 2 次印刷
ISBN 978-7-5671-4065-3/I·609　定价　280.00 元

版权所有　侵权必究
如发现本书有印装质量问题请与印刷厂质量科联系
联系电话:025-57718474

序　言

赵教授早已是著作等身的大学者、大翻译家。我作为小学弟，受邀为其新译作序，惶恐可想而知。我想起《艾子杂说》里的一则寓言，猎人把鸭子当鹰使，令其抓兔，鸭子笨手笨脚，结果不言而喻。我跟赵教授婉述此意，赵教授说："劲翮利爪，正堪搏击！"受此鼓励，我仿佛鸭脚上长出了利爪，竟有了"搏击"的冲动。

一

赵译杜甫全集完成后将是世界上第二个杜甫诗歌全集英译本。第一个全集英译本是 2008—2009 年美国 Create Space 公司出版的四卷本《墨菲的杜甫》(murphy's du fu)。也许是为了显得与众不同，《墨菲的杜甫》全书使用小写字母，包括人名、地名。译者墨菲（James R. Murphy）曾是纽约的一位中学老师，平时喜欢诗歌，出过个人诗集；退休后翻译并自助出版了《墨菲的杜甫》。据学者李特夫研究，《墨菲的杜甫》很可能译自德文版杜甫全集 Tu Fu's Gedichte(1952)，其英译的准确性不算高，诗美效果也不算很好。我搜寻相关材料，发现墨菲自己也承认："书中诗歌不是真正的杜甫诗歌英译，而是我对杜诗的反应。英语世界尚无杜诗全集，本人所为，权当抛砖引玉。"（what follows are not true translations, more they are reactions in kind. but as i said there is no individual english voice for the complete du fu and these murphy versions of poems are a paltry beginning to such an enormous task.)《墨菲的杜甫》封底）因此，在很大程度上，赵译杜甫全集可被视为世界上第一个杜甫全集英译本。

赵教授英译过很多古典诗词，如《诗经》、《三字经》、《曹操诗全集》、《英韵宋词百首》、《英韵唐诗百首》、《李白诗歌全集英译》等，其中后两本，我非常认真地拜读过。我熟悉赵译的风格，深感赵教授注重诗的形式，讲究音韵和谐，用心意象传递，强调文化传播。这次，拜读了赵译《杜甫诗歌英译》之后，感觉他保持了这些翻译特点，而且在锤词炼句方面更为用心。如果结合杜甫其人其诗的特点，就可感受赵译的用心所在。

二

杜甫在世时名气不大。其诗名远在李白、王维之下，甚至还不如岑参、储光羲。杜甫一生基本上与盛唐相始终，可盛唐时的一些重要唐诗选本，如殷璠的《河岳英灵集》、高仲武的《中兴间气集》、芮挺章的《国秀集》，均没选杜诗。杜甫生前的暗淡可见一斑。

到了中唐，情况大变。元稹、白居易、韩愈等，尽管诗风各异，却一致推崇杜甫。元稹说杜甫"凡所歌行，率皆即事名篇"(元稹《乐府古题序》)；白居易赞杜甫"诗之豪者，世称李杜"(白居易《与元九书》)；韩愈也说"勃兴得李杜"(韩愈《荐士》)。中唐以后，李杜并称，成为常规。杜甫大概没有想到，他死后会声名鹊起，与李白一起成为耀眼的双子星，并辉映千秋。

更有甚者，有些人认为杜甫应该在李白之上。白居易说，杜诗"尽工尽善，又过于李"(白居易《与元九书》)；元稹认为，杜诗"铺陈终始，排比声韵，大或千言，次犹数百，词气豪迈而风调清深，属对律切而脱弃凡近，则李(白)尚不能历其藩翰"(元稹《唐检校工部员外郎杜君墓系铭并序》)。顾陶在其《唐诗类选》序中不称"李杜"，而改称"杜李"；韦庄在其《又玄集》中也认为，杜第一，李第二。

杜甫终于被供上了神坛，被人恭敬地尊为"诗圣"、"集大成者"。他的诗成了"诗史"。闻一多说他是"四千年文化中最庄严、最瑰丽、最永久的一道光彩"(莫砺锋《杜甫评传》页419)。

确实，杜甫不是凡人。首先，他是神童，"七岁思即壮，开口咏凤凰。……九龄书大字，有作成一囊"(杜甫《壮游》)。其次，他是"学霸"，"读书破万卷，下笔如有神"(杜甫《奉赠韦左丞丈》)。而且，他小小年纪，就已出道，"往昔十四五，出游翰墨场。斯文崔魏徒，以我似班扬"(杜甫《壮游》)。他一生诗风多变，沉郁、豪放、清丽、雅致、俗野，样样齐备，样样出色。另外，他还是骑马高手(吴庚舜等《杜甫诗选》前言)、行万里路的旅行家(杜甫《壮游》)、对舞、画、歌、音乐有独特体悟的艺术天才(杜甫《剑器行》、《丹青引》、《听杨氏歌》)。他甚至有志出海远航，东游扶桑(杜甫《壮游》)。

杜甫不仅很"神",而且还非常刻苦,是著名的苦吟诗人。他的"为人性僻耽佳句,语不惊人死不休",第一次将锤词炼句与人的本性和为人联系起来。可以说,他是唐代诗人中对语言的现象和本质理解最为深刻的诗人。杜甫诗歌语言的特点很多,主要有:擅做诗眼(如"好雨知时节"),注重色彩(如"碧知湖外草,红见海东云"),活用虚词(如"且尽芳樽恋物华"),灵用叠字(如"穿花蛱蝶深深见,点水蜻蜓款款飞"),雅用俗词(如"韦曲花无赖,家家恼杀人"),句式超常(如"香稻啄馀鹦鹉粒,碧梧栖老凤凰枝"),等。窃以为,最值得一说的,是他用心锤炼的"诗眼"和雅用的"俗词"。

三

先说诗眼。元代杨载说:"诗要炼字,字者眼也。如老杜诗:'飞星过水白,落月动檐虚',炼中间一字。'地坼江帆隐,天清木叶闻',炼最后一字。'红入桃花嫩,青归柳叶新',炼第二字。非炼'入''归'字,则是儿童诗。又曰'暝色赴春愁',又曰'无因觉往来'。非炼'赴''觉'字,便是俗诗"(杨载《诗法家数》页737)。诗眼多为动词。杜诗中让人过目难忘的诗眼非常多,如,"青云羞叶密,白雪避花繁"(杜甫《甘园》);"落日邀双鸟,晴天卷片云"(杜甫《秦州杂诗二十首》之十六);"感时花溅泪,恨别鸟惊心"(杜甫《春望》)等等。仔细品读赵译,我们发现赵教授对诗眼的处理非常用心。试以上面提到的名句为例:

原　文：**感时花溅泪,恨别鸟惊心。(杜甫《春望》)**
译文一：Touched by hard times, flowers shed tears;
　　　　Dispersed by war, birds cringe in fears. (Tr. Yanchun Chao)

译文二：Seeing flowers come, a flood
　　　　Of sadness overwhelms me; cut off
　　　　As I am, songs of birds stir
　　　　My heart; ... (Tr. Rewi Alley)

诗眼是"溅"和"惊"。我们知道,花不会"溅泪",鸟也不会因诗人与家人长期分离而"惊心"。杜甫此诗写于"国破山河在"的安史之乱。诗人痛感烽火连天,亲人分离,音讯全无,他的心在流泪(眼可能也在流泪),每时每刻都心惊肉跳,因而他见到的花和鸟好像跟他有同样的感受,也在"溅泪"和"惊心"。这就是中国诗学中的抒情共振原理:诗人情感起伏,景物随心有情,二者相互交融,不分你我。杜诗《登楼》中的"花伤客心"(见"花近高楼伤客心,万方多难此登临")也同此理。

既然诗眼"溅"和"惊"触发了抒情共振,那么,译文应该尽量传达这种共振。赵译很好地做到了这一点:Touched by hard times, flowers shed tears 跟原文丝丝相扣,珠联璧合,共振明显;Dispersed by war, birds cringe in fears(英文回译中文:被战争驱散的鸟,惊恐地畏缩着),主语是"鸟",同时暗指"我";这里,"鸟"、"人"不分你我,相互交融,形成共振。对比之下,艾黎(Rewi Alley)显然没注意到诗眼的作用,他的 Seeing flowers come, a flood/Of sadness overwhelms me; cut off/As I am, songs of birds stir/My heart(英文回译中文:看见迎面而来的花朵,汹涌的悲伤淹没了我。因为我与家人长期分离,鸟的叫声触动了我的心),"花溅泪"不见了,诗眼丢了;"鸟惊心(鸟自己惊心,不是鸟惊我心)"成了"鸟的叫声触动了我的心":"鸟"、"人"有互动,但没有彼此不分。因此,艾译只有诗人的情感"振动",没有花、鸟的情感"振动"。原文的抒情共振丢失,诗味折损大半。另外,上面提到的其他名句的诗眼,篇幅关系,此不详述。请读者自己品读对应的赵译,相信诸君一定能体会到赵教授的天纵才情和精心锤炼。

四

再说"俗词雅用"。元稹说,他喜欢杜甫直接将俗词俗语入诗,不让自己的思考局限在古人的词句中("怜渠直道当时语,不著心源傍古人")。宋人黄彻对杜甫擅用俗词观察更仔细,他在《碧溪诗话》中说:"数物以'个',谓食为'吃',甚近鄙俗,独杜屡用:'峡口惊猿闻一个'、'两个黄鹂鸣翠柳'、'却绕井栏添个个'。……'对酒不能吃'、'楼头吃酒楼下卧'、'但使残年饱吃饭'、'梅熟许同朱老吃'。盖篇中大概奇特,可以映带者也。"我们认为,黄彻的最后两句点评很有道理:杜诗在上下文"奇特"的情况下,将入诗的俗词"映带"得雅了;我们还认为,俗的字面与雅的含义之间的语言张力,反过来给诗带来了"奇特"之感。我们试以杜诗中的俗词"无赖"为例,观察赵教授的英译:

原文一：剑南春色还<u>无赖</u>，触忤愁人到酒边。（杜甫《送路六侍御入朝》）
译文：The spring wind in Sword South is such <u>a knave</u>,
　　　Who stirs my rue, and shakes my wine so rough.

原文二：老罢休无赖，归来省醉眼。（杜甫《闻斛斯六官未归》）
译文：Old and retired, <u>a knave</u> you are!
　　　When back at home, you sleep, a sot.

在这两例中，赵教授以俗译俗，用 a knave 译"无赖"，在很大程度上保持了原文俗与雅之间的语言张力。特别是例一，原诗将"春色"比作"无赖"，确实"奇特"，但仔细品味，我们发现这是诗人的匠心所在：当时杜甫与旧时好友马上就要分别，愁绪萦怀，再加上安史之乱的余波带给他的忧愁，他愁心满满，眼前美好的春色反倒让他觉得"触忤"，这其实符合人之常情。以乐景写愁心，正是诗人的高明之处；"无赖"是乐与愁之间的连接点。赵译基本上保留了原来"春色还无赖"的隐喻：The spring wind is a knave，进而，这个"无赖"stirs my rue, and shakes my wine，生动形象，一气呵成，很有原文的意趣。

原文三：眼见客愁愁不醒，<u>无赖</u>春色到江亭。（杜甫《绝句漫兴九首（其一）》）
译文：I find myself sad and in sadness drowned;
　　　Spring, <u>uncalled for</u>, comes to the pavilion.

原文四：韦曲花<u>无赖</u>，家家恼杀人。（杜甫《奉陪郑驸马韦曲二首》之一）
译文：In Weich'u are <u>heartless</u> flirting flowers,
　　　which at each home drive people mad.

原文五：牧竖樵童亦<u>无赖</u>，莫令斩断青云梯。（杜甫《寄从孙崇简》）
译文：E'en herdboys, wood-gatherers <u>are not true</u>;
　　　Don't let them pave a path into clouds blue.

原文六：羯胡事主终<u>无赖</u>，词客哀时且未还。（杜甫《咏怀古迹五首（其一）》）
译文：The crafty Rams and Huns <u>one can ne'er trust</u>;
　　　The poet has not come back for the times' sake.

在此四例中，赵教授根据上下文的需要，以雅译俗，"无赖"的译文各不相同，但都与上下文非常契合，整句读起来流畅、自然。译文在整体上保持了原文的诗意。

五

从1741年杜甫的一首《少年行（一）》被译成英语算起，杜诗英译已有近280年的历史。杜诗格律严谨，有很强的音乐美感。因此，杜诗格律的英译问题很值得一说。19世纪中期以前，只有几首杜诗被译成英语，就笔者所见，都是释意性翻译。杜诗的格律，译者似乎不太在意；或者，也许是汉语水平有限，他们对杜诗的音乐感没什么认识。鸦片战争后，英国人对中国文化的认识大幅提升。19世纪末至20世纪初，以英国传教士和外交官为主体的汉学家们非常重视杜诗的格律，他们基本上都采用英诗格律体翻译杜诗。著名的译者有翟理斯（Herbert A. Giles）、弗莱彻（W. J. B Fletcher）、德庇时（John Francis Davis）、庄延龄（E. H. Parker）、巴德（Charles Budd）等。我们知道，19世纪—20世纪初，古典主义诗学在英美占主导地位，维多利亚时期的文风盛行。讲究节奏音韵是英诗传统的艺术规范，也是当时英语读者喜闻乐见的诗律形式。这些汉学家的杜诗英译形式符合那个时代的审美需要。20世纪初，英美诗歌形式开始由传统向现代转型，讲究节奏和音韵被视为诗意畅快表达的束缚。后随着英美新诗运动特别是意象派的兴起，自由体成为英语诗歌的主体。这深深影响了古汉诗英译，包括杜诗英译。从20世纪30年代开始，用格律体英译杜诗日渐式微，自由体成为主流。著名的自由体杜诗英译本有（按时间顺序）：洪业（William Hung）的 *Tu Fu: China's Greatest Poet*（1952）、汉米尔（Sam Hamill）的 *Facing the Snow: Visions of Tu Fu*（1988）、欣顿（David Hinton）的 *The Selected Poems of Tu Fu*（1989）、艾黎（Rewi Alley）的 *Du Fu Selected Poems*（2001）、华兹生（Burton Watson）的 *The Selected Poems of Du Fu*（2002）、大卫·扬（David Young）的 *Du Fu: A Life in Poetry*（2008）等；英译杜诗不多，但很有名的译者有白之（Cyril Birch）、王红公（Kenneth Rexroth）等。特别值得一提的是，大名鼎鼎的David Hawkes 的 *A Little Primer of Tu Fu*（1967）是散文体。

格律体译诗虽不再是主流，但问题还有另一面。据笔者通过在澳门理工学院做过英语助教、现已返回的4位美国富布莱特青年学子在波士顿大学、纽约大学、宾夕法尼亚大学、加州大学的问卷调查，懂点汉语或修读过英语诗歌课程的大学生,更多倾向于英语格律体的杜诗英译。他(她)们认为,格律体是雅体,是比自由体更高级的文体。事实上,英语格律体的汉诗英译在英语世界依然有市场,一直坚持用格律体译古汉诗的翻译家威尔斯(Henry W. Wells)、克拉克(Robert Wood Clack)、唐安石(John A. Turner)及其各自译本依然有名,便是明证。唐安石在其 A Golden Treasury of Chinese Poetry(1976)的前言中说:"我认为,把汉语古诗译成'自由诗',对中国诗人不公平,因为汉语古诗的韵律和节奏比其他语言的诗歌更精细、更优美"(Turner, 1976: 11-12)。克拉克在其 Millenniums of Moonbeams: An Historical Anthology of Chinese Classical Poetry(1977)一书中更肯定说,"古汉诗有严格的节奏和非常严谨的韵律系统,自由体译诗完全背离了古汉诗的气韵(spirit)"(Clack, 1977: 1314)。

赵译杜诗的文体与威尔斯、克拉克、唐安石基本一致,是比自由体更高级的雅体。我们认为,这对保持中国古诗的特色和传播中国文化大有裨益。

六

"李杜文章在,光焰万丈长"。不朽的杜甫,藉赵教授的译笔,又一次优雅地走出国门。我们相信,诗圣的这次出游,一定给围观者带来久违的惊喜。

赵教授说,他译杜甫总体比较顺利。我想,这是他天生才情加上他长期磨砺而成的非凡功力所致。"看似寻常最奇崛,成如容易却艰辛"。他译笔诗情飞扬,常给人"神明偶遇"之感。在我心目中,赵也不是凡人。特按"词林正韵"填赞词一首,表达我由衷地钦佩:

鹧 鸪 天

新社桃红起意扬,灵犀通杜译高唐。
诗心三叠云天阔,独秀一枝象寄郎。
情切切,气昂昂。乾坤在臆问斜阳。
从来高士千秋业,功在东西流水长。

蒋骁华
2020年8月1日
于澳门理工学院致远楼

Introduction

Professor Chao is a very famous translator and scholar in China. As a colleague of younger age and less academic achievements, I didn't have much confidence to write a preface-like "introduction" to his *Fu Tu's Poems in Chinese and English With Annotations* (《杜甫诗歌英译》) when he sent me the invitation. My lack of confidence reminded me of a Chinese fable, in which a hunter wanted a duck to hunt as an eagle; he tried to make it catch a rabbit. The duck was clumsy, and the result was self-evident. I euphemistically explained the meaning to Professor Chao, who replied, "you have strong wings and sharp claws to catch the rabbit!" His encouragement and trust brought me back to confidence.

1. Chao's translation can be regarded as the first English version of complete Fu Tu's poems in the world.

Chao's translation *A Complete Edition of Fu Tu's Poems* will be the second English version of Fu Tu's complete poems in the world. The first complete English version is *murphy's du fu*, which was published in four volumes by Create Space Company in New York from 2008 to 2009. Lowercase letters are adopted in the books, including names of people and places. The translator James R. Murphy was a high school teacher in New York City. He liked poetry and published a collection of his own poems. After retirement, he translated and published *murphy's du fu*. According to the study of professor T'efu Li, *murphy's du fu* was probably translated from *Tu Fu's Gedichte* (1952), the German version of Fu Tu's complete poems. The accuracy of Murphy's translation is not high, and the effect of poetic beauty is not very good. I searched for relevant materials and found that Murphy himself admitted on the back cover of *murphy's du fu*: "what follows are not true translations, more they are reactions in kind. but as i said there is no individual english voice for the complete du fu and these murphy versions of poems are a paltry beginning to such an enormous task." Therefore, to a great extent, Chao's translation can be regarded as the first complete English version of Fu Tu's poems in the world.

Professor Chao has translated many classical Chinese poems into English, such as *Book of Songs in English Rhyme*, *Three-word Primer in English Rhyme*, *One Thousand Words in English Rhyme*, *Tang Poems in English Rhyme*, *Song Lyrics in English Rhyme*, *Canons for Disciples in English Rhyme*, *Cao Cao's Poems*, *Cao Zhi's Poems*, *Cao Pi's Poems*, and so on. I am familiar with the style of Chao's translation, where Chao pays much attention to the forms of poems, highlighting the harmony of meters and rhymes, and emphasizing image conveyances and cultural transmissions. This time, in his *Fu Tu's Poems in Chinese and English*, he has successfully maintained these translation characteristics and has paid more attention to weighing his words and refining his lines. Now, let's have a close look at the poet, his poems and Chao's translation.

2. Fu Tu and his poems

Fu Tu was not very famous in his life. At that time, his reputation was a far cry from Pai Li(李白) and Wei Wang(王维), furthermore, he was less well-known than Shen Ts'en(岑参) and Kuanghsi Ch'u(储光羲). Fu Tu basically lived during *shengtang* (the prime of the T'ang dynasty). However, none of his poems was selected into important poetry anthologies of that time, such as *The Collection of Mountain and River Souls*(《河岳英灵集》), *The Collection of Best Poems of the Country*(《国秀集》), which, to a great extent, demonstrates his obscurity in his life.

After his death, the situation changed greatly. Very famous poets like

Chen Yüan(元稹), Chü-e Pai(白居易) and Yü Han(韩愈) *etc*., in spite of their different poetic styles, thought highly of Fu Tu, and extolled him as an outstanding poet. Yüan says that many of Tu's poems are beau ideals; Pai praises Tu as a master of poetry; Han thinks that Pai Li and Fu Tu are China's Muses. Since then, Li and Tu have been regarded as the greatest poets in China. Fu Tu probably didn't expect that he would finally become a peer of Pai Li, and shine like a star for hundreds of years.

What's more, there were also voices that Tu should be above Li. Chü-e Pai said in "a letter to Chiu Yüan"(《与元九书》) that Tu's poems were more exquisite than Li's; Chen Yüan made a similar comment in the "epitaph" he wrote for a friend(《唐检校工部员外郎杜君墓系铭并序》). T'ao Ku(顾陶) used "Tu and Li" instead of "Li and Tu" in his preface to his book *Selected Tang Poems*(《唐诗类选》); Chuang Wei(韦庄) also believed in his book *A Selection of Excellent Poems*(《又玄集》) that Tu was the first, and Li the second.

Tu and his poems were finally put in China's Muse Shrine, where he was revered as "Sage of Poetry" and "the greatest master of poetry", and his poems were regarded as part of the history of the T'ang dynasty. Eto Wen(闻一多), a contemporary poet and prose writer, thinks so highly of Tu that he regards him as the most magnificent cultural glory in China.

Indeed, Tu was magnificent. First of all, he was a prodigy. When he was seven years old, he could write poems; when he was nine, he had already written a "bag of poems". Secondly, he was "an erudite" who read hundreds of books. Thirdly, he had God-given talent to write poems. Moreover, he was a good horse rider, a brave traveler, and an art genius who had unique understanding of dance, painting, song and music. He was by no means an ordinary person.

Tu is not only talented, but also very hardworking. He is a famous "poem perfectionist" who revises his new poem time after time through verse humming, that is, when he writes a poem, he weighs his words and refines the metric patterns again and again. It can be said that Tu is the poet who has the most profound understanding of the essence of poetic language in the T'ang dynasty. Tu's poetic language boasts of many characteristics. They can be summarized as follows: a) good "poem eyes", e.g. "Good rain knows the season（好雨知时节）"; b) good sense of color, e.g. "Green is the grass by the blue lake, red is the cloud over the shining sea（碧知湖外草, 红见海东云）"; c) flexible use of function word, e.g. "And drink Jove's nectar sup and enjoy the flowers（且尽芳樽恋物华）"; d) adequate use of reduplicated words, e.g. "Beautiful butterflies fluttering in flowers deep, fairy-like dragonflies sliding over the pond clear（穿花蛱蝶深深见, 点水蜻蜓款款飞）"; e) elegant use of vulgar words, e.g. "Weich'u has heartless flirting flowers, which at each home drive people mad.（韦曲花无赖, 家家恼杀人）"; and f) extraordinary sentence patterns, e.g. "Ears of rice, a parrot pecking; on a tree branch, a phoenix perching（香稻啄馀鹦鹉粒, 碧梧栖老凤凰枝）". In my opinion, what is especially worth discussing here are his "poem eyes" and "elegant use of vulgar words".

3. "Poem eyes" and Chao's translations

Let's start with "poem eyes". Ts'ai Yang（杨载）of the Yüan dynasty says in his book *Methods of Poetry Writing*（《诗法家数》）: "When writing a poem, one should weigh his words, especially the word that serves as the eye of a poetic line. Let's take Fu Tu's lines as examples, in '飞星过水白, 落月动檐虚', the 'eyes' are '过' and '动'; in '地坼江帆隐, 天清木叶闻', the 'eyes' are '隐' and '闻'; and in '红入桃花嫩, 青归柳叶新', the 'eyes' are '入' and '归'." From these instances we can see that the "eyes" are usually verbs, and, in most cases, they are predicates. If the "eyes" are not well refined, the poem would sound clichéd or childish. Tu is a master in making poem eyes, and many of his poem eyes are eye-catching. For instance, the "eyes" in the following lines are impressive: "青云羞叶密, 白雪避花繁", "落日邀双鸟, 晴天卷片云", "感时花溅泪, 恨别鸟惊心". If we scrutinize Chao's translation, we will find that Chao is very careful in dealing with the "eyes". For example:

ST：感时花溅泪，恨别鸟惊心。(杜甫《春望》)

TT1：Touched by hard times, flowers shed tears;
Dispersed by war, birds cringe in fears. (Tr. Yanchun Chao)

TT2：Seeing flowers come, a flood
Of sadness overwhelms me; cut off
As I am, songs of birds stir
My heart; ... (Tr. Rewi Alley)

The "eyes" are "溅" and "惊". We know that flowers do not automatically shed tears for the country's hard time, and birds do not spontaneously sympathize the poet in his sufferings. Because the poet was deeply saddened by the flames of war, the separation of relatives, and the absence of any news from his family, his heart was in tears (his eyes might also be in tears), and he was frightened at every moment. Therefore, the flowers and birds he saw seemed to have the same feeling as him: the flowers were "shedding tears" and the birds "frightened". This is the principle of lyric resonance in Chinese Poetics: a poet's emotion fluctuates, the things he or she sees automatically have the same emotional fluctuations; the personal and impersonal emotion fluctuations blend with each other, and it is often difficult for the reader to tell the difference.

Since the poem eyes ("溅" and "惊") have triggered lyrical resonance, the translation should convey this resonance. Chao's translation has done this well: "touched by hard times, flowers shed tears" is a literal translation, perfectly matching the original. It demonstrates an obvious resonance. In the second line "Dispersed by war, birds cringe in fears", the subject is "birds", which implies "I"; here, "birds" and "I" blend with each other to form lyric resonance. In contrast, Rewi Alley apparently did not notice the poetic effect of the "eyes"; in his translation "Seeing flowers come, a flood/Of sadness overwhelms me; cut off/As I am, songs of birds stir/My heart", "溅泪" ("shed tears") disappears, the first poem eye is lost; in what follows,"鸟惊心"(literally "the birds are frightened", it also means "I am frightened") becomes "songs of birds stir/My heart". Here "birds" and "I" are not blended with each other, the former being the emotion giver, and the latter the receiver. Therefore, Alley's translation has only the poet's emotional "vibration", not emotional "vibration" of the flowers and birds. In other words, the lyric resonance of the original text is lost, and the poetic flavor is lost. In regard to the poem eyes in the other poetic lines mentioned above, I hope readers will check Chao's corresponding translations, and appreciate his talent and hard work involved.

4. Translation of vulgar words in poems

Now let's talk about "elegant use of vulgar words". Chen Yüan says that he likes Fu Tu's direct introduction of vulgar words and sayings into his poems, and his not allowing his thinking to be confined to the words and lines of the previous poets ("怜渠直道当时语,不著心源傍古人"). Ch'e Huang（黄彻）, a poem commentator of the Sung dynasty, observes in his book *Kunghsi Talk on Poetry*（《䃂溪诗话》）that Fu Tu likes using vulgar words and sayings in his poems, and he is so good at using them that the original vulgarity is tinted with an elegant tone. I agree with Huang's comments, and I believe that the language tension between the vulgar semantic meaning and the elegant associative meaning in the context brings a special flavor for the poem, which constitutes part of Tu's poetic excellence. Here is a case in point. Fu Tu uses "无赖"（a vulgar term, meaning "knave", "rascal", "rogue", etc.) in at least six of his poems. Now let's observe how Chao translates this vulgar term:

ST1：剑南春色还<u>无赖</u>,触忤愁人到酒边。(杜甫《送路六侍御入朝》)
TT：The spring wind in Sword South is such <u>a knave</u>,
　　Who stirs my rue, and shakes my wine so rough.

ST2：老罢休无赖，归来省醉眼。（杜甫《闻斛斯六官未归》）
TT：Old and retired, a knave you are!
　　When back at home, you sleep, a sot.

In these two examples, Chao translates "无赖" into "a knave", which largely maintains the original language tension between vulgarity and elegance. If we have a close look at the original lines, we'll feel that it is indeed a big surprise that the poet compares the beautiful "spring scenery" to a "rogue". However, a careful examination will enable us to find that this is the poet's ingenuity: in the context, Fu Tu's old friend was about to leave for a remote place, and he felt very sad for it. In addition, the aftermath of *Anshi* rebellion brought him great sorrow. He was full of melancholy, and the beautiful spring scenery in front of him was "offensive" to his heavy heart. And it is the poet's ingenuity to depict a "melancholic" heart with "happy" scenery, and "a rogue" or "a knave" serves as the nexus between happiness and melancholy. Chao's translation basically retains the original metaphor of "the spring wind is a knave", and keeps the language tension. Furthermore, the knave "stirs my rue, and shakes my wine", which is as vivid and impressive as the original.

ST3：眼见客愁愁不醒，无赖春色到江亭。（杜甫《绝句漫兴九首（其一）》）
TT：I find myself sad and in sadness drowned;
　　Spring, uncalled for, comes to the pavilion.

ST4：韦曲花无赖，家家恼杀人。（杜甫《奉陪郑驸马韦曲二首》之一）
TT：In Weich'u are heartless flirting flowers,
　　which at each home drive people mad.

ST5：牧竖樵童亦无赖，莫令斩断青云梯。（杜甫《寄从孙崇简》）
TT：E'en herdboys, wood-gatherers are not true;
　　Don't let them pave a path into clouds blue.

ST6：羯胡事主终<u>无赖</u>，词客哀时且未还。（杜甫《咏怀古迹五首（其一）》）
TT：The crafty Rams and Huns <u>one can ne'er trust</u>；
　　The poet has not come back for the times' sake.

In these four cases, Chao refines the vulgar term "无赖" in English with elegance according to the needs of the context. The translations of "无赖" are different, but they all fit the contexts very well. Each of the lines reads smoothly and naturally. On the whole, the translations have maintained the poetic flavors of the original texts.

5. Translation of Fu Tu's poetic metrical patterns

It has been about 280 years since one of Fu Tu's poems was translated into English in 1741. Most of Tu's poems boast of rigorous metric patterns, and give the reader a strong sense of musical beauty. Therefore, how Tu's metric patterns are translated into English is worth talking about. Before the mid-19th century, only a few of Tu's poems were translated into English. As far as I've seen, they are all interpretive translations. It seems that the translators didn't care much about the metrical patterns of Tu's poems; or, perhaps due to the limited level of their Chinese, they didn't know much about the musical beauty of Tu's patterns. After the Opium War, British scholars' understanding of Chinese culture was greatly improved. At the turn of the 19th century to the 20th century, British sinologists, mainly missionaries and diplomats, attached great importance to the metric patterns of Tu's poems. They basically adopted the metric patterns of English poetry to translate Tu's musical beauty in poems. Famous translators include Herbert A. Giles, W. J. B Fletcher, John Francis Davis, E. H. Parker, Charles Budd, *etc*. As we know, from the 19th century to the early 20th century, classical poetics was dominant in Britain and America, and the Victorian writing style was prevailing. Paying attention to rhythms and rhymes is not only the traditional artistic norm of

English poetry, but also the poetic form loved by English readers at that time. The metric patterns that the sinologists adopted for the translations of Tu's poems were in line with the aesthetic tastes of the English readers at that era. At the end of the early 20th century, the form of British and American poetry began to transform from traditional style to modern one, and highlighting rhythms and rhymes was regarded as shackles for free and natural poetic expression. Later, along with new poetry movements, especially imagism, free verse became the main body of English poetry writing. This has deeply influenced the English translation of classical Chinese poetry, including Tu's poetry. Since the 1930s, the translation of Tu's poems in metrical style has been declining day by day, and the free style has become the mainstream. The well-known free-style English translations of Tu's poems are (in chronological order): William Hung's *Tu Fu: China's Greatest Poet* (1952), Sam Hamill's *Facing the Snow: Visions of Tu Fu* (1988), David Hinton's *The Selected Poems of Tu Fu* (1989), Rewi Alley's *Du Fu Selected Poems* (2001), Burton Watson's *The Selected Poems of Du Fu* (2002), David Young's *Du Fu: A Life in Poetry* (2008), etc. Very famous translators are David Hawkes, Cyril Birch and Kenneth Rexroth.

  Although metrical-style poetry translation is no longer the mainstream, there is another side to the question under discussion. According to the questionnaire survey I conducted in Boston University, New York University, University of Pennsylvania and University of California via four American Fulbright university graduates who once worked as English teaching assistants in Macao Polytechnic Institute and now are back in the United States, it is found that university students who have some knowledge of Chinese or have taken English poetry courses tend to like Tu's poems in English metrical style. They think that metrical style is an elegant style, which appears noble and more literary. As a matter of fact, classical Chinese poetry translation in English metrical style still has a market in the English world, which is evidenced by the fact that translators such as Henry

W. Wells, Robert Wood Clack, John A. Turner and their metrical-style translations are still famous in English-speaking countries, especially the United States and England. John A. Turner says in his foreword to his *A Golden Treasury of Chinese Poetry* (1976) that it is unfair to Chinese poets if we translate classical Chinese poetry into free-style English poetry, because the rhythms and rhymes of classical Chinese poetry are much more refined and beautiful than those in other languages. In his book *Millenniums of Moonbeams: An Historical Anthology of Chinese Classical Poetry* (1977), Robert Wood Clack speaks in an assertive tone that classical Chinese poetry has very strict metrical systems, and free-style English translations have completely deviated from the verve and spirit of classical Chinese poetry.

  The style of Chao's translation of Tu's poetry is basically the same as that of Wells, Clack and Turner, which is more elegant than the free style. We believe that this elegant style is more suitable for Tu's poetry, and better for Chinese culture transmission.

6. Concluding remarks

  Professor Chao told me that his translation of Tu's poems was generally smooth. I think this is owing to his God-given talent and his excellent translation skills which have been honed for a long time. His reader-oriented translation of Tu's poems is beautiful, readable and enjoyable. In my mind, Chao is an extraordinary translator and scholar. Here is my poem of praise in a classical Chinese metrical pattern to express my sincere admiration of Professor Chao:

To the Tune of "The Partridge Sky"
Your pride is enhanced in peach blossoms pink;
The saint's gold age to pass on needs your link.
Muses and Hermes for Heavens aspire;
The cosmos sees a spray shoot up, shoot higher.

The universe turns; sideburns dyed with frost.
Heaven and earth the setting sun accost.
A true scholar aims at the greatest cause;
His merits flow from an endless resource.

Hsiaohua Chiang
August 1, 2020
Macao Polytechnic Institute

译者自序

问你：哪个朝代的诗歌最伟大？你可能毫不犹豫：唐朝。要问你谁是唐朝最伟大的诗人，你可能不好回答，因为有好几位难以取舍。如果不选冠亚军而推举几位出类拔萃者便容易得多。王维、李白、杜甫、白居易无疑是最优秀的，他们造就了唐诗的高峰。

这一高峰地球人应该有足够的认识，然而翻译绝非易事，而且误区颇多。最核心的是"道"的缺失。

"形而上者谓之道，形而下者谓之器。"这是《易经》对人类一切知识体系的高度而精准的概括，是人类知识的坐标系，是人类智慧的坐标系。然而，西方启蒙时代打开了思想的"潘多拉魔盒"，将"道"瓦解于无形——诚如《论语》所言："天下之无道也久矣。"在西方学术出现了多次转向之后，中华传统文化的复兴已然发生——集结号已经吹响，"道"的光辉已出现在东方的地平线上。

人类思想的大变革、大繁荣大多肇始于翻译——比如东方的佛经翻译、西方的《圣经》翻译，以及近代以来的西学东渐所带动的种种翻译。中华经典外译始于明朝末年，译者多是西方汉学家、外交家和教会人士。清朝末年以后出现了一些华人译者。

但我们遗憾地发现，诗性的中国经典和诗本身的神采在很大程度上被遮蔽了，正应了罗伯特·弗罗斯特那句话：诗就是翻译中丢掉的东西。

在诸多类别的翻译实践中，文学翻译是最复杂、最难以应对的一种类型，而诗歌翻译又是文学翻译中最值得关注的对象。

人是诗性的存在；诗是人类的家园；诗是人类的表征。作诗与译诗都是以诗来表征我们自身，来表征我们的世界。诗的文学特性在于以有形的文字铺排映现无形的灵魂的跃动，"有形"表现为诗的文字载体或织体特征以及押韵、节奏构成的格律，"无形"即意外之意。诗应和着宇宙的递归性，可表现为符号之符号，它表达意义，又表达意义之意义，言有尽而意无穷。

中国是诗的国度。历史的遗存可以追溯到黄帝时代的《弹歌》。《弹歌》是二字格，是四言体的先驱。四言体古诗在公元前六世纪盛行，随之骚体诗、五言体古诗、七言体古诗和杂言古诗等相继成型；进入唐朝，中华民族迎来了诗歌大繁荣，出现五言律体诗、七言律体诗和六言律体诗。

　　唐朝（公元618—907年）是盛世中的盛世，文学艺术在唐朝达到鼎盛，尤其是在诗歌方面达到了中国文学的巅峰。关于唐朝有多少诗人以及他们写了多少首诗，今人已无法统计，清朝编纂的《全唐诗》共收录四万九千四百零三首，所涉作者共有二千八百七十三人。仅从这些遗存，我们也可以看到唐代文人以体量巨大的诗歌记录了文人风骨和浩荡的盛唐气象。王维、李白、杜甫、白居易无疑是唐朝灿如明珠的诗人中最为耀眼的四人。闲逸如"诗佛"王维，寄情山水，禅意尽见于遣词造句中。浪漫如"诗仙"李白，才情恣意挥洒于诗行间；深刻、沉郁如现实主义诗人杜甫，忧国忧民之思倾注在一字一句中；真诚、清醒如白居易，所思所感皆可见于诗行。四人所作唐诗传世甚多，各领风骚，向后人展示了大唐气象和时代特征。这四位诗人能够代表中国诗歌的高度，在世界文学中也享有崇高的地位。为此，我觉得很有必要把他们留下的六千首诗完整地译成英诗。

　　西方最早大力进行唐诗英译的是18世纪英国汉学家、诗人詹尼斯（S. Jenyns），译作有《唐诗三百首选读》(Selections from the 300 Poems of the Tang Dynasty)和《唐诗三百首选读续集》(A Further Selections from the 300 Poems of the Tang Dynasty)。小畑薰良（S. Obata）最早英译了唐代诗人专集，比如1922年在纽约出版的《李白诗集》(The Works of Li Po, the Chinese Poet)。其他为唐诗英译做出贡献的英译家还有戴维斯爵士、翟理斯、理雅各、韦利、柳无忌、欧文等等。反观国内，自二十世纪八十年代以来，我国学者、翻译家翻译的唐诗译本有杨宪益与戴乃迭（Gladys）合译的《唐宋诗文选译》(Poetry and Prose of the Tang and Song)、徐忠杰翻译的《唐诗二百首新译》(200 Chinese Tang Poems in English Verse)、王守义与诺弗尔（J. Neville）合译的《唐宋诗词英译》(Poems from Tang and Song Dynasties)、吴钧陶翻译的《杜甫诗英译（一百五十首）》(Tu Fu One Hundred and Fifty Poems)、许渊冲翻译的《唐诗三百首新译》(English-Chinese 300 Tang Poems A New Translation)、《李白诗选译》(Selected Poems of Li Bai)、《唐诗一百五十首英译》(150 Tang Poems)等。可见，唐诗的英译版本虽然相对较多，然文言文的晦涩和唐诗独有的文学性为唐诗英译设置了重重障碍，回顾现有的翻译作品，唐诗英译成果并不成系统，译本多零散且译文质量参差不齐，偏离原文甚远，自然传播效果也不甚理想。本该灿如明星的唐诗反而由于翻译的精准程度不匹配而被拉下神坛，中华文化的神采在译文中被遮蔽、被消解。远游的诗神是一个蒙灰的形象，哲学内涵也被误解、被埋没。在当代文明大潮交汇的新形势下，唐诗英译亟待寻求新的翻译方法论作为指导，亟须开辟新思路以走出困局。

翻译虽然基本上表现于文字转换，实质上却蕴含着大学之道。翻译始终以言语系统之间的"易"即言语单位的切换与调变来传情达意，同时也以其与宇宙之间的全息律（holographics）表征着"davar""Brahma""道"。翻译是不乏理论的，但纵观形形色色的西方翻译理论，由于没有形而上的统领和关照，其认识是庞杂的、肤浅的、碎片化的，甚至有的理论竟是颠覆本原、本质以借翻译理论之名行解构翻译理论之实，而传统的准则，比如忠实、对等，乃至文本本身都成了负面的模因而被解构了，翻译成了是其所非的荒谬和无所不是的弥散。

笔者 2005 年著《翻译学归结论》一书，逆西方潮流而动，以《周易》指向，从众说纷纭的混沌中祭出一个明确的范式，这是摆脱混乱和无定的一个企图。它说：翻译是一个由原则统领的、译者借此进行参数调变与否决的动态系统。由此，译/易的本质是类比的、可拓逻辑的，即化矛盾为不矛盾，变不可译为可译。正如唐朝的贾公彦云："译即易。谓换易言语使相解也。"语言符号是对抽象语义的表征，无论采取何种表征方式，只要能达到对等的目的即可。翻译的最根本的目的是要传递原汁原味的原文精髓，这绝不是改写，不是操控，更不是通过直译、意译或零翻译就能解决的。它需要译者设身处地，体会原作作者的审美情调和意图，通过合理有效的调控，使译文最大限度地贴近原文，最大限度地实现形美、音美和意美的有机统一，即实现译文中各个变量间的平衡与相互制约，使译文自给自足，达致善译。译文虽然在语形和语义上与原文有所差别，但在意旨上又和原文保持高度一致。

自提出翻译学归结论后，笔者在典籍外译实践中就始终以翻译学归结论为理论指导，坚守悬置法则（ceteris paribus rule）即其他条件等同（other things being equal）下的语码转换。大道至简，这是最高效的方法论的起点。在其外围便是翻译生态——翻译伴随翻译生态环境而生。翻译与生态环境，犹如阴阳两种力量，相摩相荡，相生相克，交感成和，生生不息。

具体到诗歌翻译而言,诗的"有形"与"无形"为诗歌翻译带来了避无可避的翻译困境。在中西方诗歌体裁中,诗可以分为散体诗和格律诗两大类:散体诗强调自然、不拘束;格律诗是一种编排,照应生命的律动,在严谨中书写诗意,天各一方的民族还不约而同地造就了格律。世界范围内,英汉诗歌又占据世界诗歌的大半。英诗的格律由四种基调格(抑扬格、扬抑格、抑抑扬格和扬抑抑格)、两种变格(抑抑格和扬扬格)和不同音步数组合而成,再辅以交替韵、搂抱韵和重叠韵构成多种经典诗体。汉语古诗则以极富乐感的方块字写成,它的格律主要涉及四个方面,即押韵、节奏、平仄和歌唱或吟诵行为,通过押韵和平仄实现古诗的表情达意,或热烈欢快,或文静雅致。格律诗的诗体特征之鲜明,直接造成格律诗翻译的壁障。即使诗歌翻译艰难如此,就格律诗的翻译而言,我也是绝不含糊的——这样的诗不允许含糊,此乃格律之谓也。

虽说诗无达诂、译无定法,译者在翻译诗歌时也不可过度夸大主观能动性,更不可任意妄为、随意解构,诗人的思想性和诗的文学性需得到足够的重视,译诗必须为诗。诗歌翻译首先要受到押韵、节奏这一形式因素的制约,甚至说还要满足演唱并可以适当发挥的需要。当然,这只是一个显性的要求。为保证作品的品位,语言、美学、哲学等层面的隐性因素都需要全盘考虑。笔者近年来着力进行典籍英译,其中一大类别就是中国古代诗歌英译。在翻译时,我始终践行的翻译原则就是"以诗译诗,译经如经,是其所是"。

译诗是高度辩证的制衡机制与审美行为。关于翻译标准,我认为:所谓辩证,它是不忠而忠、不等而等的调配;所谓制衡,它是依权重而逐层否决的仲裁;所谓审美,它是以可视、可感、可唱、可听的意象营造而直入心境。翻译必须被赋予一定的自由度。译者可以根据目的或意图的需要,在不影响大体的前提下增加译文的可读性或可唱性,甚至必要时可以做些许改动或牺牲,这样反而能使译文符合原文的初衷。翻译虽然多变,但绝不是没有标准,只是它的标准不是机械的、僵死的、一成不变的,它的最高标准其实就一个字:美。

译好一首诗或一部作品首先要统摄原文要旨和神采,然后用另一种文字恰如其分地再现。何谓再现?再现不是字词的简单对应而是语篇的功能对等——译文与原文在逻辑关系、审美构成和语用意图等各个层面的对应。可见,在诗歌翻译中,逼近原则是首要的——这是翻译及评判的起点和根据;逼近的同时也为达到最佳效果进行灵活调变,以直译尽其可能,意译按其所需的辩证性为旨归。

翻译中国古代诗歌尤其是格律诗时，秉承着"以诗译诗"的翻译原则，笔者首先就要"保留"格律，绝不能以"自由"为托词对其格律任意阉割而损伤诗美。当然，我也不提倡因声损义的凑韵，或为了押韵而把句子搞得怪里怪气，这比平庸还低廉。韵律来自语义或语境，它是构成织综的重要成分，与之不可分割——分割了就不是这首诗了。它服务于整体效果，牵一发而动全身。具体来说，"译诗如诗"即译者在认识到诗的形式是诗的格式或模板的基础上，首先有必要对译文在形式上进行限定。译为无韵的散文体或有韵的参差不一的诗行不符合我的审美取向。译诗虽然无强制性的要求，但在实践中也能提取出便于操作和评估的一般准则。比如英语的一个音步一般为两个音节，而五个音步一般为十个音节，与汉语的七言在形式和内容上可以达到最佳匹配。所以为了便于操作我做了类比性的设定：将汉语三言类比为五音节；将汉语四言类比为六音节；将汉语五言类比为八音节；将汉语六言类比为九音节；将汉语七言类比为十音节；将汉语八言类比为十二音节；将汉语九言类比为十四音节。

其次，由于英汉诗歌中韵诗又占绝大比例，在译汉语韵诗时，译诗也必须押韵且有节奏，"以诗译诗，是其所是"在翻译韵诗时就包括"以韵译韵"，这一点不能妥协，但如何押韵以及采用何种韵式则可以由译者自己调整。由于韵或韵式都是类比的，除了特殊的诗体，译诗中的韵式可以相对灵活。我多用偶韵和交叉韵或隔行韵；英诗绝大部分都是抑扬格，也会根据表意的需要夹杂扬抑格、抑抑扬格、扬抑抑格等，译诗也会求诸此类格律。在英译过程中，始终注重翻译的形意张力，避免因韵害义，同时又保证原诗风格的完整再现及诗歌情感、意境、意象等内涵的高度传达，最大化地实现翻译的效度与信度。英诗的格律不像中国的格律诗那样严格，总的原则是音韵和谐。好的译诗必须是不蔓不枝，自然天成的。

再者，除了对诗体、诗韵的保留与再现手段，中国古代诗歌翻译的另一重难点在于对文化名词的翻译处理。中华文化是一个复杂的大系统，内涵深厚，博大精深，可分为形形色色的模块，比如梅兰竹菊、琴棋书画、三皇五帝、三纲五常都是特定文化的产物。并且同一名词在不同文化语境中能够呈现不一样的内涵，中华风物可被赋予不同的内容。在中国古代诗歌英译实践中，一个负责任的译者不可忽视对这类名词的内涵和意义的解释和传达，因为翻译的目的就是不同文明之间的理解互通。对文化名词的妙用往往能体现并塑造文人的个人风格，李白的浪漫主义诗风瑰丽绚烂，白居易、杜甫等诗人的现实主义诗风发人深省,王维的田园山水诗风清新脱俗。译诗也重在译味(translating the taste)。如果仅是简单地释义,这便不是文学翻译而是文字翻译。因此,好的译诗也当一如原诗,文本自足,同时与原文的文学风格最大限度地映现。

对于在英语中无法完全找到对等表达的汉语文化名词时,笔者选择了以注释的形式扩展相关知识。不过,对于译文而言,注释属于副文本(paratext)即独立于译文的另一个文本,背景知识就语篇而言是缺省值(default value),尽管在一定程度上也会影响读者对文本的认知,但对于正文而言不是文本的必要成分,它只是揭示本族语者可能具有的默认知识。而对于英语读者而言,注释却可以在不影响译诗结构和表达的条件下,成为可辅助英语读者理解译文的、有效且必要的文本。作注和译诗是不同的路径,译者不需要想象,不需要发挥,不需要浪漫,但需要查阅、考证、取舍和提炼;同时译者还要借鉴最近的考古发现,如此才能做到用最简练的语言来概括某一注释所需的完整历史的文化要素。对译者而言,作注还能再次验证译文的准确程度,起到查漏、勘误作用,反过来提高翻译质量。

在翻译和作注的过程中,译者对于专有名词必然有很多纠结,担心信息会有所遗漏、扭曲或冗余。笔者认为:为了保全原文信息和可读性,译者在翻译中应尽量避免音译;即便音译,也要照顾西方的阅读习惯,可采用西方读者和海外华人熟悉的威氏拼音;更重要的是翻译要避免编码的夹生,比如中国文化的层级体系的编码是从大至小,而英语则是从小至大,比如"蓝田山石门精舍"译成英语则应该把"蓝天山"的译文置后,如 Stonegate Vihara at Mt. Blue Field,而译作 at Mt. Blue Field Stonegate Vihara 则怪异。同理,"李白"姓李名白,译作"Li Pai"就违反了英语的编码规律,正如把"卡尔·马克思"译作"马克思·卡尔"那样悖谬,而译作"Pai Li"才符合英语的规范。

对于有些特有的中华文化概念如精卫、后羿、颛顼、秀才等,如果音译便过滤掉了中国文化的特有意义。译者还需要基于汉语词源和英语构词法在译文中进行合理创译,仿拟汉语的构词法,尽力把词素所表达的意义译出来,这等于向英语输入词汇,利用词汇在文化系统中的互文性,从而帮助英语读者通过上下文推断该词的意义所指。比如"秀才"译作"xiu cai"或"hsiu ts'ai"对于英文读者而言是毫无意义的,而重新编码为"showcharm",读者则可以产生相应的联想,而随着认知语境的增强,则可以达到等同于原文的认知效果。通过以上翻译策略,译诗可以尽可能保留原诗用典情况,并用脚注形式注释其中出现的历史典故、神话传说、文化习俗等,使读者能够迅速了解诗歌中的典故及文化内涵。可见,注释文本为达成文化互通这一翻译的最终目的也起到了积极的推手作用,一定程度上弥补了语言系统客观差异所带来的文化缺省的难解现象。

言而总之,译者如若在中国古代诗歌英译实践中,贯彻"以诗译诗,是其所是"和逼近原则,尽可能在诗体、诗韵上做到还原和再现,且以注释辅助文化名词的翻译,译诗才能一如原文,做到浅而不白、质而不俗,达成形美、意美、音美的辩证统一,这便逼近等值、等效了。如此说来,在诗歌翻译实践中,译文比肩乃至超越原文是可能的——这取决于如何操控"言尽意"与"言不尽意"的悖论和如何破解翻译的斯芬克斯之谜。

目前放眼译界,译者由于欠缺形而上的元理论意识,对翻译本体论以及语言本体论认识不足,同时欠缺语言各分相学科的系统知识,大多还拘泥于话语层次的静态的语码转换,其译文难免失真、异化。纵观典籍外译,翻译之敝不仅遮蔽了中华文化的神采而且还割裂了中西文化一体性,不仅没能促进文明互通,反而还弄巧成拙,造成更大的"隔阂"。

笔者基于对翻译本体论和语言本体论的深刻认识,以扎实的中华文化经典英译实践为佐证,提出:典籍外译新局面的突破口在于方法论的革新。译者须从翻译本体论出发,将词源学、句法学、语义学乃至哲学、神学等领域融会贯通,突破机械的二元论,以整全的、全息的眼光审察翻译这一悖论性的辩证系统,系统调和可译/不可译等矛盾,在形意张力逼近与趋同当中追求文化、文本的自恰,以期翻译理论的涅槃,使经典外译焕发勃勃生机。

受惠于中华文化复兴这个伟大时代所提供的机遇,我们拥有了便于利用的知识宝库,而国学双语研究也进入了新境界,促进了经典文化翻译的创新。在此背景下,笔者多年来一直思考翻译理论的创新并付诸翻译实践。笔者希望王维、李白、杜甫、白居易的英译可以展示唐诗的面貌,也希望与笔者已出版的其他中华文化典籍尤其是诗歌的英译作品形成呼应,继续提供经得起海内外读者检验、品读的系列译作,为中华文化"走出去"尽一份绵薄之力。

赵彦春

2020 年 9 月 1 日

于上海大学

Introduction by the Translator

If asked which dynasty is the greatest in poetry, you may reply without hesitation: the T'ang dynasty; if further asked who is the greatest poet in the T'ang dynasty, you may feel it uneasy to answer, because there are several poets too hard to rank. If not required to list the first or second but the best ones, it is much easier. Wei Wang, Pai Li, Fu Tu and Chü-e Pai, no doubt, are among the best. It is they who made the pinnacle of T'ang poetry.

This pinnacle should be well known to all earthlings. But translation is never an easy task and not without traps and fallacies. The most crucial of all is the loss of the Word.

"What is high above is the Word; what is down below is the vessel." This is a detached and exact recapitulation by *The Book of Changes* of the whole system of human knowledge, a coordinate of human knowledge and a coordinate of human wisdom. However, the Enlightenment in the West opened the Pandora's Box of thought and disintegrated the Word into dirt, as is said in *Analects*, "The world has gone astray from the Word for long." While after many turns in the West's academics, the renaissance of traditional Chinese culture has started off. The call to action has been tooted and the dawning of the Word has touched the horizon with a streak of red.

In a large sense, the great revolution or great prosperity of human thought began with translation, for example, the translation of Buddhist scriptures in the East, the translation of the Bible in the West and other kinds of translation brought about by the Eastward Spread of Western Culture in the modern era. The translation of Chinese classics started in the late Ming dynasty and translators at that time were mainly sinologists, diplomats and missionaries, and in the late Ching dynasty, some Chinese translators joined in this undertaking.

Unfortunately, we have come to find that the charm of poetic Chinese classics and poetry itself have been eclipsed to a very large extent, which happens to correspond to Robert Frost's dictum, "Poetry is what gets lost in translation."

Of all kinds of translation practice, literary translation is the trickiest and most complicated, and poetry translation is the most noteworthy kind of translation of all literary genres.

Humans are poetic beings, and poetry is the homeland of humans as well as a representation of humans. Poetry creation and poetry translation are both means of representing ourselves and representing our world. The literariness of poetry is a matter of mapping between the arrangement of visible words and the movement of invisible human souls: its visibility is manifested in what we can see, like words, texture and prosody formed by rhythm and rhyme; its invisibility refers to the meaning out of meaning. Poetry is in correspondence with the recursion of the universe and is embodied as a chain of signs or a sign of signs; it expresses meaning, and even expresses the meaning of meaning. As an old saying goes, words are finite but the meaning beyond words is infinite.

China is a nation of poetry. Its history of poetry can date back to *Song of the Catapult* in the age of Lord Yellow. *Song of the Catapult*, two characters or two syllables a line, is a forerunner of the four-character verse, i.e., verse of four characters or four syllables a line. The four-character verse flourished in the sixth century B.C., and then more types of verse came into being, such as the Woebegone form, the five-character old verse, the seven-character old verse and the varying-character old verse. The T'ang dynasty ushered in a golden age of poetry, when there appeared metrical poems with five characters a line, six characters a line and seven characters a line.

The T'ang dynasty (A.D. 618 - A.D. 907) is the most golden period among all golden times, the pinnacle of achievements in Chinese literature and arts, especially in poetry. In regard of the quantity of poets and poems in T'ang, there is no exact number yet. While it can be seen from *A Complete Collections of T'ang Poems*, a book compiled in the Ching dynasty, there are 49,403 poems produced by 2,873 poets in the T'ang dynasty. From these remains, we can also see that litterateurs then showed their charm and recorded the magnificence of that great age in a great multitude of poems. Wei Wang, Pai Li, Fu Tu and Chü-e Pai are, no doubt, the brightest representative figures of all pearl-like poets in the T'ang dynasty. Detached and delighted in nature, Wei Wang pursued the great Word through wording line by line; romantic and unrestrained, Pai Li implanted his sentiments and talents into poetic lines; incisive and realistic, Fu Tu showed his worries over the nation and people in his poems; sober and percipient, Chü-e Pai expressed his great concerns over his kin, friends and homeland. Their abounding poems, though distinctive in style, altogether mirror the history in different stages of that age. These four poets can represent the pinnacle of Chinese poetry and should have been given a stature in world literature. For this reason, I think it necessary to render their poems, 6,000 in total, into English.

The first sinologist who took pains to translate T'ang poetry is S. Jenyns, a British poet in the eighteenth century, with the fruition of *Selections from the 300 Poems of the Tang Dynasty* and *A Further Selections from the 300 Poems of the Tang Dynasty*. The first one to translate the collected works of a T'ang poet is S. Obata, renowned for *The Works of Li Po, the Chinese Poet* published in New York in 1922. Other pioneers are Sir Davis, H. Giles, J. Legge, A. Waley, Wu-chi Liu, Owen and so on. Chinese translators began to translate T'ang poetry in the 1980s, and representative translated works include *Poetry and Prose of the Tang and Song* by Hsien-e Yang and Gladys Yang, *200 Chinese Tang Poems in English Verse* by Chungchieh Hsu, *Poems from Tang and Song Dynasties* by Shou-e

Wang and J. Neville, *Tu Fu One Hundred and Fifty Poems* by Chunt'aoWu, *English-Chinese 300 Tang Poems: A New Translation* by Yüanch'ung Hsu, *Selected Poems of Li Bai* by Yüanch'ung Hsu, and *150 Tang Poems* by Yüanch'ung Hsu. As it can be seen, the obscurity of classical Chinese writings and the unique literariness of T'ang poems set many obstacles for the translation of T'ang poetry, existing translated works, though in a relatively large quantity, are far from ideal in quality and are fragmented rather than systematic in scale. So, these translations, too far away from their originals in form and meaning, have resulted in an obviously poor communication effect worldwide by now. T'ang poetry that should have been as luminous as bright stars is now being pulled down from its summit by bad translations, and the glory of Chinese civilization gets dimmed and diminished by bad translations. It also means that the images of Chinese Muses travelling afar are covered with a veil of dust, and that Chinese philosophy has been misunderstood and undermined. Against the background of cultural exchanges, a new methodology is in dire need to guide the rendering of T'ang poetry into English, so that translators can find a way out of the current plight.

Translation, a process of text transformation by and large, has an implication in the Word of the universe. It always includes the transformation between two linguistic systems to convey meanings and express emotions, and also mirrors the universal holographics to represent "davar", "Brahma" or the Word. Though there is no lack of translation theories, we can find no directions from metaphysics for translation studies in Western translation theories. The viewpoints expressed in the so-called theories can be judged as sprawling, shallow and fragmented. Some of them have even overthrown the thing-in-itself of translation and have actually deconstructed the basics of translation. Classic norms such as fidelity, equivalence and the text itself are regarded as negative memes and are deconstructed. Translation has run into a state of what it is not, with the dispersion of its essence into being anything but itself.

In 2005, I published a book *A Reductionist Approach to Translatology*, a book that goes in the opposite direction of Western translation theories. With the guidance of *The Book of Changes*, the book aims to set a clear paradigm out of all current chaos and melee, trying to lead translation studies out of disorder. As it proposes, translation is a dynamical system guided by principles, and translators can take advantage of the mechanism of checks and balances to modulate and veto parameters in the process. Hence, the essence of "trans" conforms to analogy and extenic logic, which means converting contradictoriness into compatibility and untranslatability into translatability. Just as the T'ang Confucian Scholar Kungyen Chia put it, "'yi' (falling tone, meaning trans) is equal to 'yi' (falling tone, meaning changing), namely changing from one parole into another to ensure mutual understanding". Linguistic symbols are just representations of abstract semantic meanings, and all representations can reach the same goal, different they may be. The fundamental purpose of translation is to convey the quintessence of the source text in an original way; and definitely, it is not merely what rewriting or manipulation can achieve, and even far beyond the scope of what is called literal translation, free translation or zero translation. According to *A Reductionist Approach to Translatology*, translators are required to be empathetic enough to comprehend the original's aesthetic perception and intention, and then to reasonably modulate parameters to make the translations approximate to the original as much as possible, so that the beauty in form, sound and meaning can be achieved to the largest extent, that is to say, checks and balances among all variables can be realized, and self-consistent as well as high-quality translations can be produced. Translations, though still different from the original in linguistic symbols, are very likely to be highly consistent with it in semantic meaning and motif.

Since the establishment of the reductionist approach to translatology, it has been the theoretical guide throughout my translation practice, especially that of Chinese classics, abiding by the ceteris paribus rule, namely, transcoding in the condition of other things being equal, and insisting that the great Word is the simplest and is the starting point of a methodology of the highest efficiency. Besides, translation also concerns outer communicative environment, in other words, translation exists, concurrent with it. Translation and the communicative environment, just like the two forces Shine and Shade, which endlessly collide with each other, reinforce each other and counteract each other, two in one and united in one.

In terms of poetry, its visible and invisible poetic features bring inevitable obstacles to translation. Chinese poetry and Western poetry can be generally classified into free verse and rhythmic verse. The former highlights naturalness and freedom in verse, while the latter is a fruit of many nations though far apart, featuring rhythmic rules to represent the rhythm of life itself and the poetic atmosphere behind this restriction of rhythmic rules. Chinese poetry and Western poetry can boast of more than half of all poems ever produced. In respect of Western poetry, there are basic meter patterns including four basic meter patterns (Iambus, Trochee, Anapaest and Dactyl) and two variant meter patterns (Pyrrhic and Spondee), metrical foot patterns and three common rhyming schemes (alternate rhyme as abab, enclosing rhyme as abba and distich as aa), which are the most adopted classical patterns. As for Chinese poetry, it is written in Chinese characters characterized by musicality, and the rhythmic verse features in four aspects, that is, rhyming, rhythm, tone pattern (piânn-tseh) and its chanting style for poets to convey meanings and express emotions, ardent or refined. These clear-cut poetic features of metrical verses directly challenge translators. Despite the difficulty and complexity, I show no perfunctoriness, and perfunctoriness is not allowed in metrical verses.

Admitting that "no final interpretation for literary texts, no definite translation of them either", while translating poetry, translators should not over-exaggerate their initiative, let alone wantonly interpreting and deconstructing original texts. An author's ideology and the literariness of a poem should be given enough emphasis, and its translation should still be a poem in itself. Poetry translation is firstly subject to the need of representing the original's poetic forms like rhyming and rhythm, and then to the needs of chanting or other purposes. Certainly, the requirements above are just overt ones, and to ensure the literariness of the original in the translation, invisible connotations of language, philosophy and aesthetics should all be considered. For years I have been devoted to English translation of Chinese classics, ancient poetry in particular. The ultimate translation principle I have long implemented is "translating poesie into poesie and classic into classic, translating it as it is".

Poetry translation is a highly dialectical system of checks and balances and an aesthetic activity. Speaking of translation criteria, as I see it, being dialectical lies in the modulation of parameters for dynamic fidelity and equivalence through seeming infidelity and in equivalence; checks and balances requires translators to decide whether an element should be preferred or sacrificed layer by layer based on its right weight; in aesthetic terms, poetry translation is expected to create visual and acoustical poetic imagery to impress readers. Translators should be given some independence, hence enabled to enhance the readability of a translated text according to pragmatic purposes without affecting the overall arrangements, and even to change or sacrifice some elements, if necessary, to better represent the original's intention. Translation, though ever-changing in the process, can never do without criteria, and criteria should not be mechanical, rigid or immutable. Its highest standard actually is just one word: beauty.

To produce a quality translation of poetry or literature in general, translators firstly need to fully comprehend the original's motif and style, and then appropriately represent it in another language. What is representation? It is not simple word-to-word equivalence but functional or dynamic equivalence in terms of discourse, namely, the equivalence of the original and the translated text in layers such as logical relationship, aesthetic component and pragmatic intention. This shows that in poetry translation, the principle of proximity is primary, which is the starting point and the basis for translation practice and translation criticism. Translators can flexibly modulate elements to achieve the best possible effect, aiming at the maxim "as literal as is possible, as free as necessary".

When translating ancient Chinese poetry, especially Chinese metrical poems, abiding by the principle of "translating poesie into poesie", I firstly retain the original's metrical features and never misuse a translator's freedom to arbitrarily abandon the original's metrical features at the expense of damaging its poetic beauty. Also, I don't advocate translators to unnaturally pile up rhymes at the cost of damaging meanings and twisting poetic structures. After all, going beyond the limit is as bad as falling short. Rhyme and rhythm are rooted in meaning or context, and as a significant part of poetic structure, they should not be sacrificed. They contribute to the overall poetic effect and will affect the whole body if ignored. Specifically speaking, "translating poesie into poesie" is in the condition that translators have realized the role of poetic form as a poem's base or template, at first fixing the translation's form as a poem. Translating a Chinese poem into an English blank verse or an English rhymed poem uneven in length does not conform to my aesthetic orientation. Though there is no compulsory limit for poetry translation, general translation techniques that are useful for specific performance and evaluation can be summarized from translation practice. For instance, in English, one foot generally consists of two syllables, and accordingly five feet equals ten syllables in English, which can tentatively match seven Chinese characters both in form and content. By analogy, I have set a set of rules below: translating a Chinese three-character line into a pentasyllabic line in English, a Chinese four-character line into a hexasyllabic line, a Chinese five-character line into an octosyllabic line, a Chinese six-character line into an enneasyllabic line, a Chinese seven-character line into a decasyllabic line, a Chinese eight-character line into a twelve-syllable line, and a Chinese nine-character line into a fourteen-syllable line and so on.

In the second place, as rhymed poems account for the largest part of poems, when translating rhymed Chinese poems, the translations must be in rhyme, as the principle of "translating poesie into poesie, translating it as it is" entails "translating rhyme into rhyme". It is something that a translator should never make a concession to. Of course, a translator can decide which rhyme or which rhyming scheme to use. Since rhymes are something of analogy, except some unique poetic styles or subgenres, the rhyming schemes applied in a translation can be relatively flexible. The commonly used rhyming schemes in my translations include couplets (aa), alternate rhymes (abab) or interlacing rhymes (abcb). Most English poems use Iambus as the meter pattern along with auxiliaries such as Trochee, Anapaest and Dactyl, relevant to the requirement of meaning. A translation can do likewise. During the process, a translator should constantly focus on form-meaning tension, avoid the misuse of rhymes at the cost of damaging meaning, and ensure that the translated poem can possibly represent the original's style, emotion and imagery and then can achieve the validity of, and fidelity to, the original to the largest extent. Metrical patterns of English poetry, unlike those of Chinese metrical poems, are less strict. And the general principle is being harmonious in rhyme. A high-quality translation of a poem should be pithy, smooth and natural.

In the third place, apart from the representation of the original's poetic forms and metrical patterns, one more difficulty for translation is how to translate culture-loaded words. Chinese culture is an ancient civilization of great complexity, incomparable in profoundness and exclusively rich in dimension. It consists of diverse motifs such as plant images and art images, such as "wintersweets, orchids, bamboos and chrysanthemums", "zither, go, calligraphy and painting", "Three Kings and Five Lords", and "Three Canons and Five Constants", all of which are outcomes of Chinese culture, and a single image can convey different meanings in different contexts and can be given a new content according to a certain language use. In the English translation of practice of Chinese ancient poetry, a responsible translator must never escape from interpreting these images and conveying their connotations in translation, for the reason that the purpose of translation is exactly to promote mutual understanding among all civilizations rather than a dialogue of the deaf. The use of culture-loaded words frequently manifests and shapes a poet's unique style, such as Pai Li's style of romanticism, Chü-e Pai's and Fu Tu's style of realism and Wei Wang's style of naturalism. Poetry translation also centers on the aesthetics of translating the taste. Simple literal translation is none but translation of words, not translation of literature. In this sense, excellent translations of poems should be as self-consistent as the original as well, and should mirror the original's literary style.

When faced with the occasions of culture default in the English translation of Chinese ancient poems, I choose the way of annotation to provide additional information outside the translated poems. However, in regard of translation, annotations belong to the type of paratext, namely, another text independent of the main body. For Chinese readers, background information of a Chinese ancient poem is a default value, and is not an essential part for the original though it affects Chinese readers' comprehension to some extent. Annotations in Chinese contexts can only reveal hidden knowledge some Chinese readers may need to know while reading, while for English readers, annotations in a translated text can be of great use and significance for them to comprehend the translation, which is an integral whole. Annotating is different from translating in the operational method. While providing annotations, a translator does not need to be imaginative, creative or sensitive, and instead he needs to investigate and verify messages, to select those useful out of all and finally to summarize them into definitions. Meanwhile, a translator needs to refer to most recent archaeological findings to ensure that an annotation is able to contain complete and required historic and cultural elements with the most precise expressions. In turn, annotations can verify the degree of accuracy of translations, help translators to check and correct errors, and enhance the quality.

During the process of translation and annotation, translators must be concerned about culture-loaded words, lest some information be lost, distorted or redundant. As far as I can see, to ensure the fidelity to the original's information and readability of its translation, transliteration should be avoided as much as possible; if there is no better method than transliteration, translators should fully attend to westerners' reading habits, for example, I adopt the Wade-Giles romanization, for it has been popular with westerners and overseas Chinese. What is crucial is to avoid the hybridity of recodification, for example, the encoding of the hierarchy of Chinese culture is top-down while in English it is a bottom-up direction, just the opposite, for example, "Stonegate Vihara at Mt. Blue Field", which shows a bottom-up arrangement, is good English while "at Mt. Blue Field Stonegate Vihara" is absurd. Similarly, in "Pai Li", "Pai" is first name while "Li" is family name or surname, it is good English, while "Li Pai" violates the rule of English, just like the case we call Karl Marks "Marks Karl", so preposterous. So, "Pai Li" is the right address.

As for those salient and peculiar words in Chinese culture like Ching Wei, Hou E, Chuan Hsü and hsiuts'ai, considering that their cultural connotations will vanish in translations if transliteration is applied, I suggest that translators coin English words based on Chinese etymology and English word-formation, so as to reveal the original's word origin and introduce new eastern cultural connotations to the English world. This use of lexicon's intertextuality in cultural systems can assist English readers to deduce the signified of a culture-loaded word from the translated context. For example, the word "xiu cai" or "hsiu ts'ai" makes no sense to English readers, while the recodification, like "showcharm" can trigger off similar associations, and as the target reader's cognitive environment is improved, he may have the same cognitive effect as source text readers. Through translation strategies mentioned above, a translator will be able to retain the original's allusions in the translated text to the largest extent, and provide annotations via footnotes to explain historical stories, myths, legends, and customs in the original and to delve into their connotations. So to speak, annotations play a positive role in achieving the goal of mutual understanding and compensating for the unintelligibility of cultural default brought about by the facsimiles of translation.

All in all, if a translator abides by the principle of "translating poesie into poesie, translating it as it is" and the principle of proximity while rendering Chinese ancient poetry into English, attempts to represent the original's poetic form and rhyming patterns, and provides annotations to assist translations of culture-loaded words, a translated poem can be concise and insightful, well-worded and refined, achieving the dialectical unity of beauty in form, meaning and musicality, just like the original. In this way, a translated poem can be approximate and equal to the original. Hence, in poetry translation, translations are likely to match and even exceed the original, and it depends on how a translator solves the explicability-unexplicability paradox and how he solves the riddle of Sphinx in translation.

Throughout the current translation studies and practices, it can be seen that most translators are still trapped in the static transformation of language codes at discourse level, due to the lack of a metaphysical metatheory, the ontology of translation and the ontology of language. Inevitably, their translations are unfaithful and distorted. Looking back at the course of translation of Chinese classics, translations at present have overshadowed the glory of Chinese civilization, split the oneness of the East and the West, failed to promote cultural exchanges and ironically turned out to be a barrier for cultural communication.

On the basis of a deep understanding of the ontology of translation and the ontology of language and taking substantial English translation of Chinese classics as solid evidences, I call for the innovation in translation methodology for finding a way out of the *status quo*. I suggest that translators start from the ontology of translation, synthetically apply etymology, syntax, semantics, philosophy and even theology in translation practice, and thus break through mechanical dualism. They are also expected to look upon translation as a dialectical system full of paradoxes from a holistic and holographic viewpoint. In this way, they may systematically reconcile contradictions like the translatability-untranslatability paradox; and they may pursue self-consistence of cultures as well as texts during the process of approximation and convergence in form and meaning. We look forward to the nirvana of translation theories and a refreshed look of translation of Chinese classics.

Thanks to the encouragement of the age, an age of the renaissance of traditional Chinese culture, we have access to the great treasures of knowledge. Along with bilingual studies of Chinese classics stepping into a new stage, we are experiencing the renewal of translation of Chinese classics. In this context, I have been committing myself to academic researches and translation practices for many years. I hope that the translated works of Wei Wang, Pai Li, Fu Tu and Chü-e Pai will give a true picture of what T'ang poetry is like, and that along with my other translated works of Chinese classics, these translations will keep on offering reliable resources for readers in China and overseas and will help Chinese culture to "go global" in a way.

Yanchun Chao
September 1, 2020
Shanghai University

目 录
Contents

1   序言
      Introduction

1   **译者自序**
      Introduction by the Translator

1   曲江二首(其一)
      Drinking Vis-à-vis the Bent River (No. 1)

2   春望
      A View of Spring

3   江畔独步寻花
      Looking for Flowers Alone on the Bank

4   赠花卿
      To Hua, a General

5   绝句二首(其一)
      A Quatrain Minor (No. 1)

6   绝句二首(其二)
      A Quatrain Minor (No. 2)

7   月夜忆舍弟
      Missing My Brothers on a Moonlit Night

9   旅夜书怀
      Traveling at Night

10   客至
      A Friend's Visit

11   绝句漫兴(其一)
      A Quatrain Impromptu (No. 1)

12	绝句漫兴（其三）	
	A Quatrain Impromptu（No. 3）	
13	绝句漫兴（其七）	
	A Quatrain Impromptu（No. 7）	
14	戏为六绝句（其六）	
	Six Quatrains for Fun（No. 6）	
15	漫成一首	
	An Impromptu	
16	不见	
	It's Long Since I Saw Him	
18	后游	
	A Revisit	
19	秋兴八首（其三）	
	An Impulse on an Autumn Day, Eight Poems（No. 3）	
21	玉台观	
	The Celestial Wordist Abbey	
23	倦夜	
	A Tired Night	
24	孤雁	
	The Wild Goose Astray	
25	望岳	
	Looking at Mt. Arch	
26	游龙门奉先寺	
	Visiting Sage-Adoring Temple at Dragongate	
27	登兖州城楼	
	Climbing the Gate Tower of Yanchow	
29	题张氏隐居二首	
	On Chang's Hermitage, Two Poems	
31	刘九法曹郑瑕丘石门宴集	
	Liu of the Law Section and Cheng of Hsiachiu Hold a Banquet at Mt. Stonegate	
32	与任城许主簿游南池	
	Visiting South Pool with Assistant Magistrate Hsu of Jench'eng	

34	对雨书怀走邀许主簿	

34 对雨书怀走邀许主簿
Writing My Feelings Facing the Rain, I Rush to Send Off an Invitation to Assistant Magistrate Hsu

35 巳上人茅斋
The Thatched Study of Reverend Ssu

36 房兵曹胡马
The Hun Horse of Fang, an Officer of the War Section

38 画鹰
A Painted Hawk

39 过宋员外之问旧庄
A Visit to Ministry Councilor Chihwen Sung's Former Estate

40 夜宴左氏庄
A Night Banquet at Ts'o's Estate

41 临邑舍弟书至，苦雨，黄河泛溢，堤防之患，簿领所忧，因寄此诗用宽其意
A Letter Arrives from My Brother at Lin-e; the Rain Causes the Yellow River to Overflow; the Officials Are Worried About the Dikes. Therefore I Send this Poem to Appease Him.

44 假山
An Artificial Mountain

46 李监宅二首（其一）
Librarian Li's House (No. 1)

48 赠李白
Presented to Pai Li

50 重题郑氏东亭
Another Inscription for Cheng's Eastern Pavilion

51 陪李北海宴历下亭
In the Company of North Sea Li, Feasting in Lihsia Pavilion

53 同李太守登历下古城员外新亭
A Companion Piece to Governor Li's *Climbing to the Ministry Councilor's New Pavilion by the Old Wall of Lihsia*

55 暂如临邑至鹊山湖亭奉怀李员外率尔成兴
Going to Lin-e for a While, I Reach the Lake Pavilion at Mt. Magpie, and Think of Ministry Councilor Li, Hence My Inspiration

57 赠李白
Presented to Pai Li

58 与李十二白同寻范十隐居
Going to Find Fan Ten's Hermitage with Pai Twelve Li

60 郑驸马宅宴洞中
Adjunct Groom Cheng's House, a Banquet in the Grotto

61 冬日有怀李白
Missing Pai Li on a Winter Day

63 春日忆李白
Missing Pai Li on a Spring Day

65 送孔巢父谢病归游江东兼呈李白
Seeing Off Ch'aofu Kung, Who Has Resigned on Account of Illness and Will Go Back to Visit East of the Long; Also for Pai Li

67 今夕行
This Evening: A Ballad

69 赠特进汝阳王二十二韵
Presented to the Prince of Youshine, Lord Specially Advanced

73 赠比部萧郎中十兄（甫从姑子也）
To Director of the Bureau of Review Hsiao Ten (I am the son of his father's uncle's sister)

75 奉寄河南韦尹丈人
Respectfully Sent to My Senior Wei, Governor of Honan

78 赠韦左丞丈济
Presented to Chi Wei, Vice-Director of the Left

80 奉赠韦左丞丈二十二韵
Respectfully Presented to Senior Wei, Vice-Director of the Left, a Verse of 44 Lines

84 饮中八仙歌
Song of Eight Drinking Immortals

87 高都护骢马行
Governor-General Kao's Dapple Gray

89 冬日洛城北谒玄元皇帝庙
Paying My Respects at the Temple of Emperor Dark One in Loshine on a

Winter Day

93　故武卫将军挽歌三首
Three Elegies for the General of the Palace Guard

96　赠翰林张四学士
Given to Academician Chang of the Brushwood

98　乐游园歌
Song of Pleasure Park

100　同诸公登慈恩寺塔
Climbing the Pagoda of Grace Temple with Various Gentlemen

103　投简咸华两县诸子
Sending a Note to Those in the Two Counties Allshine and Flower

105　杜位宅守岁
New Year's Eve in Wei Tu's House

107　敬赠郑谏议十韵
Respectfully Presented to Remonstrant Cheng

109　兵车行
The Chariot: A Ballad

113　前出塞九首
First Series of Going Out the Passes, Nine Poems

122　送高三十五书记
Seeing Off Secretary Kao Thirty-Five

126　奉留赠集贤院崔、于二学士（国辅、休烈）
Respectfully Left to Be Presented to Two Academicians of the Academy of Worthies, Kuofu Ts'ui and Hsiulieh Yü

129　贫交行
Friendship in Poverty: A Ballad

130　送韦书记赴安西
Seeing Secretary Wei Off to Pacified West

132　玄都坛歌寄元逸人
A Song of Dark Capital Altar, Sent to Hermit Yüan

134　曲江三章章五句
Three Stanzas on the Bent River (each stanza has five lines)

137 奉赠鲜于京兆二十韵
Respectfully Presented to Hsienyü, Governor of the Capital Region

141 白丝行
White Silk: A Ballad

143 陪郑广文游何将军山林十首
Visiting General Ho's Mountain Wood in the Company of Instructor Cheng, Ten Poems

153 丽人行
Fair Ladies: A Ballad

156 九日曲江
Double Ninth on the Bent River

158 奉陪郑驸马韦曲二首
Respectfully Accompanying Adjunct Groom Cheng in Weich'u, Two Poems

161 重过何氏五首
Revisiting General Ho's, Five Poems

167 陪诸贵公子丈八沟携妓纳凉晚际遇雨二首
Taking Singing Girls to Enjoy the Cool at Ten-Eight Trench in the Company of Childes and at Dusk It Rains, Two Poems

170 醉时歌
Singing When Drunk

173 城西陂泛舟
Boating on the Slope West of the Town

175 渼陂行
Goodslope: A Ballad

178 渼陂西南台
The Terrace Southwest of Goodslope

181 与鄠县源大少府宴渼陂（得寒字）
Feasting at Goodslope with Senior Yüan, Sheriff of Hu County

183 赠田九判官
To Judge Liang Tien Nine

185 投赠哥舒开府翰二十韵
Presented to General Han Koshu

190	寄高三十五书记	
	To Secretary Kao Thirty-Five	
191	送张十二参军赴蜀州因呈杨五侍御	
	Seeing Off Adjutant Chang on His Way to Shu, Presented to Censor Yang	
193	赠陈二补阙	
	Presented to Chen Two, Remonstrant	
195	病后过王倚饮赠歌	
	After Being Sick, I Visited E Wang for a Drink and Presented Him This Song	
198	送裴二虬作尉永嘉	
	Seeing Off Chiu P'ei Two to His Post as Sheriff in E'erfair	
199	赠献纳使起居田舍人澄	
	Presented to Ch'eng Tien, Petition Commissioner and Imperial Servant	
200	崔驸马山亭宴集	
	A Banquet at Adjunct Groom Ts'ui's Mountain Pavilion	
201	示从孙济	
	Shown to My Grandnephew Chi	
204	九日寄岑参	
	On the Double Ninth: to Shen Ts'en	
207	叹庭前甘菊花	
	Sighing over Sweet Chrysanthemums in the Yard	
209	承沈八丈东美除膳部员外，阻雨未遂驰贺，奉寄此诗	
	Sir Tungmei Shen Great Eight Has Been Made Vice-Director of the Catering Department; I Am Not Able to Gallop Off to Congratulate Him Due to the Rain. So Respectfully I Send Him This Poem	
212	苦雨奉寄陇西公兼呈王征士	
	The Pain of the Rain: Respectfully Sent to Lord West Bulge and Presented to Recruit Wang	
215	秋雨叹三首	
	Sighing over Autumn Rain, Three Poems	
219	奉赠太常张卿二十韵	
	Respectfully Presented to Chang, Chamberlain for Ceremonials	

223	上韦左相二十韵（见素）	
	Presented to Chiensu Wei, Premier of the Left	
227	沙苑行	
	Sand Park: A Ballad	
230	桥陵诗三十韵因呈县内诸官	
	Poem on Bridge Hill, to Be Shown to the Officials of the County	
236	送蔡希鲁都尉还陇右因寄高三十五书记	
	Seeing Commander Hsilu Ts'ai Off on His Return to Bulge Right, Thereby I Write to Secretary Kao Thirty-Five	
239	醉歌行	
	A Drunken Song	
242	陪李金吾花下饮	
	Accompanying Li Drinking Amid Flowers	
243	官定后戏赠	
	Playfully Presented After My Post Was Decided	
244	去矣行	
	Gone	
245	夜听许十诵诗爱而有作	
	Listening to Hsu Ten Chanting a Poem at Night and Writing Mine as I'm Perturbed	
248	戏简郑广文虔兼呈苏司业源明	
	A Playful Message to Dr. Chien Cheng, Delivered to Yüanming Su, Director of Studies, as Well	
250	夏日李公见访	
	Visited by Lord Li on a Summer Day	
252	天育骠骑歌	
	A Song for the Mount of the Imperial Stables	
254	骢马行	
	The Dappled Gray	
257	魏将军歌	
	Song for General Wei	
260	白水明府舅宅喜雨（得过字）	
	Happy with the Rain at the House of My Uncle, Magistrate of Whitewater	

261	九日杨奉先会白水崔明府	
	On the Double Ninth Yang, Magistrate of Fenghsien County, Meets with Ts'ui, Magistrate of Whitewater County	
263	自京赴奉先县咏怀五百字	
	My Trip from the Capital to Fenghsien County, a Hundred Lines	
271	甘园	
	The Orange Orchard	
272	秦州杂诗二十首（其十六）	
	Miscellanies of Ch'inchow, Twenty Poems (No. 16)	
273	春夜喜雨	
	A Blessing Rain on a Spring Night	
274	咏怀古迹（其一）	
	Chanting Historical Sites (No. 1)	
276	寄从孙崇简	
	Sent to My Grandnephew Ch'ungchien Tu	
278	闻斛斯六官未归	
	Hearing That the Official Hussu Has Not Returned	
279	送路六侍御入朝	
	Seeing Off Attendant Censor Lu Six to Court	
280	江上值水如海势聊短述	
	By the River I Come on Water Looking Like a Sea: A Short Account	
281	中宵	
	Midnight	
282	晓望	
	A Dawn View	
284	奉酬李都督表丈早春作	
	Respectfully to My Uncle, Governor Li's *Written in Early Spring*	
285	**译者简介**	
	About the Translator	

曲江二首(其一)

一片花飞减却春，
风飘万点正愁人。
且看欲尽花经眼，
莫厌伤多酒入唇。
江上小堂巢翡翠，
苑边高冢卧麒麟，
细推物理须行乐，
何用浮名绊此身。

Drinking Vis-à-vis the Bent River (No. 1)

The beauty of spring fades as blossoms fly;
The petals in the wind make me repine.
Do enjoy the blooms while they pass the eye;
Mind not how much you drink, do drink your wine;
In the tower riverside kingfishers nest.
By Park unicorns sleep on the tomb mound;
By nature, of life we should make the best;
Why should we by ranks or fame be bound?

* the Bent River: Ch'uchiang if transliterated, a royal park of T'ang, located in the southeast of Long Peace, the capital.
* kingfisher: also called halcyon, a mythical bird, said to have nested on the sea at the time of the winter solstice, when the sea was supposed to become calm.
* unicorn: a fabulous deer-like animal with one horn, a symbol of saintliness and divinity in Chinese culture. Confucius lamented the death of a unicorn captured and hence stopped compiling *The Spring and Autumn Annals* and died before long.

春　望

国破山河在，
城春草木深。
感时花溅泪，
恨别鸟惊心。
烽火连三月，
家书抵万金。
白头搔更短，
浑欲不胜簪。

A View of Spring

The state broken, the land we keep;
The spring grass in the town grows deep.
Touched by hard times, blossoms shed tears;
Dispersed by war, birds cringe in fears.
For months the beacon fires have run;
News from home's warmer than the sun.
Scratching my head, I feel hair thin,
Which could not hold up my hat pin.

* hard times: referring to Lushan An's Rebellion. In the eleventh moon of A.D. 755, Lushan An turned traitor and captured cities and forts in a few months, forcing the emperor to flee to Ssuch'uan.
* beacon: a prominent building set on a wall or hill or a similar position, as a guide or warning to garrison generals or others.

江畔独步寻花

黄四娘家花满蹊，
千朵万朵压枝低。
留连戏蝶时时舞，
自在娇莺恰恰啼。

Looking for Flowers Alone on the Bank

Myriad blossoms weigh down the twigs;
Sis Huang's place is strewn with petals.
The butterflies flutter in hued figs;
"Chat, chat", a charming bird rattles.

* the Bank: referring to the Flower Washing Stream by Fu Tu's Thatched Cottage.
* Sis Huang: Fu Tu's neighbor when he lived in Silkton, i.e. Ch'engtu.
* butterfly: any of various families of lepidopteran insects active in the day-time, having a sucking mouthpart, slender body, rope-like, knobbed antennae, and four broad, usually brightly colored, membraneous wings.

赠 花 卿

锦城丝管日纷纷，
半入江风半入云。
此曲只应天上有，
人间能得几回闻。

To Hua, a General

In Silkton there the tune of flutes or strings
Half to a river wind, half to clouds rings.
Such music should be a Heavenly tune;
One can only hear once in a blue moon.

* Hua: General Hua under Kuangyin Ts'ui, Mayor of Ch'engtu.
* Silkton: the other name of Ch'engtu for it was a town of silk.

绝句二首(其一)

迟日江山丽,
春风花草香。
泥融飞燕子,
沙暖睡鸳鸯。

A Quatrain Minor (No. 1)

Spring paints all, the stream and the hills;
The breeze blows fragrance to expand.
Swallows fly with mud in their bills;
Mandarin ducks sleep on warm sand.

* quatrain minor: a Chinese four-line poem with five characters each line, tetrameter by analogy in its English translation. A quatrain major is one with seven characters each line, pentameter in its equivalent English.
* swallow: a passerine bird, with short broad, depressed bill, long pointed wings, and forked tail, noted for fleeting flight and migratory habits. In Chinese culture, swallows are welcome to live with a family with their nest on a beam of a sitting room.
* mandarin ducks: web-footed, short-legged, broad-billed water birds that always appear in loving pairs; once one of a couple is caught, the other will die for having lost its mate. It is an entrenched metaphor for couples in Chinese culture.

绝句二首(其二)

江碧鸟逾白,
山青花欲燃。
今春看又过,
何日是归年?

A Quatrain Minor (No. 2)

The river blue, birds are more white;
The mountain green, flowers would burn.
The springtime is now on the flight;
Which year on earth can I return?

月夜忆舍弟

戍鼓断人行，
边秋一雁声。
露从今夜白，
月是故乡明。
有弟皆分散，
无家问死生。
寄书长不达，
况乃未休兵。

Missing My Brothers on a Moonlit Night

Watch drum on and off, traffics cease;
The border hears shrills of wild geese.
Autumn dew turns frost from tonight;
My town should see the moon so bright.
My brothers were driven asunder;
"Are they alive or dead?" I wonder.
It's long for news to come to hand,
And now the war fire sears my land.

* my brothers: Fu Tu had four brothers: Ying Tu, Kuan Tu, Feng Tu and Chan Tu.
* watch drum: a drum on a watch tower.
* wild goose: an undomesticated goose that is caring and responsible, taken as a symbol of benevolence, righteousness, good manner, wisdom, and faith in Chinese culture.
* Autumn dew turns frost from tonight: referring to White Dew, the fifteenth of the twenty-four terms of the year.

* the moon: the satellite of the earth, an important image in Chinese literature or culture as it can evoke many associations such as solitude and nostalgia on the one hand, and purity, brightness and happy reunions on the other. In traditional times, there used to be a "moon-viewing party" at which people sat quietly on a moonlit night, particularly under a full moon, and thought of a loved one or loved ones far away, inside the vast reaches of China proper and even overseas, who might themselves be sitting sharing the same moon at the same time, in the same reverent silence.
* the war fire: referring to the battle between Shihming Shih, the rebel, and Kuangpi Li, a T'ang general.

旅 夜 书 怀

细草微风岸，
危樯独夜舟。
星垂平野阔，
月涌大江流。
名岂文章著，
官应老病休。
飘飘何所似，
天地一沙鸥。

Traveling at Night

Thin grass ashore stirs with a blast;
My boat sails at night, a high mast.
The stars hang low o'er the broad plain;
The moonlit river pours amain.
One's not famed from a writing quill;
He should retire when old and ill.
Drifting, drifting, where shall I lie,
A seagull between sea and sky?

* seagull: a kind of sea bird, any gull or large tern, a symbol of clean integrity. The seagulls in the Wordist book *Sir Line* (Liehtzu) are particularly sensitive to impurity of motive and will make friends only with the completely guileless and disinterested. It is also used as a metaphor for drifting.

客　　至

舍南舍北皆春水，
但见群鸥日日来。
花径不曾缘客扫，
蓬门今始为君开。
盘飧市远无兼味，
樽酒家贫只旧醅。
肯与邻翁相对饮，
隔篱呼取尽馀杯。

A Friend's Visit

The spring water north and south of my hut,
Day in day out but seagulls come to view.
I've never swept my petal-strewn path but
Today my thatched gate is opened for you.
Town off, I've no dainties to entertain;
All I have to drink is home-brewed wine.
Drink with my old neighbor if you would fain,
I'll invite him across the fence to dine.

* a friend: referring to Magistrate Ts'ui.
* seagull: a kind of sea bird, any gull or large tern, a symbol of clean integrity. The seagulls in the Wordist book *Sir Line* (Liehtzu) are particularly sensitive to impurity of motive and will make friends only with the completely guileless and disinterested. It is also used as a metaphor for drifting.
* All I have to drink is home-brewed wine: Fu Tu was expressing his guilt that he could not treat his friend with better wine.

绝句漫兴(其一)

眼见客愁愁不醒,
无赖春色到江亭。
即遣花开深造次,
便教莺语太丁宁。

A Quatrain Impromptu (No. 1)

I find myself sad and in sadness drowned;
Spring, uncalled for, comes to the pavilion.
It makes flowers burst all over the ground,
And bids orioles babble all that jargon.

* the pavilion: the one at the Flower Washing Stream.
* oriole: golden oriole, one of the family of passerine birds, which looks bright yellow with contrasting black wings and sings beautiful songs.

绝句漫兴(其三)

熟知茅斋绝低小,
江上燕子故来频。
衔泥点污琴书内,
更接飞虫打着人。

A Quatrain Impromptu (No. 3)

The swallows come in again and again,
Well knowing so small my thatched cottage be.
The mud in their bills drops to my book stain,
And more, chasing flying bugs, they bump me.

* swallow: a passerine black bird, with short broad, depressed bill, long pointed wings, and forked tail, noted for fleeting flight and migratory habits. In Chinese culture, swallows are welcome to live with a family with their nest on a beam.

绝句漫兴(其七)

糁径杨花铺白毡,
点溪荷叶叠青钱。
笋根雉子无人见,
沙上凫雏傍母眠。

A Quatrain Impromptu (No. 7)

The path is strewn with white poplar catkins;
The lotus leaves o'erlap like green coins.
The young bamboo shoots nobody can see;
By their mother the ducklings asleep be.

* poplar catkin: catkin from dioecious trees and bushes of the willow family called poplars common in China.
* bamboo shoots: tender bamboo sprouts, which may be dried for storage, are used as a delicacy in China.

戏为六绝句(其六)

未及前贤更勿疑,
递相祖述复先谁。
别裁伪体亲风雅,
转益多师是汝师。

Six Quatrains for Fun (No. 6)

Sure, we've ne'er surpassed the old sages,
Because our cliches o'erfill the pages.
Distinguish what is false and what is true;
Learn from all, copy none, and you'll well do.

* Distinguish what is false and what is true: follow the tradition kept in *The Book of Songs*, which reproves what is false and eulogizes what is true.

漫 成 一 首

江月去人只数尺，
风灯照夜欲三更。
沙头宿鹭联拳静，
船尾跳鱼拨剌鸣。

An Impromptu

The moon downstream shines a few feet away;
The boat lantern glows to herald the day.
The egrets snuggle on the shoal, all serene;
A fish jumps aft, a-splashing with its fin.

* egret: a heron characterized, in the breeding season, by long and loose plumes drooping over the tail, usually white plumage.

不　见

不见李生久，
佯狂真可哀。
世人皆欲杀，
吾意独怜才。
敏捷诗千首，
飘零酒一杯。
匡山读书处，
头白好归来。

It's Long Since I Saw Him

It's long since I saw Pai Li last;
How sad he feigns to run insane.
All men have a mind to him blast;
My fond feelings for him remain.
A thousand poems he's produced;
Drifting, he has a cup in hand.
At Mt. Square books he perused;
Now old, do come back to your land.

* Pai Li: One of the greatest poets in High T'ang. He was born in A.D. 701, as many historians agree, and died in A.D. 762, as was recorded. Saliently, he was a poet, then a drunkard, then a swordsman, a traveler, a recluse, and so on. God of Wine he called himself, Fallen Immortal his friend called him, and Fairy of Poetry we all call him. He is a miracle and mystery, as his poems may reveal.
* It's long since I saw Pai Li last: Fu Tu and Pai Li left each other in A.D. 745, and when Fu Tu wrote this poem, they had not met for sixteen years.

* All men have a mind to him blast: Pai Li was jailed in Bankshine and then exiled to Nightboy because it was believed that he committed treason for having joined Prince E'er's clique, the rebels against T'ang during the Lushan An Rebellion.
* Mt. Square: about 25 kilometers from Green Lotus, Pai Li's hometown, and Pai Li studied and practiced swordplay for ten years in the Mt. Square Academy here.

后　　游

寺忆新游处，
桥怜再渡时。
江山如有待，
花柳更无私。
野润烟光薄，
沙暄日色迟。
客愁全为减，
舍此复何之。

A Revisit

The temple old I recollect;
The bridge lovely I recall.
Rivers, mountains do me expect,
Flowers, willows, not mean at all.
The mist nurtures the barren fields;
The eve sun sets the sand aglow.
My mood to natural charm yields;
How lovely, where else can I go?

* a revisit: In A.D. 761, Fu Tu visited Meditation Temple in Newford (now Under Ssuch'uan Province) and wrote *A Visit to Mediation Temple*, and in the same year he came here again, hence the poem.
* willow: any of a large genus of shrubs and trees related to the poplars, having generally smooth branches, and often long, slender, pliant, and sometimes pendent branchlets, which seem to be bidding farewell or sweeping amorously.

秋兴八首(其三)

千家山郭静朝晖，
日日江楼坐翠微。
信宿渔人还泛泛，
清秋燕子故飞飞。
匡衡抗疏功名薄，
刘向传经心事违。
同学少年多不贱，
五陵衣马自轻肥。

An Impulse on an Autumn Day, Eight Poems (No. 3)

All households in the hills bask in dawn light;
Each day sitting upstairs I face the hill.
The fishermen float and float through the night;
The swallows fly and fly in autumn chill.
Like Square, I remonstrated but woe is me!
Like Hsiang, I'd collate books but failed like that.
My schoolmates remain in power, care-free;
At Fivehills, in fur, they ride high steeds fat.

* swallow: a passerine black bird, with short broad, depressed bill, long pointed wings, and forked tail, noted for fleeting flight and migratory habits. In Chinese culture, swallows are welcome to live with a family with their nest on a beam.
* Square: Scale Square, Heng K'uang if transliterated, a Confucian scholar in Western Han dynasty and a prime minister.

* Hsiang: Hsiang Liu (cir. 77 B.C.– 6 B.C.), a Confucian classicist, bibliographer, and litterateur in the Han dynasty.
* Fivehills: near Long Peace.

玉台观

浩劫因王造,
平台访古游。
彩云萧史驻,
文字鲁恭留。
宫阙通群帝,
乾坤到十洲。
人传有笙鹤,
时过此山头。

The Celestial Wordist Abbey

The Abbey was by Prince T'eng built;
To Plain Mound I've come a long way.
Flute Man all those colored clouds gilt;
The Prince's poems last till today.
The abbey, to meet gods, towers high;
The world with all the fresco fills.
One oft hears the flute and crane cry
And the player pass the north hills.

* the Celestial Wordist Abbey: in Langchung County under today's Ssuch'uan Province, built by Prince of T'eng, i.e. Yüanying Li (A.D. 628 – A.D. 684), Emperor Grandsire's younger brother, famous for his revelry.
* Plain Mound: name of an old place northeast of Shangchiu, here a metaphor for the Celestial Wordist Abbey.
* Flute Man: a legendary flute player in the Spring and Autumn period. Lord Solemn married his daughter, Jade Player, to him. The couple became immortals and went to

Heaven, the man riding a dragon and his wife riding a phoenix.
* colored clouds: referring to those on the fresco.
* One oft hears the flute and crane cry: an allusion to Prince of Front who rose to the sky astride a crane while playing the flute.
* crane: one of a family of large, long-necked, long-legged, heron-like birds allied to the rails, a symbol of integrity and longevity in Chinese culture, only second to the phoenix in cultural importance.

倦　　夜

竹凉侵卧内，
野月满庭隅。
重露成涓滴，
稀星乍有无。
暗飞萤自照，
水宿鸟相呼。
万事干戈里，
空悲清夜徂。

A Tired Night

The bamboo cold invades my bed;
Much moonlight is to the yard shed.
Bit by bit drips the heavy dew;
There twinkle stars, but just a few.
In the dark fireflies alone glow;
The water birds each to each coo.
The war haunts me once and again;
The night passes like this in vain.

* a tired night: This poem was composed in A.D. 764, when the Lushan An's Rebellion was just quieted down and Tibetans molested Mid Plain and took over Long Peace.
* bamboo: a tall, tree-like or shrubby grass in tropical and semi-tropical regions, a symbol of integrity and altitude, one of the four most important images in Chinese literature, which are wintersweet, orchid, bamboo and chrysanthemum.
* firefly: any of a family (*Lampyridae*) of winged beetles, active at night, whose abdomens usually glow with a luminescent light.

孤　　雁

孤雁不饮啄，
飞鸣声念群。
谁怜一片影，
相失万重云？
望尽似犹见，
哀多如更闻。
野鸦无意绪，
鸣噪自纷纷。

The Wild Goose Astray

The wild goose has no mood for food
And shrieks loud for the flock: oh, nay.
Its shadow who pities? Who would?
From the cloud it has gone astray.
It seems to have seen them afar
And heard their cries and whoops so sad.
The ravens don't know how things are,
Making a din, cawing like mad.

* The Wild Goose Astray: This poem was composed when Fu Tu sojourned in K'uichow.
* wild goose: an undomesticated goose that is caring and responsible, taken as a symbol of benevolence, righteousness, good manner, wisdom and faith in Chinese culture.
* raven: a large omnivorous, crow-like bird (*Corvus corax*), having lustrous black plumage, with the feathers of the throat elongated and lanceolate.

望 岳

岱宗夫如何，
齐鲁青未了。
造化锺神秀，
阴阳割昏晓。
荡胸生曾云，
决眦入归鸟。
会当凌绝顶，
一览众山小。

Looking at Mt. Arch

Behold Mt. Arch, how high it stands!
Its green o'er Ch'i and Lu expands.
The nature's made it a great one,
Shade as its moon, shine as its sun.
Unto my chest thick clouds arise;
And homing birds fly to my eyes.
When I reach the top to view all,
All mountains under me are small.

* Mt. Arch: one of the Five Mountains in China, located in Shantung Province, along with Mt. Ever in Shanhsi, Mt. Scale in Hunan, Mt. Flora in Sha'anhsi, and Mt. Tower in Honan. Mt. Arch is the most sacred of the five, because 72 sovereigns in prehistoric China made sacrifices to the god of the mountain and 12 emperors made sacrifices from the Ch'in dynasty to the Ch'ing dynasty, clearly recorded in history books.
* Ch'i and Lu: The north side of Mt. Arch was the ancient State of Ch'i; its south side was the State of Lu.

游龙门奉先寺

已从招提游，
更宿招提境。
阴壑生虚籁，
月林散清影。
天阙象纬逼，
云卧衣裳冷。
欲觉闻晨钟，
令人发深省。

Visiting Sage-Adoring Temple at Dragongate

To the temple here I have been
And now stay o'ernight on the scene.
The shady vale utters void air,
The moonlit wood sways twigs fair.
Constellations hang low, behold;
My clothes in clouds feel cold.
I hear the dawning bell toll there
While more and more I am aware.

* Dragongate: one of the four most famous grottoes in China, located in Loshine under today's Honan Province.

登兖州城楼

东郡趋庭日，
南楼纵目初。
浮云连海岱，
平野入青徐。
孤嶂秦碑在，
荒城鲁殿馀。
从来多古意，
临眺独踌躇。

Climbing the Gate Tower of Yanchow

In East Lu's yard I've come to stay.
From south tower I look far away.
Clouds drift to Mt. Arch and the blue,
The vast moors spread to Ch'ing and Hsu.
The Ch'in Stele's there on the cliff tall,
Ruins of the Lu palace, the ruined wall.
With so many thoughts of the past,
I pace alone, my glance down cast.

* East Lu's yard I've come to stay: Fu Tu's father held a minor position at Yanchow, and this was his base for Fu Tu's travels in eastern China.
* East Lu: referring to Yanchow, but in the Han dynasty, East Lu was nine of the prefectures under Yanchow.
* Mt. Arch: one of the Five Mountains in China, located in Shantung Province, along with Mt. Ever in Shanhsi, Mt. Scale in Hunan, Mt. Flora in Sha'anhsi, and Mt. Tower in Honan. Mt. Arch is the most sacred of the five, because 72 sovereigns in prehistoric

China made sacrifices to the god of the mountain and 12 emperors made sacrifices from the Ch'in dynasty to the Ch'ing dynasty, clearly recorded in history books.
* the blue: referring to Surge Sea (Pohai).
* Ch'ing and Hsu: two realms or areas of the nine realms of China, made clear by Worm.
* Ch'in Stele: a tablet for the recording of Emperor First's merit when He toured Mt. Peaks (Mt. E) in today's Shantung Province.
* the cliff: referring to Mt. Peaks.
* the Lu palace: Lu Soul Bright Hall built by Prince of Kung, a son of Emperor Scene's in the Han dynasty, in Chockfull (Ch'üfu).

题张氏隐居二首
On Chang's Hermitage, Two Poems

其 一

春山无伴独相求，
伐木丁丁山更幽。
涧道馀寒历冰雪，
石门斜日到林丘。
不贪夜识金银气，
远害朝看麋鹿游。
乘兴杳然迷出处，
对君疑是泛虚舟。

No. 1

To spring mountains for you alone I go,
The axe hewing wood, the mountains grew still.
Chill on the creek-by road, ice and snow,
The stonegate overlooks your wooded hill.
Not greedy, the night sees auras there are,
Far from harm, the dawn looks on deer about.
I forget office on my whim afar;
An empty boat adrift you are I doubt.

---

* the stonegate: the stone gate of the Chi River in Lin-e County. And it may refer to Mt. Stonegate, a famous mountain in Good E'er. When Lingyün Hsieh governed Good E'er, he once visited Mt. Stonegate and composed poems there.

其 二

之子时相见，
邀人晚兴留。
雾潭鳣发发，
春草鹿呦呦。
杜酒偏劳劝，
张梨不外求。
前村山路险，
归醉每无愁。

No. 2

This gentleman often meets me,
Invited, until late I stay.
A pool neaththe skies, sturgeon be;
Among the spring plants the deer play.
He truly urges on me Tu's wine;
Chang's pears I do not seek elsewhere.
The village-hill roaddoes entwine;
Going home drunk, I'm free of care.

* sturgeon: also called Northern snakehead, which is about two meters long and can be as long as five meters, any of a family of large, edible, primitive bony fishes having rows of spiny plates along the body and a projecting snout.
* Tu's wine: Fu Tu's homemade wine.
  Chang's pears: a famous produce from Chang's Grand Dale according to *Yueh Pan's Ode to Idle Life*, here referring to the pears produced by another Chang, Fu Tu's friend.

刘九法曹郑瑕丘石门宴集

秋水清无底，
萧然静客心。
掾曹乘逸兴，
鞍马去相寻。
能吏逢联璧，
华筵直一金。
晚来横吹好，
泓下亦龙吟。

Liu of the Law Section and Cheng of Hsiachiu Hold a Banquet at Mt. Stonegate

This autumn waters deep and clear,
The briskness makes the guests all cheer.
The captain follows his own mind;
Astride a horse someone he'd find.
An able clerk meets the paired jade;
This banquet costs much, a gold paid.
Now it's late, good is the flute tune;
The dragon in the flood does croon.

* gold: a monetary unit used in ancient China. One gold is about 60 grams of gold.
* dragon: a fabulous serpent-like giant winged animal that can change its girth and length, a totem of the Chinese nation, a symbol of benevolence and sovereignty in Chinese culture, the totem of all Chinese across the world.

与任城许主簿游南池

秋水通沟洫，
城隅集小船。
晚凉看洗马，
森木乱鸣蝉。
菱熟经时雨，
蒲荒八月天。
晨朝降白露，
遥忆旧青毡。

Visiting South Pool with Assistant Magistrate Hsu of Jench'eng

Autumn in the field makes a pool,
We board a small boat at the wall.
The horses groomed in the dusk cool;
The thick trees have cicadas call.
Rain-blessed water chestnuts ripe grow,
Mid-autumn sees reeds that rank are.
The dawn brings down the shining dew,
And brings me the green felt afar.

* South Pool: a pool southeast of Jench'eng at that time.
* Jench'eng: Jench'eng County, today's Chining, Shantung Province.
* cicada: a homopterous insect that sings its song of summer and shrills in autumn, a symbol of death and resurrection in Chinese culture because of its metamorphosis and recycle. Therefore, in ancient China, a jade cicada figure was put in the mouth of a dead body with such an intention of eternal life.

* water chestnut: the hard horned edible fruit of an aquatic plant.
* reed: the slender, frequently jointed stem of certain tall grasses growing in wet places or in grasses themselves. A frosted reed is an image of the white hair of one getting old or suffering a mishap.
* green felt: a Confucian scholar's heritage from older generations. According to *Chin Book* , when a thief stole into the calligrapher Hsienchih Wang's room, the latter said: "Please leave that green felt; it's my heirloom. You can take anything else." Therefore, green felt is used as a synonym of heritage or heirloom.

对雨书怀走邀许主簿

东岳云峰起,
溶溶满太虚。
震雷翻幕燕,
骤雨落河鱼。
座对贤人酒,
门听长者车。
相邀愧泥泞,
骑马到阶除。

Writing My Feelings Facing the Rain, I Rush to Send Off an Invitation to Assistant Magistrate Hsu

Clouded peaks rise at the East Hill,
Then they billow the Void to fill.
Peals of thunder makes swallows shrink,
A shower causes the fish to sink.
The sage's wine faces where I wait;
My senior's car comes to the gate.
Of all the mire I do feel shame;
You ride to my steps all the same.

* the East Hills: located in today's Shaohsing, Chechiang Province, the hills where An Hsieh (A.D. 320 - A.D. 385), a statesman and litterateur with high reputation, lived with ease and kept declining official positions until he was in his forties. It is often used as a metaphor for reclusion.
* the Void: a Wordist term meaning nothingness, the beginning of everything and the use of everything.

巳上人茅斋

巳公茅屋下，
可以赋新诗。
枕簟入林僻，
茶瓜留客迟。
江莲摇白羽，
天棘蔓青丝。
空忝许询辈，
难酬支遁词。

The Thatched Study of Reverend Ssu

Neath the thatched roof of Master Ssu,
One may compose good verses new.
In the woods laid pillow and mat,
O'er melon and tea the guests chat.
Lotuses their white plumes display;
Asparagales their foliage sway.
I feel shy to stay with Hsun Hsu;
It's hard to answer Flee Free, too.

* asparagale: formally called *asparagus cochinchinensis*, perennial herb of the lily family.
* Hsun Hsu: an Eastern Chin writer, Buddhist and a representative of metaphysical poetry, listened to the famous monk Flee Free expound sutras. Everyone thought that Hsun Hsu would be unable to raise any objections; but when Hsun Hsu in turn offered an objection, they thought Flee Free too could not answer. The two kept on in dialogue. Fu Tu modestly claims not to be the equal of Hsun Hsu, while Reverend Ssu is comparable to Flee Free.
* Flee Free: Flee Free (A.D. 314 - A.D. 366), a high monk and litterateur in the Eastern Chin dynasty.

房兵曹胡马

胡马大宛名，
锋棱瘦骨成。
竹批双耳峻，
风入四蹄轻。
所向无空阔，
真堪托死生。
骁腾有如此，
万里可横行。

The Hun Horse of Fang, an Officer of the War Section

The Hun horse, of Ferghana fame,
So sharp-edged, its thin bones show might.
Bamboo pared, its two ears jut,
Wind enters its four hooves light.
Where it heads, no space is too vast;
For life it could be trusted right.
Since it bounds on like this with might,
It can fly a thousand leagues right.

* Hun: war-like nomadic peoples occupying vast regions from Mongolia to Central Asia in Chinese history, especially during the Han dynasty. They were a headache and a constant menace on China's western and northern borders.
* Ferghana: an ancient state existing in Ferghana Basin. According to historical records, the horse from Ferghana is a precious kind. As it sprints, its shoulders swell and it sweats like bleeding.

* Bamboo pared, its two ears jut: a fine horse's ears stand upright like pared bamboo or bamboo canisters when it runs, hence "bamboo pared" is used as a metonymy for a fine horse.
* bamboo: a tall, tree-like or shrubby grass in tropical and semi-tropical regions, a symbol of integrity and altitude, one of the four most important images in Chinese literature, which are wintersweet, orchid, bamboo and chrysanthemum.

画 鹰

素练风霜起，
苍鹰画作殊。
㩍身思狡兔，
侧目似愁胡。
绦镟光堪摘，
轩楹势可呼。
何当击凡鸟，
毛血洒平芜。

A Painted Hawk

Frosty winds rise from plain white silk,
A gray hawk, so wondrously drawn.
Perked up, it aims at the sly hare,
It looks sidelong, like a sad Hun.
One could grasp light from its tie-ring,
On the porch poised it can remain.
When will it strike the common birds?
Blood and feathers sprinkling the plain.

* hawk: a diurnal bird of prey, notable for keen sight and strong flight, usually used as a metaphor for one who takes military means in contrast with a dove, one who tries to find peaceful solutions.
* Hun: nomadic barbarians west and north of China, who had no trade but battle and carnage, no fields or ploughlands but only wastes where white bones lay scattered over yellow sands.

过宋员外之问旧庄

宋公旧池馆，
零落守阳阿。
枉道祇从入，
吟诗许更过。
淹留问耆老，
寂寞向山河。
更识将军树，
悲风日暮多。

A Visit to Ministry Councilor Chihwen Sung's Former Estate

Lo, Lord Sung's former pool and lodge
In Mt. Firstshine's folds lonely lie.
I turn and enter on my own,
To chant again, can I stop by?
I linger, asking the old folks,
Facing rivers and mountains high.
The general's tree I also know;
At dusk a sad wind does fast blow.

* Chihwen Sung: Chihwen Sung (cir. A.D. 656 – A.D. 712), a famous and important T'ang poet before Fu Tu's generation.
* Firstshine: Mt. Firstshine, located in today's Weiyüan County. It is the highest of all mountains there, so it is the first to receive sunshine, hence the name, and it is famous because two princes from the State of Lonebamboo called Bowone and Straightthree died of starvation here for their rectitude.

夜宴左氏庄

林风纤月落,
衣露静琴张。
暗水流花径,
春星带草堂。
检书烧烛短,
看剑引杯长。
诗罢闻吴咏,
扁舟意不忘。

A Night Banquet at Ts'o's Estate

The moon sees wind to the woods blow,
Clothes touched with dew, a calm lute's strung.
On the flowered path, unseen streams flow;
O'er the thatched hall spring stars are hung.
I check books, candle flickers on,
Swords viewed, the cups are passed to all.
A verse is read in Wu once done,
Whilst my small canoe I recall.

临邑舍弟书至,苦雨,黄河泛溢,堤防之患,簿领所忧,因寄此诗用宽其意

二仪积风雨,
百谷漏波涛。
闻道洪河坼,
遥连沧海高。
职司忧悄悄,
郡国诉嗷嗷。
舍弟卑栖邑,
防川领簿曹。
尺书前日至,
版筑不时操。
难假鼋鼍力,
空瞻乌鹊毛。
燕南吹畎亩,
济上没蓬蒿。
螺蚌满近郭,
蛟螭乘九皋。
徐关深水府,
碣石小秋毫。
白屋留孤树,
青天失万艘。
吾衰同泛梗,
利涉想蟠桃。
却倚天涯钓,
犹能掣巨鳌。

A Letter Arrives from My Brother at Lin-e; the Rain Causes the Yellow River to Overflow; the Officials Are Worried About the Dikes. Therefore I Send this Poem to Appease Him.

The Two Norms gather wind and rain,
All the valleys o'erfilled remain.
I've heard if the river breaks through,
It'll reach afar and raise the blue.
Those in charge with illness come down,
All domains complain, all in woe.
My brother's a poor job downtown,
A dike clerk doing work like so.
Days ago a letter came along:
To work the plank dyke they remain.
Like tortoise and lizards, they're strong;
One looks for magpie down in vain.
South of Yan o'er fields it blows down,
By the Chi it drowns all the grass.
Conches and oysters fill the town,
Dragons mount o'er Nine Bogs, alas.
Hsu Pass flooded due to the rain,
The rock's a small wisp in fall frost.
By poor houses lone trees remain,
Ten thousand boats neath the blue lost.
In my decline I am a stick afloat,
The Isles is "good to go", I'm told.
But I will trust a fishing boat,
And giant turtles could be controlled.

* In A.D. 741 there was a great flood in the Honan region covering 24 prefectures. Fu Tu's brother was a secretary in neighboring Shantung, where the Yellow River had flooded the levees.
* the Yellow River: the second longest river in China, flowing through Loess Plataeu, hence yellow water all the way. 5,464 kilometers long, with a drainage area of 752,443 square kilometers, it has been regarded as the cradle of Chinese civilization. As legend goes, the river derived from a yellow dragon that, couchant on Midland Plain, ate yellow soil, flooded crops, devoured people and stock, and was finally tamed by Great Worm, the First King of Hsia (21 B.C.- 16 B.C.).
* the Two Norms: referring to Heaven and earth.
* tortoise: a turtle, especially one that lives on earth, as any of a worldwide family.
* lizard: any of various reptiles, as an agama, basilisk, chameleon, geko, glass snake, horned toad, iguana, monitor, or skink.
* conch: the large, spiral, univalve shell of any of various marine mollusks, often used as a trumpet.
* oyster: any of various bivalve mollusks with an irregularly shaped, unequal shell, living attached to rocks, other shells, etc., and widely used as food.
* dragon: Though variously understood as a large reptile, a marine monster, a jackal and Satan incarnate, it is also a kind protector in folklore and myth in Western culture, a mascot on the national flag of Wales. And in the East, it has been represented as a fabulous serpent-like giant winged animal that can change its length and girth, a totem of the Chinese nation and a symbol of benevolence and sovereignty in Chinese culture.
* Nine Bogs: a bending and twisting marshland.
* the Isles is "good to go": "good to go" is a positive judgment in the hexagrams of the classic of *Changes*. Fu Tu playfully suggests that he may be swept away, but it might carry him to the Fairy Isles on East Sea.
* turtle: referring to a tortoise-like beast in mythology. In China, tablets of great importance were usually carried on the back of a turtle-like creature, which is said to be a figure of the sixth son of the dragon, who is strong and keen on carrying a heavy load.

假　　山

天宝初，南曹小司寇舅于我太夫人堂下垒土为山，一匮盈尺，以代彼朽木，承诸焚香瓷瓯，瓯甚安矣。旁植慈竹，盖兹数峰，嵚岑婵娟，宛有尘外数致。乃不知兴之所至，而作是诗。

一匮功盈尺，
三峰意出群。
望中疑在野，
幽处欲生云。
慈竹春阴覆，
香炉晓势分。
惟南将献寿，
佳气日氛氲。

An Artificial Mountain

At the beginning of the Heaven-blessed Reign, my uncle (on my mother's side), the Vice-Director of the Organization Department, heaped earth into a mountain beside my grandmother's hall. A basketful of earth a full foot high took the place of the rotten wood of a censer stand, and it held all the bowls for burning incense, which were steady indeed. Beside it he planted bamboo (*sinocalamus*). The peaks, craggy heights, and lithe bamboo convey the quality of transcending the dust world. So, I write this poem, not realizing how I am carried away.

One basketful, a foot of grace,
Three peaks, his conception plan grand.

I seem in the wild as I gaze,
Clouds will rise from the lonely land.
Kind bamboo will veil it with spring,
The Censer's dawn form is discerned.
The South Hill will to her bliss bring,
With daily blessed vapors up turned.

* Heaven-blessed: the title of Emperor Deepsire's reign which lasted from the first moon of A.D. 742 to the seventh moon of A.D. 756, during which broke out the Lushan An Rebellion.
* kind bamboo: The bamboo is a tall, tree-like or shrubby grass in tropical and semi-tropical regions, a symbol of integrity and altitude, one of the four most important images in Chinese literature. The kind bamboo is a species of bamboo growing in Wu and Shu in China. As recorded, in the third year of Emperor Letter of Han's reign, a kind of bamboo put forth in front of White Tiger Hall, and the ministers wrote verse about it, and it came to be known as kind bamboo.
* the Censer: one of the peaks of Mt. Lodge, so-called because its clouds were like smoke. Fu Tu here is clearly playing on the function of the artificial mountain as a censer stand.
* the South Hill: also known as the South Mountains, Mt. Great One, Mt. Earthlungs, the mountains south of Long Peace, a great stronghold of the capital of the T'ang Empire, towering in the middle of Ch'in Ridge and rolling about 100 kilometers. It is the birthplace of Wordist culture, Buddhist culture, Filial Piety culture, Longevity culture, Bellheads culture and Plutus culture and is praised as the Capital of Fairies, the crown of Heavenly Abode and the Promised Land of the World.

李监宅二首(其一)

尚觉王孙贵,
豪家意颇浓。
屏开金孔雀,
褥隐绣芙蓉。
且食双鱼美,
谁看异味重。
门阑多喜色,
女婿近乘龙。

Librarian Li's House (No. 1)

The airs of the peer one could feel,
The pride of families so blessed.
The peacocks gold their tails reveal;
On embroidered cushions we rest.
Now we dine on the paired fish, great,
Who would expect such unique food?
Happiness is great at your gate
As your daughter's wed a man good.

* Librarian Li: a member of the imperial family and the Director of the Imperial Library. He is renowned for his extravagance and for being a gourmand.
* peacock: the male of a gallinaceous crested bird (genus *Pavo*), which has the tail coverts enormously elongated, erectile, and marked with ocelli or eyelike spots and the neck and breast of an iridescent greenish blue.
* The peacocks gold their tails reveal: according to *The Old Book of T'ang*, Tou drew two peacocks on a screen and gave two arrows to each of those who made a marriage

proposal to his daughter, and promised to marry his daughter to the one who could succeed in hitting the target. Yüan Li, who later became Emperor Highroot of T'ang, shot both peacocks, therefore became Tou's son-in-law.

赠 李 白

二年客东都，
所历厌机巧。
野人对腥膻，
蔬食常不饱。
岂无青精饭，
使我颜色好。
苦乏大药资，
山林迹如扫。
李侯金闺彦，
脱身事幽讨。
亦有梁宋游，
方期拾瑶草。

Presented to Pai Li

For two years I've stayed at East Town,
A tall craft and guile I do frown.
A man of the wilds can eat meat;
There's no enough greens I can eat.
Of course, I have green essence food;
I will keep healthy as I could.
Of much elixir I'm in need;
In woods my trail's swept off indeed.
Lord Li, you're a talent like gold,
Discharged, you seek knacks manifold.
I will travel Liang and Sung too

　　　　To look for ganoderma true.

* *Presented to Pai Li*: Presumably the earliest of Fu Tu's poems to Pai Li (A.D. 701 - A.D. 762), his elder friend, who at this point had been relieved of his position as a Brushwood Attendant (politely represented in this poem as Pai Li's escape). Shortly thereafter Fu Tu was to go off to the region around Kaifeng (Liang), where he had the company of Pai Li and Shi Kao (A.D. 701 - A.D. 765).
* For two years I've stayed at East Town: Fu Tu stayed at Loshine, keeping company of his father's tomb. Loshine has been named Lochow, East Capital and so on.
* Green essence food: a part of the Wordist dietary regimen in which rice is steamed in a broth made from the leaves, stalks, and husks of the grain.
* elixir: a hypothetical substance sought by medical alchemists to change base metals into gold or prolong life indefinitely.
* discharged: Pai Li offended Lishih Kao, the eunuch chamberlain, who backbitten him to Lady Yang, i.e. Jade Ring, Emperor Deepsire's most favored imperial concubine, therefore he was discharged from his sinecure in Brushwood Academy.
* Liang: what is today's Kaifeng, Honan Province.
* Sung: what is today's Shangchiu, Honan Province.
* ganoderma: *Ganoderma Lucidum Karst* in Latin, a grass with an umbrella top, a pore fungus, used as medicine and tonic in China.

重题郑氏东亭

华亭入翠微，
秋日乱清晖。
崩石欹山树，
清涟曳水衣。
紫鳞冲岸跃，
苍隼护巢归。
向晚寻征路，
残云傍马飞。

Another Inscription for Cheng's Eastern Pavilion

The arbor stands on the green lea;
Disarrayed is the autumn view.
A dropped rock leans on a hill tree,
Ripples pull sheets of algae hue.
Lavender scales vault to the bank;
A gray hawk returns to its nest.
With tattered clouds by horse's flank,
It's dark, I must go without rest.

* This poem was composed for Escort Commander Cheng's Eastern Pavilion in A.D. 744, when Fu Tu was in Loshine, newly married.
* algae: any of several divisions of simple organisms having no true root, stem, or leaf, found in water and damp places and include edible seaweed or pond scum.
* lavender scales: a metaphor for fish.
* hawk: a diurnal bird of prey, notable for keen sight and strong flight, usually used as a metaphor for one who takes military means in contrast with a dove, one who tries to find peaceful solutions.

陪李北海宴历下亭

东藩驻皂盖，
北渚凌清河。
海右此亭古，
济南名士多。
云山已发兴，
玉佩仍当歌。
修竹不受暑，
交流空涌波。
蕴真惬所遇，
落日将如何。
贵贱俱物役，
从公难重过。

In the Company of North Sea Li, Feasting in Lihsia Pavilion

The East Fence Lord halts his black tile;
He crosses the river at North Isle.
West of the sea this kiosk is old,
Chinan boasts great scholars, behold.
The cloudy mountains stir our trill;
Those with jadeite pendants sing still.
Tall bamboo do not let in the heat,
The waves of the streams surge to meet.
I'm content with those of renown,
What'll happen once the sun goes down?

  Nobles and commons put to test,

  Hard, I must leave you as your guest.

* This poem was written in A.D. 745, when Fu Tu, on his way to Lin-e to see his brother Ying Tu, visited Yung Li in Chinan.
* North Sea Li: referring to Yung Li (A.D. 678 – A.D. 747), an official and calligrapher in the T'ang dynasty. He was once prefect of North Sea, today's Ch'ingchow, Shantung Province. He was killed by Premier Linfu Li (A.D. 683 – A.D. 753) out of schemes and intrigues.
* Lihsia: Lihsia was near Chi'nan in Shantung.
* East Fence Lord: referring to Yung Li.
* North Isle: a shoal near Lihsia Pavilion.
* Chinan: a city south of the Chi River, today's Chinan, Shantung Province.

同李太守登历下古城员外新亭

新亭结构罢，
隐见清湖阴。
迹籍台观旧，
气冥海岳深。
圆荷想自昔，
遗堞感至今。
芳宴此时具，
哀丝千古心。
主称寿尊客，
筵秩宴北林。
不阻蓬荜兴，
得兼梁甫吟。

A Companion Piece to Governor Li's Climbing to the Ministry Councilor's New Pavilion by the Old Wall of Lihsia

There's been built the pavilion new;
The lake south shore is a dim view.
Among old temples is its site;
Vapors dim hill and sea from light.
The lotuses recall their past;
The battlements stay long to last.
A feast has been prepared, now done,
The mournful strings call back what's gone.
Our host toasts to his honored guest,

In Northern Wood we cheer and rest.
A spur a shack-dweller does bring,
With them, *Ode to Father Liang* I sing.

* This poem was composed in A.D. 745, when Fu Tu met Pai Li and North Sea Li in Chinan.
* the pavilion: built by Chihfang Li, the Ministry Councilor, who had come to Chinan as an assistant (although there is some debate about this). Chihfang Li is the host of this gathering, and Yung Li, the Governor of North Sea, is the honored guest in this poem.
* NorthernWood: a grove out of the town of Lihsia.
* Father Liang: a hill at the foot of Mt. Arch, a place that a large number of corpses were buried together.
* *Ode to Father Liang*: alias *O Father Liang*, a folk tune used as an elegy.

暂如临邑至鹊山湖亭奉怀李员外率尔成兴

野亭逼湖水，
歇马高林间。
鼍吼风奔浪，
鱼跳日映山。
暂游阻词伯，
却望怀青关。
霭霭生云雾，
惟应促驾还。

Going to Lin-e for a While, I Reach the Lake Pavilion at Mt. Magpie, and Think of Ministry Councilor Li, Hence My Inspiration

Pavilion in the wilds, near the lake,
I halt my horse in the tall grove.
Crocodiles roar, waves surge to break;
Fish leap, the sun lights hill and cove.
To the poet I would say good-bye,
But to Blue Pass there he has gone.
Now clouds and haze appear on high;
May he come back, come back anon.

* Mt. Magpie: a mountain where the renowned physician Magpie was buried, hence the name, near the north bank of the Yellow River.

* crocodile: any of a subfamily of large, flesh eating, lizard-like reptile living in or

around tropical streams and having thick skin, horny skin composed of scales and plates, a long tail, and a long, narrow, triangular head with massive jaws.
* Blue Pass: the name of pass, which is probably Solemn Ridge Pass in Hsuchow.

赠 李 白

秋来相顾尚飘蓬，
未就丹砂愧葛洪。
痛饮狂歌空度日，
飞扬跋扈为谁雄。

Presented to Pai Li

Autumn comes to you with dandelion down;
A shame to Ko, I've gained no cinnabar.
Drinking, singing, you pass your days in vain;
Fly into rage, who are heroes? Who are?

* This poem was written around A.D. 745 when Fu Tu travelled Ch'i and Chao and Pai Li, repelled by the crafty eunuch, left Long Peace to travel Ch'i and Lu. The two poets met and sighed over their failure and drifting.
* dandelion: any of several plants of the composite family, common weeds with jagged leaves, often used as greens, and yellow flowers.
* Ko: Surge Ko (Hung Ko), a hermit in the Chin dynasty, who refined cinnabar at Mt. La Phu.
* cinnabar: a crystallized red mercuric sulfide, HgS, the chief ore of mercury, the raw mineral material for elixir in Wordist alchemy.

与李十二白同寻范十隐居

李侯有佳句，
往往似阴铿。
余亦东蒙客，
怜君如弟兄。
醉眠秋共被，
携手日同行。
更想幽期处，
还寻北郭生。
入门高兴发，
侍立小童清。
落景闻寒杵，
屯云对古城。
向来吟橘颂，
谁欲讨莼羹。
不愿论簪笏，
悠悠沧海情。

Going to Find Fan Ten's Hermitage with Pai Twelve Li

Lord Li has the best lines to glare,
Resembling K'eng Yin everywhere.
I'm a sojourner in East Meng, too,
Like a brother I feel for you.
Drunk, in autumn we share a quilt,
We walk along, by the sun gilt.

We'd visit a secluded spot,
Our Master Northtown then we sought.
Into his gate, we felt great joy,
Waiting on, stood a serving boy.
In dim light we heard cold spell call,
Massed clouds faced the ancient wall.
Ode to the Orange you just croon,
Who'd seek soup of water shield soon?
He won't look for a position,
Those feelings of his blue ocean!

* K'eng Yin: K'eng Yin (A.D. 511 – A.D. 563), a prominent poet in the Liang and Chen dynasties of the Southern and Northern Dynasties period.
* East Meng: the area of Lu County, that is, today's Yanchow Shantung Province.
* Northtown: usually referring to a hermit.
* *Ode to the Orange*: a Ch'u verse authored by Yüan Ch'ü (340 B.C.- 278 B.C.), a great patriotic poet and official of Ch'u.

郑驸马宅宴洞中

主家阴洞细烟雾，
留客夏簟青琅玕。
春酒杯浓琥珀薄，
冰浆碗碧玛瑙寒。
误疑茅堂过江麓，
已入风磴霾云端。
自是秦楼压郑谷，
时闻杂佩声珊珊。

Adjunct Groom Cheng's House, a Banquet in the Grotto

O'er Cheng's grotto mist does entwine;
The mats for guests are of green serpentine.
Cups of spring wine thick, strong, like amber gold,
Bowls of ice, emerald, their agate cold.
The thatched shack is beyond the bank, I doubt;
On its breezy stairs, I'm in clouds throughout.
To Cheng's valley the tower of Ch'in towers close;
One hears her pendants tinkling as she goes.

* Cheng: Chienyao Cheng, the emperor's son-in-law, Count of Jungshine.
* the tower of Ch'in: an allusion to the princess, Jade Player, who was married to Flute Man by his father, Marquis Solemn of Ch'in. The couple played the flute on the tower every day. One day a phoenix alighted to the tower and the couple rose to the sky astride the phoenix.

冬日有怀李白

寂寞书斋里，
终朝独尔思。
更寻嘉树传，
不忘角弓诗。
短褐风霜入，
还丹日月迟。
未因乘兴去，
空有鹿门期。

Missing Pai Li on a Winter Day

In the still stillness of my room,
All morning I miss you in gloom.
I hunt down the tale of the tree;
The poem *Horny Bow* haunts me.
Wintry chill your homespun clothes bear;
Your cinnabar's protracted there.
I've no way to go on my whim;
In vain Deergate does wait for him.

* *Horny Bow*: a poem from *The Book of Songs*, the first stanza of which reads like this: Drawn is the horny bow; / If loosened, it will back go. / If brothers dear stay fast, / Affection will long last. According to *Ts'o's Annals*, this poem was composed by Sir Declare of Han, a minister of Chin, when he visited the State of Lu to express the mutual love between two brother states, and then paid a visit to Sir Martial of Chi, Prime Minister of Lu, who had a fine tree in his estate. When the tree was praised by Sir Declare of Han, Sir Martial of Chi said would take good care of the tree to

commemorate the poem *Horny Bow*.
* Deergate: insinuating hermitage. In Later Han dynasty, Master P'ang gathered medicinal herbs at Deergate, declining invitations to the officialdom.

春日忆李白

白也诗无敌，
飘然思不群。
清新庾开府，
俊逸鲍参军。
渭北春天树，
江东日暮云。
何时一樽酒，
重与细论文。

Missing Pai Li on a Spring Day

Pai Li it is, poet without peer,
Just like wind-borne, a different mind.
A Commander Yü, fresh and clear,
Like Adjutant Pao, so refined.
I, north of the Wei, neath spring trees,
You, east of the Long, in dusk hue.
Is there a cup of wine to please?
I'd discuss a verse fine with you.

* Commander Yü: Hsin Yü (A.D. 513 – A.D. 581), a general and a famous litterateur in the Northern and Southern Dynasties period.
* Adjutant Pao: Chao Pao (A.D. 416 – A.D. 466), a litterateur in the Southern Dynasties period.
* the Wei: the River Wei, the biggest tributary of the Yellow River.
* east of the Long: the areas of Southern Chiangsu and Northern Chechiang, where Pai Li was travelling then.

* the Long: the longest river in China, regarded as Mother of Chinese culture, originating from the T'angkula Mountains on Tibet Plateau, flowing through 11 provincial areas, more than 6,300 kilometers long, the third longest river in the world.

送孔巢父谢病归游江东兼呈李白

巢父掉头不肯住，
东将入海随烟雾。
诗卷长留天地间，
钓竿欲拂珊瑚树。
深山大泽龙蛇远，
春寒野阴风景暮。
蓬莱织女回云车，
指点虚无是征路。
自是君身有仙骨，
世人那得知其故。
惜君只欲苦死留，
富贵何如草头露。
蔡侯静者意有馀，
清夜置酒临前除。
罢琴惆怅月照席，
几岁寄我空中书。
南寻禹穴见李白，
道甫问信今何如。

Seeing Off Ch'aofu Kung, Who Has Resigned on Account of Illness and Will Go Back to Visit East of the Long; Also for Pai Li

Ch'aofu shakes his head, unwilling to stay;
To East Sea, he plans to go on his way.
Between earth and sky his poems will all please,

His fishing pole touches those coral trees.
Lurch in mountains and swamps all dragons will;
The scene of the wild goes dim in spring's chill.
The Weaver of the Isles turns her cloud cart,
And points at the void, for which you'll depart.
For sure, you've immortal bones, with all bliss;
How could earthly people understand this?
We want to give our all to make you stay;
All wealth and honor will fade, will decay.
With patience and love Ts'ai's waiting for you;
He's wine laid in the porch, a night view.
The strings stop, the mats face the lonely moon;
Will you send me a letter very soon?
At Worm's Cave if you meet him anyhow
Say I miss him and care how he is now.

* According to *The Old Book of T'ang*, Ch'aofu Kung, Pai Li and other four lived in reclusion in the Ts'ulai Mountains in Shantung, and came to be known as Six Free Men.
* East Sea: what is known as East China Sea today.
* coral: the hard, stony skeleton secreted by certain marine polyps and often deposited in extensive masses forming reefs and atolls in tropical seas. Corals are considered marvels, and Ch'aofu Kung's imagines that ocean journey will take him into the realm of the immortals.
* Weaver: a goddess, usually in a constellation, but here living on the Isles, the isles of gods and immortals. As a constellation she governs the astral region of Wu and Yüeh, where Kung is going.
* the void: the state of nothingness, described by *Sir Lush* as some place that is barren and boundless.
* Ts'ai: unidentified.
* Worm's Cave: referring to where Worm, the founding lord of the Kingdom of Hsia, was buried.

今 夕 行

今夕何夕岁云徂,
更长烛明不可孤。
咸阳客舍一事无,
相与博塞为欢娱。
冯陵大叫呼五白,
袒跣不肯成枭卢。
英雄有时亦如此,
邂逅岂即非良图。
君莫笑
刘毅从来布衣愿,
家无儋石输百万。

This Evening: A Ballad

What evening is this? —the year is gone, bore;
Night lasts with the candle, not to ignore.
In the hostel in Allshine nothing's done;
We come together to cast dice for fun.
In excitement, loudly, crying "Five white!"
Half stripped, I can't get a throw all right.
Sometimes even heroes are just like this;
Taking chance shouldn't be thought as amiss.
Don't laugh now.
To join common folks Ee Liu does aspire;
A million cash lost, he's no rice, in mire.

* Allshine: the ancient capital of Ch'in, present-day Hsienyang, Sha'anhsi Province. It was so called because all its rivers and mountains could get sunshine from all around. It was built in 350 B.C. and Ch'in moved its capital here the next year from Oakshine (Liyang).
* five white: a good throw in the game.
* Ee Liu: a gambling partner of Yü Liu(A.D. 356 – A.D. 422), the founder of the Liu-Sung. He famously wagered fortune he did not have. Ee Liu later opposed Yü, was defeated, and ended up killing himself.

赠特进汝阳王二十二韵

特进群公表，
天人夙德升。
霜蹄千里骏，
风翮九霄鹏。
服礼求毫发，
惟忠忘寝兴。
圣情常有眷，
朝退若无凭。
仙醴来浮蚁，
奇毛或赐鹰。
清关尘不杂，
中使日相乘。
晚节嬉游简，
平居孝义称。
自多亲棣萼，
谁敢问山陵。
学业醇儒富，
辞华哲匠能。
笔飞鸾耸立，
章罢凤骞腾。
精理通谈笑，
忘形向友朋。
寸长堪缱绻，
一诺岂骄矜。
已忝归曹植，
何知对李膺。
招要恩屡至，

崇重力难胜。
披雾初欢夕,
高秋爽气澄。
尊罍临极浦,
凫雁宿张灯。
花月穷游宴,
炎天避郁蒸。
砚寒金井水,
檐动玉壶冰。
瓢饮唯三径,
岩栖在百层。
且持蠡测海,
况挹酒如渑。
鸿宝宁全秘,
丹梯庶可凌。
淮王门有客,
终不愧孙登。

Presented to the Prince of Youshine, Lord Specially Advanced

The prince, Advanced, does all lords lead;
He's Heaven's man, heavenly grace.
Frosty hooves, a thousand-league steed,
Wind-borne wings, Roc of the high race.
You follow rites, all details known,
So loyal, you forget your own.
The Most High's keen on you at court;
When you leave, he's no good support.
Floating lees are brought to sweet wine,

Rare feather on a hawk may shine.
All free of dust is your pure gate,
Court envoys come early or late.
Your pleasure outings reduced much,
Filial and right, you're praised as such.
To you the kinship of all is great;
Who'd dare ask for a royal treat?
Your learning rates second to none;
Your style's splendor is the best one.
Your brush waved, like a phoenix cries,
Your verse done, like a dragon flies.
Your profound reason's well conveyed;
Your cordial friendship's best displayed.
Full of love, you show love intact,
Your word kept, you ne'er rashly act.
Unworthy to join Chih Ts'ao's school,
How could I enter Ying Li's pool?
Through invitations, you've moved me;
In such high state I should not be.
That foggy night I was with you, peer;
The high autumn skies saw air clear.
All cups looked out on the far shore;
Wild geese slept with the lamp and oar.
Flowers and moonlight, all feasts and plays,
Shunning the heat of summer days.
Inkstone chilled with water cold made,
Eaves stirred with ice from pots of jade.
A poor man, I have three ways mere;
I dwell a cliff, the hundredth tier.
I've taken a gourd to plumb the sea,
Thanks to one who pours wine to me.

> How can a treasure be kept from all?
> I may climb the red ladder tall.
> Our Prince of Huainan has his men,
> I won't feel shy before Sun then.

* the Prince of Youshine: Chin Li, Emperor Deepsire's nephew, was given the honorary title Lord Advanced in A.D. 744.
* Roc: a legendary enormous powerful bird of prey. In Chinese mythology, it was transformed from a fish in North Sea. *Sir Lush* reads like this: There in North Sea is a fish called Minnow, whose body spans about a thousand miles. When transformed into a bird, it is called Roc, whose back spans about a thousand miles. With a burst of vigor, it flies up, whose wings are like clouds hemming the sky. This bird, skimming tides, flies to South Sea. And this South Sea is called the Pool of Heaven.
* hawk: a diurnal bird of prey, notable for keen sight and strong flight, usually used as a metaphor for one who takes military means in contrast with a dove, one who tries to find peaceful solutions.
* Chih Ts'ao: Chih Ts'ao (A.D. 192 – A.D. 232), Making by courtesy name, Ts'ao Ts'ao's third son, a famous litterateur, a representative of Making Peace Literature. His *Verse to Moon Girl* has been best remembered throughout history. Chih Ts'ao here represents Prince of Youshine, Chin Li.
* Ying Li: Ying Li (A.D. 110 – A.D. 169), a wise and upright statesman of the Eastern Han. A close friend of Mi Tu, they were called "Li-Tu". Fu Tu is modestly stating that he is unworthy to recreate the "Li-Tu" pairing.
* wild geese: The wild goose is an undomesticated goose that is caring and responsible, taken as a symbol of benevolence, righteousness, good manner, wisdom and faith in Chinese culture.
* Prince of Huainan: probably An Liu (179 B.C. – 122 B.C.), who had *Sir Huainan* compiled by his thousands of hangers-on.
* Huainan: an area in the drainage basin of the Huai River, first an eastern barbarian area governed by a vassal state of Chough called Choulai in Western Chough period, enfeoffed as Kingdom of Huainan in the Han dynasty.
* Sun: referring to Teng Sun. The third-century recluse Teng Sun met Kang Hsi (223 – 262) and judged him to have great talent but inadequate wisdom, fearing that he would come to harm. Kang Hsi later got into political trouble, and before he was executed, he wrote a poem with the line "Now I am ashamed before Teng Sun." With this allusion, Fu Tu expresses that he will follow the Prince's advice.

赠比部萧郎中十兄（甫从姑子也）

有美生人杰，
由来积德门。
汉朝丞相系，
梁日帝王孙。
蕴藉为郎久，
魁梧秉哲尊。
词华倾后辈，
风雅霭孤骞。
宅相荣姻戚，
儿童惠讨论。
见知真自幼，
谋拙愧诸昆。
漂荡云天阔，
沈埋日月奔。
致君时已晚，
怀古意空存。
中散山阳锻，
愚公野谷村。
宁纡长者辙，
归老任乾坤。

To Director of the Bureau of Review Hsiao Ten (I am the son of his father's uncle's sister)

A paragon there, of those best,
From a great household of the crest.

To the peers of Han his line's traced,
And to Emperor of Liang graced.
A director for long, well-bred,
Grand, wise, so praised, he goes ahead.
His speech does all youngsters outshine,
His poems his altitude refine.
House geomancy praised you, the boy;
Your knowledge I, small, did enjoy.
Since childhood I've felt your esteem,
But, inept, I'm ashamed I deem.
So swept along through the vast sky,
I sink as days and months go by.
Too late to serve you though I'm fain,
Old virtues stay with me in vain.
K'ang Chi to Hillshine did retire;
Fool Man did a village desire.
How could I share the old men's cart?
I'll go home, let God play His part.

* the Bureau of Review: a bureau under the Department of Penalty.
* Emperor of Liang: Emperor Martial of Liang (A.D. 464 – A.D. 549), the founder of Liang in the Southern and Northern Dynasties period.
* house geomancy: according to The book of Chin, Shu Way lost his father when small and lived in his maternal grandmother's house. A house geomant predicted to his grandmother that her grandson would make a great success, and indeed Shu Way became a high official later. In this poem Shu Way is used as metaphor for Director Hsiao.
* K'ang Chi: K'ang Chi (A.D. 224 – A.D. 263), a thinker, musician and litterateur in Three Kingdoms period. When he was appointed Grand Master of Palace Leisure; he refused to take up his appointment and went to Hillshine where he worked as an amateur ironmonger.
* Hillshine: Yüehyang if transliterated, a city in today's Hunan Province.
* Fool Man: a metaphor for a hermit.

奉寄河南韦尹丈人

有客传河尹，
逢人问孔融。
青囊仍隐逸，
章甫尚西东。
鼎食分门户，
词场继国风。
尊荣瞻地绝，
疏放忆途穷。
浊酒寻陶令，
丹砂访葛洪。
江湖漂短褐，
霜雪满飞蓬。
牢落乾坤大，
周流道术空。
谬惭知蓟子，
真怯笑扬雄。
盘错神明惧，
讴歌德义丰。
尸乡馀土室，
难话祝鸡翁。

Respectfully Sent to My Senior Wei, Governor of Honan

I'm told Governor of Honan
Asks of Jung Kung, meeting a man:

Does he still in the mountains rest
Or does he go from east to west?
Dining from cauldrons makes all rates,
The verse continues *Airs of the States*.
Seeing on none he can depend,
I, rash, think he's at a dead end.
I seek out Lord Glee for thick wine,
With Ko I'd cinnabar refine.
In plain clothes I'd go without care;
Frost and snow fill my tangled hair.
Lonely on the dome of the blue,
I roam around, void of the True.
As brilliant I could not be seen,
I fear being laughed at as mean.
E'en gods fear you're so smart and wise;
Your virtue all would eulogize!
An earthen hut still in Corpse there,
Reminds one of Chicken Man's flair.

* When Fu Tu wrote this poem, he had just failed to pass the examination (in which, notoriously, the minister Linfu Li had all the candidates failed). Soon afterward Chi Wei was recalled to Long Peace and given a post in the central government.
* Jung Kung: Jung Kung (A.D. 153 – A.D. 208), a litterateur in Eastern Han, one of "Seven of Making Peace", a nineteenth-generation descendant of Confucius.
* *Airs of the States*: the first section of *The Book of Songs* which is the first collection of Chinese poetry.
* Lord Glee: Lingyün Hsieh (A.D. 385 – A.D. 433), a highborn poet, Buddhist, idyllist and traveler, famous for landscape poems, inherited the title Lord Glee from his grandfather, Hsuan Hsieh (A.D. 343 – A.D. 388), a famous general of Eastern Chin.
* Ko: referring to Surge Ko (Hung Ko), a famous hermit in the Chin dynasty.
* brilliant: an allusion to an Eastern Han Wordist adept who was treated well by grandees.
* mean: an allusion to Man Yang's drafting of *Great Void*. His imitation of *Changes* was

mocked for the enterprise.
* Corpse: the name of a place in ancient China, west of Yanshi under today's Loshine.
* Chicken Man: an ancient chicken keeper. He raised chickens for a hundred years and had more than a thousand chickens at a time, and named all of them. When he called, the chickens would come to him.

赠韦左丞丈济

左辖频虚位，
今年得旧儒。
相门韦氏在，
经术汉臣须。
时议归前烈，
天伦恨莫俱。
鸰原荒宿草，
凤沼接亨衢。
有客虽安命，
衰容岂壮夫。
家人忧几杖，
甲子混泥途。
不谓矜馀力，
还来谒大巫。
岁寒仍顾遇，
日暮且踟蹰。
老骥思千里，
饥鹰待一呼。
君能微感激，
亦足慰榛芜。

Presented to Chi Wei, Vice-Director of the Left

The Left Aide is oft a void mere;
An old-style scholar comes this year.

Ministers o'erfill the Wei clan;
Skills in the Classics need a Han.
All ascribe this to forebears yet,
Your kin could not join you, regret.
On Wagtail Plain, last year's plants stay,
Phoenix Pool connects with Broad Way.
You have one content with the time,
Looking old, hardly in his prime.
Everyone cares about his bud,
Dropped to a puddle mixed with mud.
I don't claim that I'm the elect;
A greater shaman I respect.
In the cold year I see your smile;
At day's end I pause for a while.
Old steeds for a thousand miles pry;
Starving eagles wait for one cry.
If you can be e'en faintly stirred,
You may console one with one word.

* Chi Wei: Chi Wei (A.D. 687 – A.D. 754), a minister and poet in the T'ang dynasty.
* the Left: the Left Prime Ministeror the Left Office of the Privy Council.
* Ministers o'erfill the Wei clan: Chi Wei's father, Ssuli Wei, and his elder uncle Ch'engch'ing Wei were once prime ministers.
* Skills in the Classics need a Han: Hsien Wei and Yuanch'eng Wei in the Han dynasty became prime ministers because of their knowledge in Confucian classics.
* Wagtail Plain: the name of a plain, named after a line in *The Book of Songs*: In need a wagtail's made; / His brothers run to his aid. / Good friends only stand by. / Seek their help? You but sigh.
* On Wagtail Plain, last year's plants stay: alluding to the death of Chi Wei's brother.
* Phoenix Pool: referring to the Secretariat, of which Chi Wei is one of the Vice-Directors. The line suggests that this is the way to even higher positions.

奉赠韦左丞丈二十二韵

纨绔不饿死,
儒冠多误身。
丈人试静听,
贱子请具陈。
甫昔少年日,
早充观国宾。
读书破万卷,
下笔如有神。
赋料扬雄敌,
诗看子建亲。
李邕求识面,
王翰愿卜邻。
自谓颇挺出,
立登要路津。
致君尧舜上,
再使风俗淳。
此意竟萧条,
行歌非隐沦。
骑驴十三载,
旅食京华春。
朝扣富儿门,
暮随肥马尘。
残杯与冷炙,
到处潜悲辛。
主上顷见征,
欻然欲求伸。
青冥却垂翅,

蹭蹬无纵鳞。
甚愧丈人厚,
甚知丈人真。
每于百僚上,
猥诵佳句新。
窃效贡公喜,
难甘原宪贫。
焉能心怏怏,
只是走踆踆。
今欲东入海,
即将西去秦。
尚怜终南山,
回首清渭滨。
常拟报一饭,
况怀辞大臣。
白鸥没浩荡,
万里谁能驯?

Respectfully Presented to Senior Wei, Vice-Director of the Left, a Verse of 44 Lines

Rich boys are of starvation free;
A scholar's cap makes one amiss.
Just listen, sir, quietly to me;
A poor fellow could tell you this.
When I was young in the days gone,
With Scan, high guests I looked upon;
I've worn out ten thousand scrolls read;
When writing, I've an inspired head.
For I think o'er Hsiung I can win;

In verse I regard Chih as kin.
Yung Li seeks to know me by face,
Han Wang wants to live near my place;
I thought that I would well out stand;
A crucial job I could command.
I'd make my lord greater than Mound,
And cause our customs to be sound.
In the end these thoughts became bleak,
I tried singing, not feeling meek.
I rode anass for thirteen years,
And dined in the capital's spheres.
At dawn I knocked at nobles' doors,
At dusk I'd follow a plump horse.
With dregs of food and goblets cold,
Where'er I went, pains I'd withhold.
Lately summoned by the Most High,
In an instant I'd try to fly.
But in the dark my wings gave in,
I lost footing, failed, weak and thin.
Your kindness, sir, puts me to shame,
And I understand your high aim.
E'er, before all the hundred peers,
You recite my new lines for cheers.
I'd emulate Lord Kung's delight;
It's hard to accept Hsien Yüan's plight.
How can my heart so painful stay?
All I could do is run away.
I'd wish to go east to the blue,
And leave Ch'in in the west there too.
I cherish the South Hill so dear,
And turn my head to the Wei clear.

Always that one meal I'd repay,
And from that man I'd go away.
The white gull's gone to the wild vast;
So far there, who can tame it fast?

* This poem was composed in A.D. 748 when Fu Tu was 37, sojourning in Long Peace and was thought highly by Chi Wei, Vice Director of the Left. As Fu Tu was failed in Grand Test by Prime Minister Linfu Li, he was depressed and would go out for a tour, so he wrote this to bid farewell to Chi Wei.
* the Left: the Left Prime Ministeror the Left Office of the Privy Council.
* Scan: Kuan if transliterated, one of the hexagrams in *Changes*, meaning to observe. Its reference to "high guest" was an archaic way of referring to examination candidates. Fu Tu sat in for the Civil-Service Examination in Loshine at 24.
* Chih: Chih Ts'ao, the most famous poet of the early third century.
* Mound: Mound (2377 B.C.- 2259 B.C.), Yao if transliterated. Divine and noble, Mound has been regarded as one of Five Lords in ancient China.
* the Most High: referring to Emperor Deepsire.
* Lord Kung: Yü Kung (127 B.C.- 44 B.C.) a high official and economist in the Western Han dynasty. He was once overjoyed at his friend Chi Wang's great success and optimistic with his own future. Fu Tu likened himself to Yü Kung in the hope that Chi Wei could recommend him to the court.
* the South Hill: also known as the South Mountains, Mt. Great One, Mt. Earthlungs, the mountains south of Long Peace, a great stronghold of the capital of the T'ang Empire, towering in the middle of Ch'in Ridge and rolling about 100 kilometers. It is the birthplace of Wordist culture, Buddhist culture, Filial Piety culture, Longevity culture, Bellheads culture and Plutus culture and is praised as the Capital of Fairies, the crown of Heavenly Abode and the Promised Land of the World.
* Always that one meal I'd repay: an allusion to Hsin Han 's repayment. Hsin Han (cir. 231B.C.- 196 B.C.) was a founding commander of the Han regime. He had been poor and shown a good endurance of humiliation. Once a young man made fun of him and forced him to crawl through his arching legs, and Han did so without changing his expression. He was once given a meal by a washer woman when in desperate straits. Later, when he rose to prominence, he wanted to repay that small kindness.
* gull: seagull, a kind of sea bird called gull or large tern, a symbol of clean integrity. The seagulls in the Wordist book *Sir Line* (Liehtzu) are particularly sensitive to impurity of motive and will make friends only with the completely guileless and disinterested.

饮中八仙歌

知章骑马似乘船，
眼花落井水底眠。
汝阳三斗始朝天，
道逢曲车口流涎，
恨不移封向酒泉。
左相日兴费万钱，
饮如长鲸吸百川，
衔杯乐圣称避贤。
宗之潇洒美少年，
举觞白眼望青天，
皎如玉树临风前。
苏晋长斋绣佛前，
醉中往往爱逃禅。
李白一斗诗百篇，
长安市上酒家眠。
天子呼来不上船，
自称臣是酒中仙。
张旭三杯草圣传，
脱帽露顶王公前，
挥毫落纸如云烟。
焦遂五斗方卓然，
高谈雄辨惊四筵。

Song of Eight Drinking Immortals

Stave rides his horse like sailing on a boat;

Blurred, he falls in a well and sleeps afloat.
Having drunk three pots, Shine goes to court now;
Mash-cart met en route, his mouth drools enow,
Sad, he can't change his fief to Wine Spring, how?
Left Minister gets up and spends like showers;
Like a whale he sucks in hours after hours;
Cup to his lips, he's the saint, shunning powers.
To Sire is carefree, with handsome young eyes,
His cup raised, his pupils raised to the skies,
Gleaming like a jade tree thru soughs and sighs.
Chin fasts before figures of Buddha men;
When he's so drunk, he tries to escape Zen.
A pot of wine drunk, Pai's verse may pour down;
He sleeps to snore in a pub of the town.
Son of Heaven calls him to go aboard;
He would not, declaring: "I am Wine Lord."
After three cups, Sunrise, Cursive Saint, leers.
Cap dropped, head bare, he stands before the peers,
Wielding his brush, hence a great piece appears.
Only after five pots does Burn there rise,
His eloquence does all at feast surprise.

* Eight Drinking Immortals: The eight who are good at drinking in Long Peace are Pai Li, Chihchang Ho, Shihchih Li, Chin Li, Tsungchih Ts'ui, Chin Su, Hsu Chang, and Sui Chiao, dubbed Eight Drinking immortals. This poem consists of eight portraits of them.
* Stave: referring to Chihchang Ho, whose first name means Knowing Staves.
* Shine: referring to Chin Li, the Prince of Youshine (Juyang), Chihchang Ho's good friend.
* Wine Spring: Spring of Wine, a city called Chiuch'üan if transliterated, in the western part of today's Kansu Province, as is said to have possessed a natural fountain of wine. According to *Myths and Marvels* (Shen-e Ching), In the wilderness of West China,

there gurgles a fountain of wine pure like jade, more than 3 meters in width and more than 10 meters in depth and, which can revive or rejuvenate a drinker to eternal life. And a folklore source says in the Western Han dynasty, Swift Huo (140 B.C.- 117 B.C.) put his wine into the spring so that there would be an adequate supply for a celebration party after their defeating a Hun invasion, hence the name.

* Left Minister: Shichih Li(A.D. 694 - A.D. 747), of the royal family of T'ang, prime minister, Emperor Grandsire's great grandson.
* To Sire: Chungchih Ts'ui, secretary, knighted Count of Ch'i.
* Chin: Chin Su (A.D. 676 - A.D. 734), from Blue Field County, a court official.
* Pai: Pai Li (A.D. 701 - A.D. 762), 12 years Fu Tu's senior, a famous poet, accorded God of Wine, Fallen Immortal, and Fairy of Poetry.
* Sunrise: Hsu Chang (cir. A.D. 675 - A.D. 750), from Wu County, once Sheriff of Wu County.
* Burn: Sui Chiao, a commoner.

高都护骢马行

安西都护胡青骢,
声价欻然来向东。
此马临阵久无敌,
与人一心成大功。
功成惠养随所致,
飘飘远自流沙至。
雄姿未受伏枥恩,
猛气犹思战场利。
腕促蹄高如踣铁,
交河几蹴曾冰裂。
五花散作云满身,
万里方看汗流血。
长安壮儿不敢骑,
走过掣电倾城知。
青丝络头为君老,
何由却出横门道?

Governor-General Kao's Dapple Gray

West Governor's Hun dapple gray, as said,
In a flash came to the east, its fame spread.
In war this horse has no rival to name,
Of one mind with its master, the same aim.
It goes where he will, having special care,
Wind from afar, Drifting Sands drifting there.
It's never received the stable's grace;

Fierce tempered, the battlefield it will race.
Like trampling iron, hooves high, ankles bound nice,
At the Link it stomps cracks in the layered ice.
Its five mane-tufts spread out to clouds afloat;
Its sweat and bleed ten thousand leagues can note.
This horse stout lads of Long Peace dare not ride;
Faster than a bolt, well known far and wide.
Harnessed in silk, for its lord it does neigh;
Where will it run when going out Cross Way?

* This poem was composed between A.D. 749 and A.D. 750. In the third month of A.D. 749, Governor-General Hsienchih Kao, one of Emperor Deepsire's best generals in the Northwestern Commandery, returned to Long Peace in victory, after having defeated Gilgit, one of the client principalities of Tibet, in today's Kashmir.
* West: literally, Pacified West, one of the major commanderies in T'ang's Central Asia.
* Hun: one of barbaric nomadic Asian peoples who frequently invaded China, a general term referring to all northern or western invaders or aliens; Hun, as an adjective or attributive, refers to something about or of Huns.
* dapple: an animal whose skin or fur is spotted, a horse in this poem.
* Drifting Sands: the desert in Northwest China.
* the Link: the Link River: the river flowing around the ancient town called Link River, built by a king of Jushi, in today Turpan, New Land (Hsinchiang), 8,150 li, i.e., 4,075 kilometers from Long Peace, T'ang's capital.
* five mane-tufts: In T'ang, the mane of a horse was often tied into five tufts.
* Long Peace: Ch'ang'an if transliterated, the capital of the T'ang Empire, with 1,000,000 inhabitants, the largest walled city ever built by man, and a cosmopolis of world religions, Buddhism, Confucianism, Wordism, Nestorianism, Zoroastrianism, and even Islamism represented by Saracens. It was the wonder of the age that reached the pinnacle of brilliance in Emperor Deepsire's reign: The main castle with its nine-fold gates, the thirty-six imperial palaces, pillars of gold, innumerable mansions and villas of noblemen, the broad avenues thronged with motley crowds of townsfolk, gallants on horseback, and mandarin cars drawn by yokes of black oxen, countless houses of pleasure, which opened their doors by night all made this city a kaleidoscope of miracles.
* Cross Way: The first northwest gate of Long Peace leading to the west regions of China.

冬日洛城北谒玄元皇帝庙

配极玄都閟,
凭高禁御长。
守祧严具礼,
掌节镇非常。
碧瓦初寒外,
金茎一气旁。
山河扶绣户,
日月近雕梁。
仙李盘根大,
猗兰奕叶光。
世家遗旧史,
道德付今王。
画手看前辈,
吴生远擅场。
森罗移地轴,
妙绝动宫墙。
五圣联龙衮,
千官列雁行。
冕旒俱秀发,
旌旆尽飞扬。
翠柏深留景,
红梨迥得霜。
风筝吹玉柱,
露井冻银床。
身退卑周室,
经传拱汉皇。
谷神如不死,

养拙更何乡。

Paying My Respects at the Temple of Emperor Dark One in Loshine on a Winter Day

For Pole Star's fete, Dark Gate is closed;
Resting on heights, the stockade goes long.
The Sire keepers strict with ritual;
The controller wards off what's wrong.
Its emerald tiles bear first chill;
Its gold pillar's by the One Air.
Mountains and rivers face the gate;
Sun and moon to its carved beams glare.
Coiling roots of the plums are large;
Splendid Orchid shining leaves sends.
His family's left out of time;
What is Worth on our Lord depends.
I value great artists of the past;
Master Wu leads the field for all.
The dense array budges Earth's axis;
Marvels stir on the compound's wall.
Our Five Saints dressed in Dragon Robes,
The officials lined like wild geese.
Crowns and tassels stand out and forth,
And pennons flutter in the breeze.
Pines and cypresses cast their shades,
Red pear trees catch the far frost white.
Wind blows pegs of the aeolian harp,
The well's silver rails frozen tight.
Having left his Word to Han's Lords,

>   He withdrew from the House of Chough.
>   The Valley God is not dead, ne'er;
>   Simple-minded, where did he go?

* In A.D. 749, Fu Tu wrote this poem when paying his respects to Emperor Dark One Temple in the east capital.
* Emperor Dark One: the title given to the deified Laocius. In the T'ang dynasty, while Confucianism remained the guiding principle of state and social morality, Wordism had gathered an incrustation of mythology and superstition and became popular with both the court and the commoners. Laocius, the founder, was claimed by the reigning dynasty as its remote progenitor and was honored with an imperial title, Emperor Supreme Dark One in A.D. 666, and entitled Emperor Mahatma Dark One in A.D. 743. Laocius's temples were built in the two capitals and all prefectures.
* Loshine: the East Capital of the T'ang Empire. The T'ang imperial house worshipped Laocius, who shared their surname Li, as a remote ancestor, thus combining religious Wordism and dynastic ancestor worship. It should be noted that Loshine, the Eastern capital, had been visited by the court frequently during Empress Wu's reign and intermittently in the first part of Deepsire's reign. Indeed, Deepsire had been born in the city. When this poem was written, however, the court had not returned to Loshine in more than a decade and, in fact, no T'ang emperor was to visit the city ever again.
* Pole Star's fete: to the deified ancestor who is counterpart of Heaven. In this case it would be Laocius. Dark Gate is the gate of Dark Capital, which is a precinct in Heaven, with its own counterpart in the earthly temple. And Dark Gate is also the Dark Gate of Long Peace, on the major road to Central Asia.
* Sire: a temple for remote ancestors. The T'ang royal house claimed descent from Laocius and instituted Laocius temples for his worship.
* One Air: the primal force of the cosmos.
* Splendid Orchid: There are two common associations of this term. It is the title of a zither song and it was the name of the palace hall in which Emperor Martial (140 B.C.-87 B.C.) was born. His father Emperor Scene saw reddish vapors all around the windows. The second association is primary here, with Deepsire being compared to Emperor Martial. We might want to translate the line as: "In Splendid Orchid Palace the huge leaf sheds light"; that is, Deepsire bears the same relation to Laocius that leaf bears to root.
* What is Worth on our Lord depends: referring to Deepsire's annotation of *The Word and the World*. Again there is a play on *The Word and the World* as both the book and

the qualities, the Word and its realizations or revelations.
* Five Saints: five ancestral emperors.
* Dragon Robe: the official robe worn by an emperor.
* crowns and tassels: crowns refer to imperial crowns or emperors, and tassels are the strings with jade that hang at the edge of the crown.
* Wind blows pegs of the aeolian harp: Although a kite seems to have often referred to wind-chimes hung from the eaves, the same was done with zithers as aeolian harps. The "pegs" in the poem suggests the possible use of a zither for this purpose.
* his Word: his wisdom to govern the world or what is said in *The Word and the World*.

故武卫将军挽歌三首

其 一

严警当寒夜,
前军落大星。
壮夫思敢决,
哀诏惜精灵。
王者今无战,
书生已勒铭。
封侯意疏阔,
编简为谁青。

Three Elegies for the General of the Palace Guard

No. 1

Strict curfew's set on a cold night;
A Vanguard star's fallen aground.
Stalwart men think on his virtue right;
The edict pities his soul profound.
Now the king has no war to fight,
Scholars have their name on the roll.
In vain his enfeoffment has been;
For whom do his script slips stay green?

---

* Vanguard: the part of an army that goes ahead of the main body, here referring to the Palace Guard.
* his script slips: This suggests that the general was also a calligrapher.

其 二

舞剑过人绝，
鸣弓射兽能。
铦锋行惬顺，
猛噬失蹄腾。
赤羽千夫膳，
黄河十月冰。
横行沙漠外，
神速至今称。

No. 2

In sword dance he did surpass all,
Shooting right with his twanging bow.
His sharp blade swayed all to enthrall;
Sharp fangs failed, he leaped to and fro.
His red feathers, fine food there passed,
The River had ice the tenth moon.
He marched beyond the desert vast;
His swiftness we praise and we croon.

* the Yellow River: the second longest river in China, flowing through Loess Plateau, hence yellow water all the way. 5,464 kilometers long, with a drainage area of 752,443 square kilometers, it has been regarded as the cradle of Chinese civilization. As legend goes, the river derived from a yellow dragon that, couchant on Midland Plain, ate yellow soil, flooded crops, devoured people and stock, and was finally tamed by Great Worm, the First King of Hsia (21 B.C.- 16 B.C.). Its fertile valleys were turned into fields of rice, barley and oscillating corn, amid gleaming streams and lakes.

其 三

哀挽青门去，
新阡绛水遥。
路人纷雨泣，
天意飒风飘。
部曲精仍锐，
匈奴气不骄。
无由睹雄略，
大树日萧萧。

No. 3

They bear him out Green Gate in pain;
By the Blaze the tomb-path is new.
People on the road shed tears like rain;
A ghostly gust of wind blows through.
His corps are as e'er keen and smart,
So that the Huns cannot grow proud.
Now we can't see his plan and art;
Each day the large tree rustles loud.

* Green Gate: the southeast gate of Long Peace.
* the Blaze: the Blaze River originating from the northwest of Mt. Blaze, which is two hundred miles from Long Peace.
* Hun: war-like nomadic peoples occupying vast regions from Mongolia to Central Asia in Chinese history, especially during the Han dynasty. They were a headache and a constant menace on China's western and northern borders, having no trade but battle and carnage, no fields or plough lands but only wastes where white bones lay scattered over yellow sands.

赠翰林张四学士

翰林逼华盖，
鲸力破沧溟。
天上张公子，
宫中汉客星。
赋诗拾翠殿，
佐酒望云亭。
紫诰仍兼绾，
黄麻似六经。
内分金带赤，
恩与荔枝青。
无复随高凤，
空馀泣聚萤。
此生任春草，
垂老独漂萍。
倘忆山阳会，
悲歌在一听。

Given to Academician Chang of the Brushwood

Brushwood's by the canopy there;
A whale's force breaks through the brine.
In Heaven, lord, you ride the air;
At court, the Han guest star does shine.
You write poems in Kingfisher Hall,
And have a feast at Cloud Pavilion.

Purple edicts, you manage all,
And pen Six Classics on hemp scrolls.
You have been granted a gold tie
And given lychee fruit, still green.
With Phoenix no more can I fly,
But o'er caught fireflies weep, so keen.
Let this life go on like spring grass;
Old, I'm duckweed drifting along.
Let's meet in Hillshine now, alas,
Listen again to my sad song.

* Academician Chang: Chi Chang, Prime Minister Yüeh Chang's second son, husband of Princess of Quiet Love (Ningch'in).
* Brushwood: formally known as Brushwood Academy, an imperial academy for literature and arts. Pai Li was once appointed to serve in Brushwood as Emperor Deepsire appreciated his talent.
* the Han guest star: referring to Academician Chang, who, as the princess's husband, was permitted to build his estate in the palace much the same as Kuang Yan slept with one of his feet on Emperor Lightmight's abdomen.
* Kingfisher Hall: a building in the palace complex.
* Cloud Pavilion: a pavilion in the palace complex.
* Six Classics: the six canonized Confucian books: *The Book of Songs*, *High Book*, *Rites*, *Changes*, *Music*, and *Spring and Autumn Annals*.
* lychee: a Chinese evergreen tree of the soapberry family, cultivated in warm climates for its fruit. Lychee was sent from south to the imperial palace by horses running by relays.
* caught fireflies: an allusion to the story of Yin Ch'e, an Eastern Chin minister. When he was young, he did reading with the light given by caught fireflies due to his poverty.
* duckweed: any of several small, disk-shaped, floating aquatic plants common in streams and ponds.
* Hillshine: the place where K'ang Chi, a famous poet in the Chin dynasty, once lived in hermitage.

乐 游 园 歌

乐游古园崒森爽,
烟绵碧草萋萋长。
公子华筵势最高,
秦川对酒平如掌。
长生木瓢示真率,
更调鞍马狂欢赏。
青春波浪芙蓉园,
白日雷霆夹城仗。
阊阖晴开昳荡荡,
曲江翠幕排银榜。
拂水低徊舞袖翻,
绿云清切歌声上。
却忆年年人醉时,
只今未醉已先悲。
数茎白发那抛得,
百罚深杯亦不辞。
圣朝亦知贱士丑,
一物自荷皇天慈。
此身饮罢无归处,
独立苍茫自咏诗。

Song of Pleasure Park

Trees in old Pleasure Park look dense and strong;
Green creepers stretch on, growing thick and long.
For the young lord's high feast, flown is the balm;

Facing our wine is Ch'in Plain like a palm.
With long-life ladles feelings true we show;
Joke over "saddled steeds", so mad we go.
Lotus Park is live with spring waves again;
Like thunder, the escort march in Walled Lane.
Heaven's Gate opes neath the skies, clear and vast,
Green tents by the Bent, silver placards cast.
Brushing waters, lingering, dancing sleeves fly;
The song through clouds, piercingly clear and high.
I then recall I was oft drunk like mad;
Now as I get drunk I may have got sad.
The strands of hair white how can I reduce?
A hundred forfeits of cups, I don't refuse.
I know a scholar's low in this saintly reign,
Though each has its own right in the domain.
Cups drunk, nowhere to go, I stand alone;
Neath the sky a verse to myself I croon.

* Pleasure Park: the highest place in Long Peace, from which one could see the entire city. On the last day of the first lunar month, it became a gathering place to enjoy early spring.
* Lotus Park: southeast of Pleasure Park, having Lotus Pool in it.
* the Bent: Ch'uchiang if transliterated, the Bent River and also a royal park of T'ang, located in the southeast of Long Peace, the capital.
* a hundred forfeits of cups: At feast games were often played, and the loser had to pay a "forfeit" of drinking a cup of wine.

同诸公登慈恩寺塔

高标跨苍穹，
烈风无时休。
自非旷士怀，
登兹翻百忧。
方知象教力，
足可追冥搜。
仰穿龙蛇窟，
始出枝撑幽。
七星在北户，
河汉声西流。
羲和鞭白日，
少昊行清秋。
秦山忽破碎，
泾渭不可求。
俯视但一气，
焉能辨皇州。
回首叫虞舜，
苍梧云正愁。
惜哉瑶池饮，
日晏昆仑丘。
黄鹄去不息，
哀鸣何所投。
君看随阳雁，
各有稻粱谋。

Climbing the Pagoda of Grace Temple with Various Gentlemen

Its high crest strides up o'er the blue,
Where a fierce wind for e'er remains.
Not in a free man's mood, it's true;
Climbing here brings a hundred pains.
Now I know the force of the Sign
Leads one to seek what underlies:
Upward we bore through Dragon's line,
And from the dark of beams we rise.
The Seven Stars in the north glow
And the Milky Way's sound flows west.
She-her whipped the bright sun to go;
Young Sky made time run without rest.
Ch'in's hills were suddenly broken to bits;
The Ching and Wei could not be found.
Looking down, I saw only vapor fits,
How could I make out the land's bound?
I turned and to Hibiscus cried,
But then clouds hung o'er Mt. Blue.
Of yore, they drank at Jade Pool's side;
As late o'er Mt. Queen the sun grew.
The brown swan goes off, on and on;
Where will it lodge with mournful cries?
Look at the geese that follow the sun!
Each has made plans for its own rice.

* the Pagoda of Grace Temple: alias Great Wild Goose Pagoda built by Dhama Master

Ts'ang Hsuan in the third year of Emperor Highsire's reign, i.e., 652.
* various gentlemen: referring to Shih Kao, Chü Hsüeh, Shen Ts'en and Kuanghsi Ch'u.
* the force of the Sign: Sakyamuni founder of Buddhism (565 B.C.- 486 B.C.) usually taught with a sign, hence Buddhism is also known as the religion of the Sign.
* Dragon's line: a narrow pathway inside the pagoda.
* Seven Stars: referring to those of the Northern Dipper.
* the Milky Way: the Silver River that Queen Mother made with her hair pin in Chinese mythology; a luminous band circling the heavens composed of stars and nebulae; the Galaxy.
* She-her: the driver of the sun wagon, the mother of the sun or the dyad of Goddess of Sun and Goddess of Calendar in Chinese mythology. As is said, She-her, drives the sun across the sky, hastening the day to its end.
* Young Sky: Shaohao if transliterated, the god in charge of autumn according to Chinese mythology.
* Ch'in's hills: referring to the South Hills, south of Long Peace.
* the Ching and Wei: the two rivers as the branches of the Yellow River.
* Hibiscus: Shun if transliterated, an ancient sovereign, a descendant of Lord Yellow, regarded as one of Five Lords in prehistoric China.
* Mt. Blue: Ts'angwu if transliterated, the mountain where Hibiscus's tomb lies. It is used as a metaphor for Emperor Grandsire's tomb.
* they drank at Jade Pool's side: The peripatetic King Solemn of Chough wandered west to Mt. Queen, the abode of the Queen Mother of the West. The pair had a famous banquet at Jade Pool before he left.
* Jade Pool: a pool on Mt. Queen.
* Mt. Queen: Mt. Kunlun if transliterated, is the one of the most sacred mountains in China. It starts from the eastern Pamir Plateau, stretches across New Land (Hsinchiang) and Tibet, and extends to Blue Sea (Ch'inghai), with an average altitude of 5,500 – 6,000 meters. In Chinese mythology, Mt. Queen is where Mother West dwells.
* brown swan: referring to the swan that is good at flying.

投简咸华两县诸子

赤县官曹拥材杰,
软裘快马当冰雪。
长安苦寒谁独悲,
杜陵野老骨欲折。
南山豆苗早荒秽,
青门瓜地新冻裂。
乡里儿童项领成,
朝廷故旧礼数绝。
自然弃掷与时异,
况乃疏顽临事拙。
饥卧动即向一旬,
敝衣何啻联百结。
君不见空墙日色晚,
此老无声泪垂血。

Sending a Note to Those in the Two Counties Allshine and Flower

Red County officials are great, behold;
Soft capes and fleet steed, snow and ice they take.
Who is in Long Peace, suffering the cold?
A Birch-leaf Pear rustic's bones seem to break.
Bean sprouts on the southern hills grow like that;
By Green Gate my melon lot's cracked, so cold.
Those county fellows in the neck grow fat;
My friends in the court to me now acts bold.

Great Nature cast off all those out of date,
Not to mention one inept everywhere.
Lying hungry, I just lie there till late;
If my clothes are worn, worn clothes I just wear
Don't espy by the bare walls the late sun glows,
In silence, this old man's silent tear flows?

* Allshine and Flower: Allshine and Flower, two counties near Long Peace.
* Red County: referring to the capital Long Peace.
* Long Peace: Ch'ang'an if transliterated, the capital of the T'ang Empire, with 1,000,000 inhabitants, the largest walled city ever built by man, and a cosmopolis of world religions.
* Birch-leaf Pear: referring to Birch-leaf Pear Ridge, Fu Tu's ancestral home, where Fu Tu himself once lived.
* a Birch-leaf Pear rustic: referring to Fu Tu, who styled himself Birch-leaf Pear Rustic.
* the southern hills: referring to the South Hill, also known as the South Mountains, Mt. Great One, Mt. Earthlungs, the mountains south of Long Peace, a great stronghold of the capital of the T'ang Empire, towering in the middle of Ch'in Ridge and rolling about 100 kilometers. It is the birthplace of Wordist culture, Buddhist culture, Filial Piety culture, Longevity culture, Bellheads culture and Plutus culture and is praised as the Capital of Fairies, the crown of Heavenly Abode and the Promised Land of the World.
* Green Gate: the southeast gate of Long Peace, where Marquis of East Ridge grew melons after the Ch'in Empire collapsed. The melons, known for their good taste, were called East Ridge Melons or Green Gate Melons.

杜位宅守岁

守岁阿戎家，
椒盘已颂花。
盍簪喧枥马，
列炬散林鸦。
四十明朝过，
飞腾暮景斜。
谁能更拘束，
烂醉是生涯。

New Year's Eve in Wei Tu's House

New Year's Eve, I'm in Cousin's house;
Pepper flowers in plates, the taste's praised.
From the mangers comes noise of steeds;
Wood crows are scared by torches raised.
Morrow, I'll be forty years old,
Near evening like the slanting sun.
Who can be so constrained, not bold?
From now, drunk and mad I will run.

* This poem comes from A.D. 751, the tenth year of Heaven-Blessed, when Fu Tu sojourned in Long Peace, remaining obscure and falling ill. Wei Tu was Tu Fu's cousin and the son-in-law of the Minister Linfu Li, who was the notorious crafty prime minister, and Wei Tu as a fawner followed by a large group of timeservers. With Linfu Li's death and posthumous disgrace in the following year, Wei Tu was exiled to Hsinchow in modern Kuangtung.
* New Year's Eve: the last day of the year according to Chinese Lunar calendar.

* pepper flowers: flowers of Chinese red pepper or Ssuch'uan red pepper. Mixing Ssuch'uan red pepper flowers with wine was a New Year's custom. In the Chin dynasty, the wife of Chen Liu, née Chen, once wrote an ode to pepper flowers, two lines of which read like this: A flushing, flushing fair, / May you live on for e'er.
* From the mangers comes noise of steeds: The mangers and steeds are a metonymy for high officials who are evidently coming to pay their respects.
* Morrow, I'll be forty years old: This echoes Confucius's dictum that one should get established in his thirties. However, Fu Tu will be entering his fortieth year, not yet established, without office.

敬赠郑谏议十韵

谏官非不达，
诗义早知名。
破的由来事，
先锋孰敢争。
思飘云物外，
律中鬼神惊。
毫发无遗恨，
波澜独老成。
野人宁得所，
天意薄浮生。
多病休儒服，
冥搜信客旌。
筑居仙缥缈，
旅食岁峥嵘。
使者求颜阖，
诸公厌祢衡。
将期一诺重，
欻使寸心倾。
君见途穷哭，
宜忧阮步兵。

Respectfully Presented to Remonstrant Cheng

A remonstrant is no bad post;
You're well known for *Songs* you review.

You've always done well, it's no boast;
To be first, who dare vie with you?
Your thoughts waft now out of the sky,
To gods and ghosts your verse is known.
You've not the least regret or sigh;
The waves of your speech sound well grown.
How could this rustic settle down?
Am I destined to go astray?
Oft sick, done with a scholar's gown,
To mystics I'll entrust my way.
I would live with immortals fair,
Dine as a traveler for years best.
An envoy seeks out Lump Face there,
But various lords Heng Mi detest.
I'd hope for the weight of a job,
Which requires one's full devotion.
At a dead end you see one sob;
Captain Juan's grabbed with emotion.

* *Songs*: *The Book of Songs*, some poems of which are strongly associated with reproof or remonstrance, like *Massive Rat*.
* Lump Face: an intelligent Wordist in *Sir Lush*.
* Heng Mi: Heng Mi (A.D. 173 - A.D. 198), an upright man in the Three Kingdoms period. When Mi was banished to Wuhan, the magistrate gave him a parrot and required him to write a verse about it, hence *Ode to the Parrot*, comparing the parrot to himself.
* Captain Juan: referring to Chi Juan (A.D. 210 - A.D. 263), a poet in the Chin dynasty, who was once a field officer.

兵 车 行

车辚辚,马萧萧,
行人弓箭各在腰。
耶娘妻子走相送,
尘埃不见咸阳桥。
牵衣顿足拦道哭,
哭声直上干云霄。
道傍过者问行人,
行人但云点行频。
或从十五北防河,
便至四十西营田。
去时里正与裹头,
归来头白还戍边。
边庭流血成海水,
武皇开边意未已。
君不见
汉家山东二百州,
千村万落生荆杞。
纵有健妇把锄犁,
禾生陇亩无东西。
况复秦兵耐苦战,
被驱不异犬与鸡。
长者虽有问,
役夫敢申恨?
且如今年冬,
未休关西卒。
县官急索租,
租税从何出?

信知生男恶，
反是生女好。
生女犹得嫁比邻，
生男埋没随百草。
君不见青海头，
古来白骨无人收。
新鬼烦冤旧鬼哭，
天阴雨湿声啾啾。

The Chariot: A Ballad

Chariots rattle, horses neigh;
Bow, arrows at the waist, men march their way.
Moms and dads, wives and kids rush to say bye;
Allshine Bridge you can't see as dust does fly.
Pulling at clothes, stamping, blocking, they cry;
Cries rise straight up to the clouds in the sky.
A passer-by asks a man on the way:
The man replies: Troops are oft called today.
At fifteen some the River north guard best;
When forty they till troop farms in the west.
When they leave, Headman gives them turbans mere;
Back home, hair white, then back to the frontier.
Blood on the frontier flows like an ocean,
Land extending is the Most High's motion.
Don't you espy
In two hundred shires east of the pass there
All villages creep with thorns in fields bare?
Sturdy wives there are to hold hoe and plow
On lanes and slopes but they can't have enow.

E'en worse for troops in the bitterest wars,
Driven on, no different from dogs and boars.
Though you may pose the question, sir,
Does a conscript dare to demur?
And now in this winter, this year
They still send troops to the frontier;
County clerks demand taxes now,
But where to get taxes, and how?
To have boys is bad, as is said,
Better to have a girl instead.
Your girl to your neighbor can be married;
Your boy will be with all grasses buried.
Don't you espy by Kokonor there
Since of yore there have been white bones lay bare?
New ghosts vent their wrongs and former ghosts weep,
It's cloudy, it's raining and insects cheep.

* The poem makes reference to the northwestern frontiers, however, many Chinese critics believe that Fu Tu's protest was actually targeted at the disastrous campaigns in the south against the Kingdom of South Summons in A.D. 751 and after. The historical record describes popular disaffection for the South Summons campaigns in terms similar to Fu Tu's. In the northwest the loss of tens of thousands of T'ang troops in the Pyrrhic capture of the almost impregnable Stone Fortress from a few hundred Tibetans was a waste—caused by Deepsire's insistence—but it did not seriously damage the large armies operating in Central Asia. The war with the Tang's old ally South Summons was initiated through arrogant political ineptness and consummated by military ineptness as well, with the destruction of two large T'ang armies and South Summons' subsequent alliance with Tibet. Fu Tu is probably not referring to any single campaign, but to the steady drain on the peasantry caused by immoderate conscription.
* Allshine Bridge: on the Wei River, built in the age of Emperor Martial of Han, the indispensable route between Long Peace and the west areas.
* the River: referring to the Yellow River, the second longest river in China, regarded as the cradle of Chinese civilization. It is 5,464 kilometers long, with a drainage area

of 752,443 square kilometers. As legend goes, the river derived from a yellow dragon that, couchant on Midland Plain, ate yellow soil, flooded crops, devoured people and stock, and was finally tamed by Great Worm, the First King of Hsia (21 B.C.- 16 B.C.).

* at fifteen some the River north guard best: young people were sent to the Yellow River to guard it well against Tibetan looters.
* Headman: A headman, a countryside leader, manages about a hundred households in the T'ang dynasty.
* the Most High: referring to Emperor Deepsire in this poem.
* two hundred shires east of the pass: referring to the two hundred and seventeen prefectures east of Case Dale Pass.
* Kokonor: also known as West Sea or Blue Sea (Ch'inghai), the great salt lake more than 3,300 meters above sea-level in today's Ch'inghai Province.

前出塞九首

First Series of Going Out the Passes, Nine Poems

其 一

戚戚去故里，
悠悠赴交河。
公家有程期，
亡命婴祸罗。
君已富土境，
开边一何多。
弃绝父母恩，
吞声行负戈。

No. 1

Fretted, fretted, I leave my town,
Going to the Link, far away.
Officials have its plans set down;
Desertion traps men to decay.
Rich in lands, our lord rules above;
How he extends the frontier!
E'er forsaking my parents' love,
Voice so choked, I shoulder a spear.

* This series gives the development of a conscript sent to the army in the Northwest. This army remained loyal in the An Lushan Rebellion.
* the Link River: the river flowing around the ancient town called Link River, built by a king of Jushi, in today Turpan, New Land (Hsinchiang), 8,150 li, i.e., 4,075 kilometers from Long Peace, T'ang's capital.

其 二

出门日已远,
不受徒旅欺。
骨肉恩岂断,
男儿死无时。
走马脱辔头,
手中挑青丝。
捷下万仞冈,
俯身试搴旗。

No. 2

It's so late when I leave the gate,
Not being bullied by my mate.
Of course, my love to kin I tie;
But any time a man can die.
I spur my horse, harness untied,
Blue silk reins I sway as I ride.
Headlong downhill, in spirits high,
To snatch the flag I crouch to try.

* horse: a large herbivorous solid-hoofed quadruped (*Equus caballus*) with coarse mane and tail, of various strains: Ferghana, Mongolian, Kazaks, Hequ, Karasahr and so on and of various colors: black, white, yellow, brown, dappled and so on, domesticated about four thousand years ago, reared as a pet, employed as a beast of draught and burden and especially for riding upon. Horses have played an important part in human civilization, widely employed in agriculture, transportation and warfare.

其 三

磨刀鸣咽水,
水赤刃伤手。
欲轻肠断声,
心绪乱已久。
丈夫誓许国,
愤惋复何有。
功名图骐驎,
战骨当速朽。

No. 3

By the Sob I sharpen my sword;
Water red, the blade's cut my hand.
The heart-breaking sounds are ignored,
But the turmoil his heart can't stand.
When a man swears to reach his aim,
What place is left for rage or care?
While Letters Hall keeps deeds of fame;
Bones left from battles crumble there.

* the Sob: alias the Bulge River, which flows like being choked with sobs. A folk song is like this: The Bulge flows and flows, / With Sobs, full of woes; / Behold the Ch'in Plain, / It's a place of pain.
* Letters Hall: also known as Unicorn Hall, a palace of the Han dynasty, implying the court.

其 四

送徒既有长，
远戍亦有身。
生死向前去，
不劳吏怒嗔。
路逢相识人，
附书与六亲。
哀哉两决绝，
不复同苦辛。

No. 4

To take troops ahead he says bye;
To far garrison we'll go there.
We go off forward to live or die,
Sergeants need not trouble to glare.
On the road I meet one I know;
By him I send my care to kin.
That we are kept apart we rue
And will never share thick and thin.

其 五

迢迢万里余,
领我赴三军。
军中异苦乐,
主将宁尽闻。
隔河见胡骑,
倏忽数百群。
我始为奴仆,
几时树功勋。

No. 5

Far and so far off the wilds spread;
Into the army we are led.
In the army some rise, some fall;
The Commander cannot hear all.
'cross the River I saw steeds Hun,
So fast, a band of hundreds run.
I'm a born slave, a slave by breed;
When can I perform a great deed?

* the River: referring to the Yellow River, the second longest river in China, the cradle of Chinese civilization. As legend goes, the river derived from a yellow dragon that, couchant on Midland Plain, ate yellow soil, flooded crops, devoured people and stock, and was finally tamed by Great Worm, the First King of Hsia (21 B.C.- 16 B.C.). Its fertile valleys were turned into fields of rice, barley and oscillating corn, amid gleaming streams and lakes.
* Hun: war-like nomadic peoples occupying vast regions from Mongolia to Central Asia in Chinese history, especially during the Han dynasty. They were a headache and a constant menace on China's western and northern borders.

其 六

挽弓当挽强，
用箭当用长。
射人先射马，
擒贼先擒王。
杀人亦有限，
列国自有疆。
苟能制侵陵，
岂在多杀伤。

No. 6

Drawing a bow, draw the one strong;
Using arrows, use the ones long.
Shooting a man, shoot his stallion;
Catching bandits, catch their chieftain.
Killing should admit of a bound;
A country should have a firm ground.
If aggression could be well stopped,
Why should so many heads be lopped?

* stallion: an uncastrated male horse, especially one used as a stud.

其 七

驱马天雨雪，
军行入高山。
径危抱寒石，
指落曾冰间。
已去汉月远，
何时筑城还。
浮云暮南征，
可望不可攀。

No. 7

We gallop, the sky threatens snow;
The army march, the mountains rise.
The paths are steep, cold rock below,
Fingers fall off to piles of ice.
Already gone far from the moon,
When shall we return, building the Wall?
Clouds drift southward: it'll be dusk soon;
We can watch but can't go at all.

* the moon: the satellite of the earth, a representative of shade or feminity of things, alluding to the belle in this poem. In a universe animated by the interaction of Shade and Shine energies, the moon is Shade visible, the very germ or source of Shade, and the sun is its Shine counterpart.

其 八

单于寇我垒,
百里风尘昏。
雄剑四五动,
彼军为我奔。
虏其名王归,
系颈授辕门。
潜身备行列,
一胜何足论。

No. 8

The Khan's devils our forts invade;
Behold, miles and miles war dust flies.
Twice or thrice our male sword is swayed,
And their troops flee before our eyes.
We'll go back, caught the chief well-known,
Their heads hung on Commander's Gate.
I'll retreat to live on my own;
One victory alone we don't rate.

* Khan: referring to the chief of a Hun nation, also called Ch'anyü.
* male sword: In ancient China, precious swords were made in pairs, male and female.

其 九

从军十年馀，
能无分寸功。
众人贵苟得，
欲语羞雷同。
中原有斗争，
况在狄与戎。
丈夫四方志，
安可辞固穷。

No. 9

I've been in army for years ten;
You may guess merits I've done some.
Chance for advantage prized by men,
I do feel shame to be like them.
War's waged in Mid Plain, rise or fall;
Many Hunters and Arms are slain.
A true man's concerns are for all;
How could I refuse to bear pain?

* Mid Plain: Central China.
* Hunters and Arms: E and Jung if transliterated, two nationalities north or west of China.

送高三十五书记

崆峒小麦熟，
且愿休王师。
请公问主将，
焉用穷荒为。
饥鹰未饱肉，
侧翅随人飞。
高生跨鞍马，
有似幽并儿。
脱身簿尉中，
始与捶楚辞。
借问今何官，
触热向武威。
答云一书记，
所愧国士知。
人实不易知，
更须慎其仪。
十年出幕府，
自可持旌麾。
此行既特达，
足以慰所思。
男儿功名遂，
亦在老大时。
常恨结欢浅，
各在天一涯。
又如参与商，
惨惨中肠悲。
惊风吹鸿鹄，

不得相追随。
黄尘翳沙漠，
念子何当归。
边城有馀力，
早寄从军诗。

Seeing Off Secretary Kao Thirty-Five

Wheat is ripe on Mt. Hollow west;
I wish our Royal Troops would rest.
Pray you ask the commander there:
What's the use of trekking wilds bare?
The starving hawk, not having its fill,
Tilting its wing, chase all at will.
Lo, you make your saddled horse prance,
Like Yu-and-Ping's lads to romance.
Clerkship and sheriff's post you fled,
So to escape the scourge and cane.
And I ask: "What's your job instead,
In Martial Might have a campaign?"
"A secretary's post", you reply;
"The lords of the realm honor me."
Men are hard to know neath the sky;
One must take care how he can be.
For ten years if you stay in post,
You can take up a flag to sway.
On this journey you can gain most,
Which can console me a big way.
One's fulfillment and great success
Can also come when one is old.

Our lapse of joys does me depress;
To our own dreams all of us hold.
Shen and Shang, each the other sees?
Gloomy, I feel sorrow at heart.
A blast of wind blows the wild geese,
They cannot do but fly apart.
Dust veils the desert far and near,
When you will return? I now brood.
With strength left in the far frontier,
Send me a war verse if you could.

* Kao Thirty-Five: Fu Tu's friend, the poet Shih Kao. He had captured the attention of Han Koshu, the commander of the Northwestern armies, and had been given a post as a secretary in his headquarters. Like a number of civil officials whose careers had stagnated, Kao found that serving with the military would indeed be a path to success.
* Mt. Hollow: a mountain in present-day Kansu Province, famous for martial arts. As is said, people here are brave and skillful at fighting battles. And it is a Wordist sanctuary, where Lord Yellow learned the Word from Sir Goodharvest. *Sir Lush* keeps a record of this inquiry, as reads: Lord Yellow had reigned nineteen years and his orders were carried out all over the land. Having heard that Sir Goodharvest lived on Mt. Hollow, he went to pay him a visit, saying: "I hear that you know the very Word. May I inquire of you about the quintessence of the very Word? I would acquire the essence of Heaven and earth to help five grains and sustain my people. And I also want to govern Shade and Shine so that all things may grow well." Because of this event, Mt. Hollow is esteemed as the first Wordist mountain in China.
* I wish our Royal Troops would rest: Earlier Tibetans had often raided at harvest time for the grain; but Han Koshu, Shi Kao's commander, had stopped the raids. Therefore, Fu Tu wishes there would be no military operations.
* hawk: a diurnal bird of prey, notable for keen sight and strong flight, usually used as a metaphor for one who takes military means in contrast with a dove, one who tries to find peaceful solutions.
* Yu-and-Ping: Yuchow in today's Hopei Province, and Pingchow in today's Shanhsi Province, the two places famous for their brave young men in history.
* Martial Might: Wuwei if transliterated, also known as Coolton in history, a prefectural city located in present-day Kansu Province, built by Emperor Martial of

Han (156 B.C.- 87 B.C.) to garrison the border, so named because Swift Huo defeated Huns and thus showed the martial might of the great Han Empire. It has been prosperous as the hub of the Silk Road and famous for wine brewage, hence styled Grape Wine Town.

* a secretary's post: Kao can get a position as a regional civil official by virtue of his long service in the army.
* Shang and Shen: They are never in the sky at the same time, a figure for those who part never to see each other again.

奉留赠集贤院崔、于二学士（国辅、休烈）

昭代将垂白，
途穷乃叫阍。
气冲星象表，
词感帝王尊。
天老书题目，
春官验讨论。
倚风遗鹢路，
随水到龙门。
竟与蛟螭杂，
空闻燕雀喧。
青冥犹契阔，
陵厉不飞翻。
儒术诚难起，
家声庶已存。
故山多药物，
胜概忆桃源。
欲整还乡旆，
长怀禁掖垣。
谬称三赋在，
难述二公恩。

Respectfully Left to Be Presented to Two Academicians of the Academy of Worthies, Kuofu Ts'ui and Hsiulieh Yü

This reign will soon see my hair white;

I cry at the palace gates in plight.
My shine strikes the stars in the sky;
My lines can stir our Most High.
The high seniors write out the theme,
The judge examines how I deem.
With the winds, I leave the ee's track,
I'd reach Dragon Gate by a creek.
I end up with serpents, alack.
But helplessly hear wrens shriek.
Staying away from the dark skies,
I won't wing my way to the blue.
By scholar's arts it's hard to rise,
But my clan's good name can still do.
In my home mountains all herbs grow,
Its good sight recalls Shangrila.
In my carriage back home I'll go,
My thoughts fly to the wall afar.
My three eufs have won your praise;
How can I say thanks to your grace?

* the Academy of Worthies: an official office in charge of the compilation and collation of books.
* the high seniors: referring to the ministers Hsilieh Chen and Linfu Li who writes the questions for Fu Tu's Grand Test.
* The judge examines how I deem: "The judge" refers to a spring officer from the Ministry of Rites, who reads and judges Fu Tu's answers.
* the ee's track: echoing a famous note in *Spring and Autumn Annals* that "six ee birds flew backwards over Sung's capital". An ee bird is like a crane, mentioned in Chinese ancient books. Fu Tu interprets this inauspicious sign as due to headwinds; in other words, he encountered adverse winds from the judgment and went backwards rather than advancing.
* Dragon Gate: According to legend, a carp that can pass over the rapids at Dragon Gate on the Yellow River turns into a dragon. This is a common figure for passing the

examination. Fu Tu fails the test due to Linfu Li's crafty manipulation.
* serpent: a snake, especially a large or poisonous one. It's usually used as a metaphor for a sneaking, treacherous person.
* wren: any of numerous small passerine birds, having short rounded wings and a short tail, symbolizing something unimportant.
* Shangrila: an ideal land free of tyranny and exploitation.
* euf: a genre of flowery prose, usually in rhyme.

贫 交 行

翻手作云覆手雨，
纷纷轻薄何须数。
君不见
管鲍贫时交，
此道今人弃如土。

Friendship in Poverty: A Ballad

Palm up they make cloud, palm down they make rain;
Like feathers air-borne, to count them why fain?
Don't you espy
Friendship of Kuan and Pao, when poor were they,
Is thrown off like dirt by people today?

---

* Kuan and Pao: Chung Kuan lived in poverty, but Shu Pao treated him very well; and when Shu Pao entered the service of the Marquess of Ch'i (645 B. C.), he recommended Chung Kuan, who eventually became Marquess Huan's chief minister.

送韦书记赴安西

夫子欻通贵，
云泥相望悬。
白头无藉在，
朱绂有哀怜。
书记赴三捷，
公车留二年。
欲浮江海去，
此别意茫然。

Seeing Secretary Wei Off to Pacified West

You, sir, have been so highly raised,
You cloud on high, and I mud waste.
White-haired, I've none to care for me;
In red, you express sympathy.
Secretary, you have come off thrice;
In Grand Test, I have been failed twice.
I'll go off and drift on the seas;
Parting now, my thoughts won't me please.

* Pacified West: often known as West Tent Office, Pacified West Tent Office, referring to the protectorate first based in Link River in A.D. 640 and then moved to Kuci (Kuqa) in A.D. 648, governing four towns in the western regions of China, covering an area as far as Persian Bay and much of today's New Land (Hsinchiang) Autonomous Region.
* in red: In the T'ang dynasty, a censor was granted a gold seal and a red gown.

Secretary Wei was also a censor, hence the expression of "in red".

* Grand Test: also called Court Test or Court Examination, the highest level of the civil-service examinations aiming at selecting qualified officials, instituted by Emperor Highsire of T'ang (A.D. 628 – A.D. 683), held every three years and the final decision of ranking was made by an emperor himself.

玄都坛歌寄元逸人

故人昔隐东蒙峰，
已佩含景苍精龙。
故人今居子午谷，
独在阴崖结茅屋。
屋前太古玄都坛，
青石漠漠常风寒。
子规夜啼山竹裂，
王母昼下云旗翻。
知君此计诚长往，
芝草琅玕日应长。
铁锁高垂不可攀，
致身福地何萧爽。

A Song of Dark Capital Altar, Sent to Hermit Yüan

My friend once lived on Meng's Peak in the east,
Wearing a sword light and a dragon gilt.
Now he dwells Meridian Vale, troubled least;
Where on its north slope a thatched hut he's built.
To his house Dark Capital Altar stands true;
Blue rocks spread far and wide, cold wind does bite.
The cuckoo cries by night to the bamboo;
Cloud flags waving, Queen Mother does alight.
I know that he plans to live there for e'er,
Ganoderma and langgan grow well, they must.

There the iron chain hangs so high in the air;
How blessed you are in Blessed Land, free of dust!

* Dark Capital Altar: the name of a Wordist Altar.
* Meng's Peak: the highest peak of Mt. Meng, which boasts almost one thousand historical attractions.
* Meridian Vale: a vale road south of Long Peace County, more than 300 kilometers from Mid-Pass (Kuanchung) to Mid-Han (Hanchung).
* cuckoo: any of a family of birds with a long, slender body, grayish-brown on top and white below, a symbol of sadness in Chinese culture. As is said, during the Shang dynasty, Cuckoo (Yü Tu), a caring king of Shu, abdicated the throne due to a flood and lived in reclusion. After his death, he turned into a cuckoo, wailing day and night, shedding tears and blood.
* bamboo: a tall, tree-like or shrubby grass in tropical and semi-tropical regions, a symbol of integrity and altitude, one of the four most important images in Chinese literature, which are wintersweet, orchid, bamboo and chrysanthemum.
* Queen Mother: Mother West, a mythological immortal in Chinese culture, a sovereign goddess living on Mt. Queen. Her appearance was originally described as human-bodied, tiger-toothed, leopard-tailed and hoopoe-haired. Mother West is regarded as a goddess in charge of women protection, marriage and procreation, and longevity.
* ganoderma: *Ganoderma Lucidum Karst* in Latin, a grass with an umbrella top, a pore fungus, used as medicine and tonic in China.
* langgan: a legendary tree bearing pearl-like fruit, a metaphor for a valuable object.
* iron chain: As legend goes, in the Chin dynasty, there was a garrison at Meridian Vale and west of the vale an iron chain hung there more than three hundred meters long, and a tiger couching on a crag deterred anyone from gaining access.
* Blessed Land: where immortals live. According to Wordism, there are 36 Heavenly Abodes and 72 Blessed Lands.

曲江三章章五句

Three Stanzas on the Bent River
(each stanza has five lines)

其 一

曲江萧条秋气高，
菱荷枯折随风涛，
游子空嗟垂二毛。
白石素沙亦相荡，
哀鸿独叫求其曹。

No. 1

The Bent's dreary, and the autumn air high.
Wind snaps water-chestnut and lotus dry
The vagrant at his grizzled hair does sigh.
White rocks and pale sands are also swept nigh,
Seeking its own kind, the sad swan does cry.

* the Bent: Ch'uchiang if transliterated, a royal park of T'ang, located in the southeast of Long Peace, the capital.
* water chestnut: the hard horned edible fruit of an aquatic plant.
* lotus: one of the various plants of the waterlily family, noted for their large floating leaves and showy flowers, a symbol of purity and elegance in Chinese culture, unsoiled though out of soil, so clean with all leaves green.
* swan: a large web-footed, long-necked bird (subfamily *Cygninae*), allied to but heavier than the goose and noted for its grace on the water, as the whooper, the trumpeter swan, and the whistling swan.

其 二

即事非今亦非古,
长歌激越梢林莽,
比屋豪华固难数。
吾人甘作心似灰,
弟侄何伤泪如雨。

No. 2

Ere me lies not today nor yesterday;
Over the woods and wilds, there rings my lay;
Roof to roof, splendor and power display.
Now I just let my heart like ash decay;
Why should my nephew with tears pine away?

其 三

自断此生休问天，
杜曲幸有桑麻田，
故将移住南山边。
短衣匹马随李广，
看射猛虎终残年。

No. 3

I have made my mind not to ask the sky;
At Tu's Bent, hemp and mulberry fields have I;
I'll move to stay by the South Mountains high.
Plainly-dressed, to follow Broad Li I'll try,
And watch him shoot fierce tigers till I die.

* Tu's Bent: a district near Long Peace, the long-standing residence of the Tu lineage.
* hemp and mulberry fields: According to T'ang law, hemp and mulberry fields are inheritable farmland, where a definite numbers of elms, date trees or mulberries are planted and a piece of land is given as a fringe benefit for planting hemp when fifty mulberries have been planted.
* Broad Li: Kuang Li if transliterated. General Li(? -119 B.C.) was a renowned general who won many battles against the Huns in the Han dynasty. Two of his descendants left deep footprints in Chinese history, Hao Li (A.D. 351 - A.D. 417), King Martial Glare of West Cool (A.D. 400 - A.D. 421) and Yüan Li (A.D. 566 - A.D. 635), the founder and first emperor of T'ang.

奉赠鲜于京兆二十韵

王国称多士，
贤良复几人。
异才应间出，
爽气必殊伦。
始见张京兆，
宜居汉近臣。
骅骝开道路，
雕鹗离风尘。
侯伯知何算，
文章实致身。
奋飞超等级，
容易失沈沦。
脱略磻溪钓，
操持郢匠斤。
云霄今已逼，
台衮更谁亲。
凤穴雏皆好，
龙门客又新。
义声纷感激，
败绩自逡巡。
途远欲何向，
天高难重陈。
学诗犹孺子，
乡赋忝嘉宾。
不得同晁错，
吁嗟后郤诜。
计疏疑翰墨，

时过忆松筠。
献纳纡皇眷，
中间谒紫宸。
且随诸彦集，
方觊薄才伸。
破胆遭前政，
阴谋独秉钧。
微生沾忌刻，
万事益酸辛。
交合丹青地，
恩倾雨露辰。
有儒愁饿死，
早晚报平津。

Respectfully Presented to Hsienyü, Governor of the Capital Region

Many knights there are in the domain;
How many of them are really good?
Rare talents should come forth again;
They must be raised, in unique mood.
Mayor Chang of the town now I see;
He holds a good place near the throne.
The Brownie steeds gallop, now free;
Hawks and falcons leave dust wind-blown.
Don't admire a count more or less;
It is your verse that brings success.
You fly aloft, higher from your dream,
With ease you forsake what's been lax.
You don't go fishing at Pan Stream,

But take up the Ying craftsman's axe.
Now you've come right next to the sky,
Who's so close to a lord of state?
In phoenix roosts chicks gladly cry;
There're new clients at Dragon Gate.
By your good name I'm stirred and led;
Though having failed, I'll try again.
This road's so long, where does it head?
To Heaven, it's hard to explain.
I studied *Songs* when I was small,
To recite, I was made a guest;
I could not match Ts'uo Chao at all
And I sighed Shen Ch'ih did me best.
My plans lax, I doubt brush and ink;
My chance missed, pure worth I recall.
With royals I try best to link;
Ushered, I've entered Purple Hall.
I followed a group of men bright,
I hoped my talent I'd reveal.
So bad, the bad judge came in sight,
Plotting, he held the potter's wheel.
This man had desired to crush me,
Hence all became bitter and sour.
You appeared to help to my glee;
Now your kindness is like a shower.
A scholar worries he'll starve soon,
Ask Count of Peace Ford for a boon.

---

* many knights: Here used is the archaic implication of what would be, in the T'ang case, many gentlemen is a phrase from the Classic of Documents.
* Chang: Ch'ang Chang. Compared is Chungtung Hsienyü to Ch'ang Chang, who held

the same office with distinction in the reign of Emperor Declare of Han (Han Hsuanti).

* Hsienyü: Chungtung Hsienyü, the right-hand man of Prime Minister Kuochung Yang. After having failed to win a post with his three poetic expositions (euf), Fu Tu is trying to get the support of an important member of Kuochung Yang's faction.
* the Ying craftsman: This comes from a fable in *Sir Lush* about an artisan of Ying, the old capital of Chu, who wielded his ax with such precision that he could swing it and remove a speck of dust from his friend's nose. This is a figure of Chungtung Hsienyü's skill and mastery.
* a lord of state: "with the ritual robes (gun) of the tiers." The "three tiers" were a constellation that corresponded with the tribune (three lords), the prime ministers of state.
* *Songs: The Book of Songs*, the first collection of Chinese poetry compiled by Confucius in Seventh Century B.C., which consists of *Airs of the States*, *Psalms*, and *Odes*.
* to recite: refers to those men recommended to take the examination. "Guest" refers to an examination candidate.
* Ts'uo Chao: a Western Han figure who was selected by Emperor Martial of Han in a court examination.
* Shen Ch'ih: a Western Chin figure who was selected in an examination.
* Purple Hall: referring to the palace.
* men bright: referring to the Academy of Scholarly Worthies, who were to judge Fu Tu's responses to topics for composition.
* bad judge: referring to Linfu Li, whose dislike of Fu Tu was said to have been the reason for failing.
* Peace Ford: Hung Kungsun, minister in Emperor Martial of Han's time and enfeoffed as Count of Peace Ford, was known for his good treatment of clients. Here it stands for Kuochung Yang.

白　丝　行

缲丝须长不须白，
越罗蜀锦金粟尺。
象床玉手乱殷红，
万草千花动凝碧。
已悲素质随时染，
裂下鸣机色相射。
美人细意熨帖平，
裁缝灭尽针线迹。
春天衣着为君舞，
蛱蝶飞来黄鹂语。
落絮游丝亦有情，
随风照日宜轻举。
香汗轻尘污颜色，
开新合故置何许。
君不见才士汲引难，
恐惧弃捐忍羁旅。

White Silk: A Ballad

Reeling silk, one needs length, not color white;
For Yüeh and Shu silk use a gauge of gold.
On the loom a fair hand throws out red bright;
Stirred are green plants and chic flowers manifold.
Sad, the plain fabric's dyed to suit the fad;
Ripped, it falls from the loom shooting red.
A belle, taking great care, irons it flat;

Cut and sewn, trace goes of needle and thread.
As clothes for spring, to please you it does dance,
Butterflies come flying, and orioles sing.
Falling floss, straying strands have their romance,
Catching sunlight as they play with the spring,
Fragrant sweat and light dust sully its face;
The new shown, the old shut, to be put where?
Don't you espy talents are hard to be given grace?
They fear bumpy travels they cannot bear.

* This seems to describe embroidery or brocade.
* Yüeh: the State of Yüeh (2032 B.C.- 222 B.C.), a vassal state in Southeast China through the ages of Hsia, Shang, and Chough.
* Shu: one of the earliest kingdoms in China, founded by Silkworm according to legend. In the Three Kingdoms period, a new Shu was established by Pei Liu, hence one of the three kingdoms in that period.
* butterfly: any of various families of lepidopteran insects active in the day-time, having a sucking mouthpart, slender body, ropelike, knobbed antennae, and four broad, usually brightly colored, membraneous wings.
* oriole: golden oriole, one of the family of passerine birds, which looks bright yellow with contrasting black wings and sings beautiful songs.

陪郑广文游何将军山林十首

Visiting General Ho's Mountain Wood in the Company of Instructor Cheng, Ten Poems

其 一

不识南塘路，
今知第五桥。
名园依绿水，
野竹上青霄。
谷口旧相得，
濠梁同见招。
平生为幽兴，
未惜马蹄遥。

No. 1

The road to South Pond I don't know,
But now I recognize Bridge Five.
The famous park rests on the blue,
Rising to blue the bamboos thrive.
Valley Mouth is a longtime friend;
Invited to Hao Bridge we are.
As a hermit, my time I'd spend;
I ne'er grudge my horse may go far.

* bamboo: a tall, tree-like or shrubby grass in tropical and semi-tropical regions, a symbol of integrity and altitude, one of the four most important images in Chinese literature, which are wintersweet, orchid, bamboo and chrysanthemum.
* Valley Mouth: the name of a hermit.

其 二

百顷风潭上，
千章夏木清。
卑枝低结子，
接叶暗巢莺。
鲜鲫银丝脍，
香芹碧涧羹。
翻疑柁楼底，
晚饭越中行。

No. 2

By a hundred-acre breezy pool,
A thousand summer trees are cool.
The bottom fruit branches bend low,
The leaves keep orioles from show.
Fresh gold carp, sliced in silver white,
Fragrant celery from a bight.
I feel I'm neath the rudder great,
Travelling in Yüeh and dining late.

* oriole: golden oriole, one of the family of passerine birds, which looks bright yellow with contrasting black wings and sings beautiful songs.
* carp: fresh water food fish (*Ciprinus carpio*) of China, now widely distributed in Europe and America, a mascot in Chinese culture, symbolizing great success and harmony. An idiom "a carp jumping over the Dragon Gate" means climbing up the social ladder or succeeding in the imperial civil service examination.
* Yüeh: the State of Yüeh (2032 B.C.- 222 B.C.), a vassal state under Hsia, Shang and Chough in Southeast China in the Spring and Autumn period. As a regime, it was first founded by Nothing Left (Wuyü), King Young Health (Shaok'ang) of Hsia' son born of a concubine.

其 三

万里戎王子，
何年别月支。
异花开绝域，
滋蔓匝清池。
汉使徒空到，
神农竟不知。
露翻兼雨打，
开坼渐离披。

No. 3

Prince of Arms from far, far away,
When did it leave Jouchih for here?
This alien flower blooms all to ray,
Lush creepers go round the pond clear.
The Han envoy got there in vain;
Of it Magic Farmer ne'er knew.
Toppled by dew, beaten by rain,
It blows, so bedraggled with dew.

* Prince of Arms: the name of an alien plant.
* Jouchih: indicating an area around Hohsi Corridor, which is 1,000 kilometers long and about 100 kilometer wide, and the nationality or language bearing the name.
* Han: China or Chinese, a metonymy adopted because of the powerful Han Empire founded by Pang Liu, King of Han before he won the war and reunified China.
* Magic Farmer: one of Three Sovereigns in remote ages, along with Hidden Spirit and Nüwa. Magic Farmer, also known as King of Corn, is regarded as the father of herb medicine and agriculture.

其 四

旁舍连高竹，
疏篱带晚花。
碾涡深没马，
藤蔓曲藏蛇。
词赋工无益，
山林迹未赊。
尽捻书籍卖，
来问尔东家。

No. 4

The cottage's close to tall bamboo,
The thin hedge holding up late flowers.
The pool's deep to drown steeds, it's true;
Rattan vines can keep snakes from showers.
My skill in verse brings me no gain;
My tracks in mountain forests are not far.
My books so held, sell them I'd fain;
Why not buy some as good they are?

* bamboo: a tall, tree-like or shrubby grass in tropical and semi-tropical regions, a symbol of integrity and altitude, one of the four most important images in Chinese literature, which are wintersweet, orchid, bamboo and chrysanthemum.
* rattan: the long, tough, flexible stem of a palm (genera *Calamus* and *Daemonorops*) growing in Asia, Africa and Australia, which can be used as material for the making of chairs and a variety of other furniture.

其　五

剩水沧江破，
残山碣石开。
绿垂风折笋，
红绽雨肥梅。
银甲弹筝用，
金鱼换酒来。
兴移无洒扫，
随意坐莓苔。

No. 5

O'erflowing water floods the Blue;
On the bare hill is a brown stone.
Green hanging, a wind snaps bamboo;
Blossoms burst, and plums are well grown.
With silver scales, the lute we play,
The golden fish exchanged for wine.
Don't sweep it off, here we can stay,
Sit on the moss as is thought fine.

* the Blue: the Blue River, an unidentified river in this poem.
* plum: a kind of plant or the edible purple drupaceous fruit of the plant which is any one of various trees of the genus *Prunus*, cultivated in temperate zones.
* moss: a tiny, delicate green bryophytic plant growing on damp decaying wood, wet ground, humid rocks or trees, producing capsules which open by an operculum and contain spores. Under a poet's writing brush, it may arouse a poetic feeling or imagination.

其 六

风磴吹阴雪，
云门吼瀑泉。
酒醒思卧簟，
衣冷欲装绵。
野老来看客，
河鱼不取钱。
只疑淳朴处，
自有一山川。

No. 6

His breezy stone steps blown with snow,
At his cloud gate flies a cascade.
On the mat from wine, I come to;
Cold, in my clothes stuff can be laid.
A rustic comes to see his guest,
but on river-fish spends no gold.
It seems a place simply the best,
With hills and rills rolling and rolled.

* with hills and rills rolling and rolled: a scene of an Edenic place or a place like Peach Blossom Source free from exploitation and depression.

其 七

棘树寒云色,
茵陈春藕香。
脆添生菜美,
阴益食单凉。
野鹤清晨出,
山精白日藏。
石林蟠水府,
百里独苍苍。

No. 7

The jujube tree, cloud color cold,
Lily and lotus in the pool.
The fresh greens are so crisp, behold;
The shade can make our food so cool.
Wild cranes come in the morning clear;
Hill sprites hide in under the sun.
Stone woods coiled round by water near,
A hundred leagues see its blue run.

* jujube: any of a genus of trees or shrubs of the buckthorn family, especially the common jujube, the lotus tree.
* lily: any of a large genus (*Lilium*) of perennial plants of the lily family, grown from a bulb, and having typically trumpet-shaped flowers, white or colored.
* lotus: one of the various plants of the waterlily family, noted for their large floating leaves and showy flowers, an important image in Chinese culture; in most cases it is associated with Buddhism, for example, Pai Li has various names, one of which is Green Lotus Buddhist.

其 八

忆过杨柳渚，
走马定昆池。
醉把青荷叶，
狂遗白接䍦。
刺船思郢客，
解水乞吴儿。
坐对秦山晚，
江湖兴颇随。

No. 8

Passing Willow Shoal, I recall,
By Queen Pond galloping my horse.
A lotus leaf held, drunk to fall,
I threw off my turban by force.
I long for a Ying man to row;
To oar, better is a Wu man.
We face Mt. Ch'in in dusky glow;
I'd enjoy nature as I can.

* the Ying man: A craftsman from Ying could cut off the powder on his partner's nose with his swift axe, but he could no longer perform it after his brave partner passed away.
* Wu man: man south of the Yangtze River, good at boating because of the abundance of water in the area.
* Mt. Ch'in: alias Mt. South, the Southern Hills, the Southern Mountains, Mt. Great One and Mt. Earth lungs, the mountains south of Long Peace, a great stronghold of the capital, towering in the middle of Ch'in Ridge and rolling about 100 kilometers.

其 九

床上书连屋，
阶前树拂云。
将军不好武，
稚子总能文。
醒酒微风入，
听诗静夜分。
绤衣挂萝薜，
凉月白纷纷。

No. 9

On his couch, books there are a lot,
Before his steps is a tall wood.
Martial things the general loves not;
At verse his children are all good.
He sobers when a breeze comes in,
Harking to verse in the still night.
His clothes, and the moss hanging green,
Cool moon, so diffused is the white.

* moss: a tiny, delicate green bryophytic plant growing on damp decaying wood, wet ground, humid rocks or trees, producing capsules which open by an operculum and contain spores. Under a poet's writing brush, it may arouse a poetic feeling or imagination.
* moon: the planet of the earth, which appears at night and gives off shining silvery light, an image of purity, solitude and nostalgia as it always looks cool and is alone.

其 十

幽意忽不惬，
归期无奈何。
出门流水住，
回首白云多。
自笑灯前舞，
谁怜醉后歌。
只应与朋好，
风雨亦来过。

No. 10

My will for seclusion does drop;
The time to go back I can't bear.
Outdoors, the flow comes to a stop;
I can see white clouds everywhere.
I laugh at my dance to the light;
Who loves the song a drunk man hums?
I should join my friends for the night
And stop my play now a rain comes.

丽 人 行

三月三日天气新，
长安水边多丽人。
态浓意远淑且真，
肌理细腻骨肉匀。
绣罗衣裳照暮春，
蹙金孔雀银麒麟。
头上何所有，
翠微匎叶垂鬓唇。
背后何所见，
珠压腰衱稳称身。
就中云幕椒房亲，
赐名大国虢与秦。
紫驼之峰出翠釜，
水精之盘行素鳞。
犀箸厌饫久未下，
鸾刀缕切空纷纶。
黄门飞鞚不动尘，
御厨络绎送八珍。
箫鼓哀吟感鬼神，
宾从杂沓实要津。
后来鞍马何逡巡，
当轩下马入锦茵。
杨花雪落覆白蘋，
青鸟飞去衔红巾。
炙手可热势绝伦，
慎莫近前丞相瞋。

Fair Ladies: A Ballad

The third day of the third moon sees fresh air,
By waters of Long Peace swarm ladies fair.
They look afar, their mood quiet, pure and true,
Their skin smooth and their build well-balanced too.
Their embroidered silk gowns shine in late spring;
Peacocks glow like gold and unicorns sing.
What do they have on their head?
Plumed and leafed tiaras matching their hair.
What do they have on their back?
Apron-adorning pearls fixed there to glare.
There propped are cloud tents for their noble kin,
With titles for the belles, like Kuo and Ch'in.
The camel hump comes from a cooking pot,
A crystal plate holds a white carp there caught.
From surfeit rhino-horn chopsticks not plied,
Thread like slices with phoenix knives not tried.
Yellow Gate sees steeds come, stirring no dust;
Royal Kitchen sends dainties to one's lust.
Lutes and flutes stir spirits for the best hour;
Waiters and guests throng—'tis the gate to power.
A saddled horse comes—leisurely like that;
The rider dismounts to the silken mat.
Catkins fall like snow to the duckweed seek;
A bluebird flies off, red scarf in its beak.
The greatest power he has, as none can share;
Don't come close to Right Minister's hot glare!

* This is a satire of the minister Kuochung Yang on the occasion of a visit to Bent River Park, with the emperor accompanied by his favorite Lady Yang, Jade Ring (Kuifei Yang), and her two sisters, the Duchesses of Kuo and Ch'in.
* the third day of the third moon: Sacrifice Day, when people go outing to commemorate their ancestors and exorcize evil spirits with orchids.
* Long Peace: referring to Ch'ang'an if transliterated, the metropolis of gold, the capital of the T'ang Empire, with 1,000,000 inhabitants, the largest walled city ever built by man, and a cosmopolis of world religions, Buddhism, Confucianism, Wordism, Nestorianism, Zoroastrianism, and even Islamism represented by Saracens. It saw the wonder of the age that reached the pinnacle of brilliance in Emperor Deepsire's reign: The main castle with its nine-fold gates, the thirty-six imperial palaces, pillars of gold, innumerable mansions and villas of noblemen, the broad avenues thronged with motley crowds of townsfolk, gallants on horseback, and mandarin cars drawn by yokes of black oxen, countless houses of pleasure, which opened their doors by night all made this city a kaleidoscope of miracles.
* peacock: the male of a gallinaceous crested bird (genus *Pavo*), which has the tail coverts enormously elongated, erectile, and marked with ocelli or eyelike spots and the neck and breast of an irridescent greenish blue.
* unicorn: a fabulous deer-like animal with one horn, a symbol of saintliness and divinity in Chinese culture. Confucius lamented the death of a unicorn captured and hence stopped compiling the Spring and Autumn Annals and died before long.
* Kuo and Ch'in: Duchess of Kuo and Duchess of Ch'in, the titles granted to the sisters of Lady Yang, Deepsire's favorite.
* camel hump: a table delicacy, especially roast camel hump that appears in the recipes of T'ang's nobles.
* Catkins fall like snow to the duckweed seek: insinuate the fornication with his cousin, Duchess of Kuo.
* catkin: a deciduous scaly spike of flowers, as in the willow, an image of helpless drifting or wandering in Chinese literature.
* duckweed: any of several small, disk-shaped, floating aquatic plants common in streams and ponds.
* bluebird: a legendary bird in Chinese mythology, Queen Mother's messenger, used as a metaphor for a messenger between a man and woman.
* Right Minister: referring to Kuochung Yang (? - A.D. 756), appointed Right Minister (Prime Minister) in November, A.D. 752.

九 日 曲 江

缀席茱萸好，
浮舟菡萏衰。
季秋时欲半，
九日意兼悲。
江水清源曲，
荆门此路疑。
晚来高兴尽，
摇荡菊花期。

Double Ninth on the Bent River

Adorning mats, cornel's well done,
Lotus dried, we drift in a boat.
Autumn's last month, time is half gone,
This Double Ninth is a sad note.
The River flows, the clear stream bends;
This course seems like that at Chaste Gate.
This evening my high spirit spends,
The chrysanthemum as my mate.

* the Bent: Ch'uchiang if transliterated, a royal river park of T'ang, located in the southeast of Long Peace, the capital.
* cornel: a kind of dogwood carried or worn on Double Ninth Day, as it can exorcize evil spirits, as is traditionally believed.
* Double Ninth: referring to the Ninth of the Ninth moon, a day observed in memory of those who have passed away in Chinese tradition.
* chrysanthemum: any of a genus of perennials of the composite family, some cultivated

varieties of which have large heads of showy flowers of various colors, a symbol of elegance and integrity in Chinese culture. It can be used as herb medicine or stuff to go with tea or as an independent drink, and it can be used as an ingredient for wine.

奉陪郑驸马韦曲二首
Respectfully Accompanying Adjunct Groom Cheng in Weich'u, Two Poems

其 一

韦曲花无赖，
家家恼杀人。
绿尊虽尽日，
白发好禁春。
石角钩衣破，
藤枝刺眼新。
何时占丛竹，
头戴小乌巾。

No. 1

Weich'u has heartless flirting flowers,
Which at each home drive people mad.
With green goblets we pass our hours,
Can white hair resist the spring fad?
Our clothes the sharp crags hook and tear;
Our eyes the fresh cane twigs attack.
When shall we take the bamboo there,
On our heads wearing small scarves black?

* Weich'u: 15 kilometers from the capital, a place for pleasure or leisure, where one could see villas and parks of nobles and celebrities of the Great T'ang Empire.

* bamboo: a tall, tree-like or shrubby grass in tropical and semi-tropical regions, a symbol of integrity and altitude, one of the four most important images in Chinese literature, which are wintersweet, orchid, bamboo and chrysanthemum.

其 二

野寺垂杨里，
春畦乱水间。
美花多映竹，
好鸟不归山。
城郭终何事，
风尘岂驻颜。
谁能共公子，
薄暮欲俱还。

No. 2

The temple looms in willow's hue;
Spring garden-plots sprawl to the rills.
Lovely flowers, set off by bamboo,
Good birds won't return to the hills.
Why be in the town in the end?
In dust how can one shiny stay?
With a childe who can his days spend
And go back towards the dusk gray?

* willow: any of a large genus (*Salix*) of shrubs and trees related to the poplars, having generally smooth branches, and often long, slender, pliant, and sometimes pendent branchlets, a symbol of farewell or nostalgia in Chinese culture.
* bamboo: a tall, tree-like or shrubby grass in tropical and semi-tropical regions, a symbol of integrity and altitude, one of the four most important images in Chinese literature, which are wintersweet, orchid, bamboo and chrysanthemum.

重过何氏五首
Revisiting General Ho's, Five Poems

其 一

问讯东桥竹,
将军有报书。
倒衣还命驾,
高枕乃吾庐。
花妥莺捎蝶,
溪喧獭趁鱼。
重来休沐地,
真作野人居。

No. 1

I ask about East Bridge bamboo,
The general writes me in reply.
My clothes inside out, a horse I ride;
It's my cottage, my pillow high.
Flowers set, orioles brush butterflies;
Otters chase fish, making a din.
He spends his days off here at rest;
Truly, a rustic I dwell in.

* bamboo: a tall, tree-like or shrubby grass in tropical and semi-tropical regions, a symbol of integrity and altitude, one of the four most important images in Chinese literature, which are wintersweet, orchid, bamboo and chrysanthemum.
* oriole: golden oriole, one of the family of passerine birds, which looks bright yellow

with contrasting black wings and sings beautiful songs.
* butterfly: any of various families of lepidopteran insects active in the day-time, having a sucking mouthpart, slender body, ropelike, knobbed antennae, and four broad, usually brightly colored, membraneous wings.
* otter: any of various furry carnivores with webbed feet used in swimming and a long, slightly flattened tail. Its lustrous fur is used as stuff for expensive vestments or costumes.

其 二

山雨尊仍在，
沙沈榻未移。
犬迎曾宿客，
鸦护落巢儿。
云薄翠微寺，
天清黄子陂。
向来幽兴极，
步屣过东篱。

No. 2

Cups still there in the mountain rain;
Sinking in sand, the beds there remain.
The dog greets a familiar guest;
A crow guards chicks dropped from the nest.
O'er Blue Mist Temple thin clouds veer;
O'er Yellow Slope the sky is clear.
So raised is my retreating soul,
As past the eastern hedge I stroll.

* Blue Mist Temple: changed from Blue Mist Palace in Great Harmony Valley south of Long Peace County.
* Yellow Slope: alias Prince's Slope in Fanch'uan.

其 三

落日平台上，
春风啜茗时。
石栏斜点笔，
桐叶坐题诗。
翡翠鸣衣桁，
蜻蜓立钓丝。
自今幽兴熟，
来往亦无期。

No. 3

The setting sun does the plain ease;
I sip my tea in the spring breeze.
At the stone rail my brush I ply;
Paulownia leaves I versify.
On the clothes-racks kingfishers sing;
Dragonflies stand on th' fishing string.
My zest to retreat is complete,
There's no fixed date to go or meet.

* paulownia: any of a genus of Chinese trees of the figwort family, with heart-shaped leaves and panicles of handsome, fragrant and purple flowers.
* kingfisher: a beautiful bird looking like a halcyon pileata.
* dragonfly: a large insect having narrow, transparent, net-veined wings and feeding most on flies, mosquitoes, etc.

其 四

颇怪朝参懒，
应耽野趣长。
雨抛金锁甲，
苔卧绿沈枪。
手自移蒲柳，
家才足稻粱。
看君用幽意，
白日到羲皇。

No. 4

How strange, you are so lax at court,
Much used to your rustic disport.
To the rain your mail you did toss;
Your lacquered spear lies on green moss.
The willows you planted sway nice,
Your household has just enough rice.
One can see your recluse's mind,
With Hidden Spirit now combined.

* willow: any of a large genus of shrubs and trees related to the poplars, having generally narrow leaves, smooth branches, and often long, slender, pliant, and sometimes pendent branchlets, a symbol of farewell or nostalgia in Chinese culture. The best image is in *Vetch We Pick*, a verse in *The Book of Songs*, which reads like this: When we left long ago, / The willows waved adieu. / Now back to our home town, / We meet snow falling down.
* Hidden Spirit: Fuhsi if transliterated, the ancestor of Chinese, the earliest documented god of creation and king of kings in Chinese culture. Sky Water (T'ianshui) in today's Kansu Province is believed to be Hidden Spirit's birthplace, as is the topographical center of China.
* with Hidden Spirit now combined: a state of being free of worries, an easy life.

其 五

到此应常宿，
相留可判年。
蹉跎暮容色，
怅望好林泉。
何路沾微禄，
归山买薄田。
斯游恐不遂，
把酒意茫然。

No. 5

You'd come and for long abide here;
It's the best place to spend a year.
Times goes slowly in the dusk haze;
To the wood and creek you long gaze.
Once you have had a meager pay,
Buy a lean field, in woods you stay.
I doubt this dream to me ne'er rays,
Cup in hand, my thoughts run, a daze.

陪诸贵公子丈八沟携妓纳凉晚际遇雨二首
Taking Singing Girls to Enjoy the Cool at Ten-Eight Trench in the Company of Childes and at Dusk It Rains, Two Poems

其 一

落日放船好，
轻风生浪迟。
竹深留客处，
荷净纳凉时。
公子调冰水，
佳人雪藕丝。
片云头上黑，
应是雨催诗。

No. 1

The sun set, it's fine to canoe;
The breeze brisk, waves rise in the pool.
We rest in the grove of bamboo;
The calm lotus sends in the cool.
The lords with ice chill their drink;
The belle cuts lotus roots snow white.
A cloud floats overhead like ink;
It's the rain urging me to write.

---

* Ten-Eight Trench: a canal 10 kilometers southwest of Long Peace for provision of drinking water and transportation. It is so called because it is ten feet wide and eight

feet deep.
* bamboo: a tall, tree-like or shrubby grass in tropical and semi-tropical regions, a symbol of integrity and altitude, one of the four most important images in Chinese literature, which are wintersweet, orchid, bamboo and chrysanthemum.
* lotus: one of the various plants of the waterlily family, provincial for their large floating round leaves and showy flowers, especially the white or pink Asian lotus, used as a religious symbol in Hinduism and Buddhism. In Chinese culture, it is a symbol of purity and elegance, unsoiled though out of soil, so clean with all leaves green, is is a common image in Chinese literature, as two lines of a lyric by Hsiu Ouyang (A.D. 1007 - A.D. 1072) read: "A thunder brings rain to the wood and pool, / The rain hushes the lotus, drips cool."

其 二

雨来沾席上，
风急打船头。
越女红裙湿，
燕姬翠黛愁。
缆侵堤柳系，
幔卷浪花浮。
归路翻萧飒，
陂塘五月秋。

No. 2

Rain drops fall on my mat, brisk, curt;
The rash wind punches on my prow.
Now wet is the Yüeh girl's red skirt;
The Yan belle lowers her sad black brow.
Near dyke willows my rope I tie;
The curtain furls while sprays feel cool.
On our way back our sails sigh, sigh;
In June, autumn falls to Slope Pool.

---

* Yüeh: the State of Yüeh (2032 B.C.- 222 B.C.), a vassal state under Chough in Southeast China in the Spring and Autumn period. As a regime it preceded Chough, first founded by Nothing Left (Wuyü), King Young Health (Shaok'ang) of Hsia's son born of a concubine.
* Yan: the State of Yan (1044 B.C.- 222 B.C.), a vassal state in the Spring and Autumn period, one of the Seven Powers in the Warring States period.
* Slope Pool: the name of a specific pond, or referring to any pond in general.

醉 时 歌

诸公衮衮登台省,
广文先生官独冷。
甲第纷纷厌粱肉,
广文先生饭不足。
先生有道出羲皇,
先生有才过屈宋。
德尊一代常坎坷,
名垂万古知何用。
杜陵野客人更嗤,
被褐短窄鬓如丝。
日籴太仓五升米,
时赴郑老同襟期。
得钱即相觅,
沽酒无复疑。
忘形到尔汝,
痛饮真吾师。
清夜沉沉动春酌,
灯前细雨檐花落。
但觉高歌有鬼神,
焉知饿死填沟壑。
相如逸才亲涤器,
子云识字终投阁。
先生早赋归去来,
石田茅屋荒苍苔。
儒术于我何有哉,
孔丘盗跖俱尘埃。
不须闻此意惨怆,

生前相遇且衔杯。

Singing When Drunk

Distinguished men rise to posts manifold;
This college man a sinecure does hold.
In mansions they're sated with meat and rice;
This college man has no meal to suffice.
This gentleman can Hidden Spirit best;
This gentleman in verse writing can crest.
His worth revered, unfulfilled is his aim;
What's the use of that with his lasting fame?
A Birch leaf Pear rustic, I'm so scorned at:
My homespun short, my locks grizzled like that.
Pints of rice from Grand Barn I buy each day;
In Old Cheng's and with friends I often stay.
When I get cash, I'll seek them out,
And will go buy wine with no doubt.
If you can drink yourself, so free;
My greatest teacher you will be.
We set the spring brew in the chilly night;
A flower rain falls from eaves to our lamp bright.
Gods come when loud we sing I am aware;
If we starve to o'erfill the ditch, we don't care.
Hsiangju, talented, washed dishes on his own;
Sir Cloud, learned, from the tower jumped, down thrown.
This gentleman wrote verse on "home to go";
His stony fields and thatched roof see moss grow.
What's the use of Confucianism to me?
Confucius or Barefoot no longer be.

> Don't feel so wretched at this, do cheer up;
> Should we meet in this life, let's raise our cup.

* Because of the bad harvest of 753 and due to heavy rain, the government sold rice at a reduced price to poor people, but kept the allotment low to prevent hoarding. By mentioning that he goes to visit Ch'ien Cheng after buying his rice ration, Fu Tu places himself among the poor, unlike those "sated with meat and rice".
* this college man: referring to Ch'ien Cheng (A.D. 691 – A.D. 759), who held a professorship at Liberal Arts College, one of the seven colleges under Imperial Academy.
* A Birch leaf Pear rustic: Fu Tu dubbed himself Birch leaf Pear Rustic.
* Hsiangju: Hsiangju Ssuma (179 B.C.—118 B.C.), a famous litterateur and poet, Wenchün's husband. His *Sir Nothing* is a masterpiece, a literary genre between verse and prose, which can be termed as euph (a coinage based on euphuism and euphemism); it has exerted great influence upon later generations of scholars.
* Sir Cloud: referring to Man Yang (53 B.C.– A.D. 18): Hsiung Yang if transliterated, a great scholar, rhymed prose writer and official in the Han dynasty. His *The Great One* is a masterpiece, a literary genre between verse and prose, which can be termed as euph (a coinage based on euphuism and euphemism); it has had a deep influence on works of later generations. According to *History of the Han Dynasty*, when other officials flattered those in power, only Man Yang kept to himself to write his philosophical work, *The Great One*.
* home to go: When Poolbright T'ao resigned from his office as Magistrate of P'engtse, he wrote a verse: *Go Back Home*.
* Confucianism: Confucianism, with Confucius as its founder and representative, is an Eastern religion/philosophy. Although it is more accurately referred to as a philosophy, books on world religions inevitably include it with other religions from Buddhism to Zoroastrianism.
* Confucius (551 B.C.– 479 B.C.) was a renowned thinker, educator and statesman in the Spring and Autumn period, born in the State of Lu, who was the founder of Confucianism and who had exerted profound influence on Chinese culture. Confucius is one of the few leaders who based their philosophy on the virtues that are required for the day-to-day living. His philosophy centered on personal and governmental morality, correctness of social relationships, justice and sincerity.
* Barefoot: Thief Barefoot, a notorious robber mentioned in *Sir Lush* as Confucius's Wordist antagonist.

城 西 陂 泛 舟

青蛾皓齿在楼船，
横笛短箫悲远天。
春风自信牙樯动，
迟日徐看锦缆牵。
鱼吹细浪摇歌扇，
燕蹴飞花落舞筵。
不有小舟能荡桨，
百壶那送酒如泉？

Boating on the Slope West of the Town

This tower boat hold white teeth and beaming eyes,
Long flutes, short pipes, sadness played to the skies.
A spring breeze blows freely to the white mast;
The sun low, we see the cables pulled fast.
Fish puff ripples to shake the singer's fan;
Swallows kick petals to the feasting man.
Had we not smaller boats to ply their oars,
How could we bring jugs of wine spring that pours?

* the slope west of the town: referring to the lake called Goodslope, formed by the confluence from the stream from Mt. South and Master Hu's Fountain, 7 kilometers in circumference.
* tower boat: a large boat that appeared before the Han dynasty, having a three-storey building like a great tower on the deck with a large space or an aisle around for the passage of carts and horses.

* singer's fan: a kind fan often used in dancing.
* swallow: a passerine bird, with short broad, depressed bill, long pointed wings, and forked tail, noted for fleeting flight and migratory habits. In Chinese culture, swallows are welcome to live with a family with their nest on a beam of a sitting room.

渼 陂 行

岑参兄弟皆好奇,
携我远来游渼陂。
天地黕惨忽异色,
波涛万顷堆琉璃。
琉璃汗漫泛舟入,
事殊兴极忧思集。
鼋作鲸吞不复知,
恶风白浪何嗟及。
主人锦帆相为开,
舟子喜甚无氛埃。
凫鹥散乱棹讴发,
丝管啁啾空翠来。
沈竿续蔓深莫测,
菱叶荷花净如拭。
宛在中流渤澥清,
下归无极终南黑。
半陂已南纯浸山,
动影袅窕冲融间。
船舷暝戛云际寺,
水面月出蓝田关。
此时骊龙亦吐珠,
冯夷击鼓群龙趋。
湘妃汉女出歌舞,
金支翠旗光有无。
咫尺但愁雷雨至,
苍茫不晓神灵意。
少壮几时奈老何,

向来哀乐何其多！

Goodslope: A Ballad

Shen Ts'en and his brother, curious they are;
They bring me to Lake Goodslope from afar.
Earth and sky dim, all colors change to pass;
Ten thousand acres of ripples, massed glass.
The glassy ripples roll, our boat set sail,
The experience strange, glee high, hence my ail.
Crocodiles gulping whales are known no more,
How the ill wind, white waves surge to my sore!
My host's brocade sails are now spread for me;
The boatman's happy, and the air dust-free.
Mallards and gulls flee as the oar sings there,
Notes of strings, pipes and chirps thru the green air.
Too deep to be gauged, and it has ne'er been;
Water-nut leaves and lotus blooms look clean.
We're midstream, where it's as clear as Surge Bay,
Receding endlessly from Mt. South gray.
The mountain's soaked by the south of the lake,
Where reflections stirred up shimmer with quake.
The gunwale in the dark heads for Cloud Fane;
The moon comes out over Blue Field Pass again.
Right now, Black Dragon is spitting forth pearls;
Peace beats the drum and wind from dragons whirls.
Hsiang Consorts and Han Maids come forth to dance;
Gold poles and green banners have their light prance.
Nearby, I worry thunderstorms will fall;
In this vast blue I can't grasp God at all.

How long is prime? We can't but grow old;
Thereby we've sorrows and joys manifold!

* Goodslope: the name of a lake in today's Sha'anhsi Province, so named because of the good taste of the water and fish in the lake.
* Shen Ts'en: Shen Ts'en(cir. A.D. 718 – 769): a frontier fortress poet in the T'ang dynasty.
* crocodile: any of a subfamily of large, flesh eating, lizard-like reptile living in or around tropical streams and having thick skin, horny skin composed of scales and plates, a long tail, and a long, narrow, triangular head with massive jaws. The crocodile mentioned in this poem refers to Chinese alligator living in the Yangtze River and the Huai River areas.
* mallards and gulls: waterfowls common in lakes and marshlands.
* Surge Bay: the ocean off the northeastern coast.
* Cloud Fane: southeast of Hu County in today's Sha'anhsi Province.
* Blue Field Pass: 34 kilometers from Blue Field County, located southeast of Goodslope Lake.
* Black Dragon: a dragon said to have precious pearls under its jaw according to an allegory in *Sir Lush*. Here it is a figure for the moon rising over Blue Field seen in reflection.
* Peace: Peace Reliance, Feng-e if transliterated, God of the Yellow River.
* Hsiang Consorts: the goddesses of the River Xiang, originally Lord Mound's two daughters married to Lord Hibiscus, which died crying over the death of their husband in Lake Cavehall.
* Han Maids: nymphs of the Han River.

渼陂西南台

高台面苍陂，
六月风日冷。
蒹葭离披去，
天水相与永。
怀新目似击，
接要心已领。
仿像识鲛人，
空蒙辨鱼艇。
错磨终南翠，
颠倒白阁影。
崷崒增光辉，
乘陵惜俄顷。
劳生愧严郑，
外物慕张邴。
世复轻骅骝，
吾甘杂蛙黾。
知归俗可忽，
取适事莫并。
身退岂待官，
老来苦便静。
况资菱芡足，
庶结茅茨迥。
从此具扁舟，
弥年逐清景。

The Terrace Southwest of Goodslope

The terrace faces the green hill;
In the sixth moon it does feel chill.
Reeds and rushes have off gone;
Heavens and waters become one.
The fresh does my eyes apprehend;
The essentials, I can comprehend.
While mermaids vague I recognize,
A skiff from haze looms to my eyes.
The verdure of Mt. South seems ground,
White Tower's shade inverted around.
What looms there is what glitters high,
There's but one hour to climb I sigh.
Yan and Cheng's merit I desire;
Chang and Ping's affairs I admire.
This world ignores e'en the best steed;
Like frogs a low life I would lead.
Now I'm going home, all can be ignored;
I just do what I can afford.
Why think of office now retired?
Old men need to be quiet, not wired.
I hope nuts and foxnuts there are
And I'll make thatched cottage afar.
From now on I will own a boat,
And to my life's clear scene, I'll float.

* Goodslope: the name of a lake in today's Sha'anhsi Province, so named because of the good taste of the water and fish in the lake.

- reed: the slender, frequently jointed stem of certain tall grasses growing in wet places or in grasses themselves. A frosted reed is an image of the white hair of one getting old or suffering a mishap.
- rush: any one of various grass-like, usually aquatic herbs.
- mermaid: a legendary marine creature having as its upper part the head and body of a lovely woman and its lower part the scaled body and tail of a fish.
- Mt. South: the Southern Hills, a sight of great significance located in Sha'anhsi Province, regarded as a holy place. It is also known as the Southern Mountains, Mt. Great One, Mt. Earth lungs, the mountains south of Long Peace, a great stronghold of the capital, towering in the middle of Ch'in Ridge and rolling about 100 kilometers. It is the birthplace of Wordist culture, Buddhist culture, Filial Piety culture, Longevity culture, Bellheads culture and Plutus culture and is praised as the Capital of Fairies, the crown of Heavenly Abode and the Promised Land of the World.
- Yan and Cheng: You Peace Yan(86 B.C.- A.D. 10) and Sir Truth Cheng, two hermits at the end of the Western Han dynasty.
- Chang and Ping: Liang Chang (250 B.C.- 186 B.C.) and Han Ping, two hermits in the Eastern Han dynasty, who resigned their offices to live in reclusion.
- nut: referring to water chestnuts in this poem.
- foxnut: an annual aquatic herbaceous plant, the fruit of which is used as medicine for diseases caused by dampness.

与鄠县源大少府宴渼陂(得寒字)

应为西陂好,
金钱罄一餐。
饭抄云子白,
瓜嚼水精寒。
无计回船下,
空愁避酒难。
主人情烂熳,
持答翠琅玕。

Feasting at Goodslope with Senior Yüan, Sheriff of Hu County

Western Slope does to all appeal;
One'd squander cash there on one meal.
We scoop rice beaming cloud-seed white,
And chew melon like crystal bright.
We won't get off, so we won't veer;
But it's hard to resist wine I fear.
I'm warm-hearted, and my host too;
Now I toast him at the bamboo.

* Hu County: southwest of Long Peace under the governance of the Capital Region, which was once a state under the Kingdom of Hsia.
* Western Slope: alias Goodslope Lake.
* melon: a trailing plant of the gourd family, or its fruit. There are two genera, the muskmelon and the watermelon, each with numerous varieties, growing in both tropical and temperate zones.

* bamboo: a tall, tree-like or shrubby grass in tropical and semi-tropical regions, a symbol of integrity and altitude, one of the four most important images in Chinese literature, which are wintersweet, orchid, bamboo and chrysanthemum.

赠田九判官

崆峒使节上青霄，
河陇降王款圣朝。
宛马总肥春苜蓿，
将军只数汉嫖姚。
陈留阮瑀谁争长，
京兆田郎早见招。
麾下赖君才并入，
独能无意向渔樵。

To Judge Liang Tien Nine

The envoy to Hollow mounts to the blue;
Kings of Ho and Bulge pledge faith to our court.
Ferghana horses get fat on clover in spring;
Our general like Swift Huo proves the best sort.
Who can compete with Yü Juan of Ch'enliu?
Tien of Long Peace was earlier summoned, crack.
Under their standards, all talents will join;
But to mountains and seas I would go back.

* After the defeat of the T'uyühun in A.D. 754, Han Koshu sent Liang Tien Nine to the capital to announce the victory to Emperor Deepsire.
* Hollow: Mt. Hollow, a mountain in present-day Kansu Province, famous for martial arts. As is said, people here are brave and skillful at fighting battles. And it is a Wordist sanctuary, where Lord Yellow learned the Word from Sir Goodharvest. Sir Lush keeps a record of this inquiry, as reads: Lord Yellow had reigned nineteen years and his orders were carried out all over the land. Having heard that Sir Goodharvest

lived on Mt. Hollow, he went to pay him a visit, saying: "I hear that you know the very Word. May I inquire of you about the quintessence of the very Word? I would acquire the essence of Heaven and earth to help five grains and sustain my people. And I also want to govern Shade and Shine so that all things may grow well." Because of this event, Mt. Hollow is esteemed as the first Wordist mountain in China.

* Ho and Bulge: referring to small states in today's West China.
* Ferghana horse: Ferghana was an ancient state existing in Ferghana Basin. According to historical records, the horse from Ferghana is a precious kind. As it sprints, its shoulders swell and it sweats like bleeding.
* Swift Huo: Swift Huo (140 B.C.- 117 B.C.), a renowned general, prominent strategist and patriotic hero in the Han dynasty. He made his first show at 17, leading 800 fierce cavalrymen to penetrate into enemy lines and defeat the Huns. Huo fought against the Huns in three major wars and each time returned with victory. He died of illness at 24, leaving his achievements as one of the highest glory for Chinese military commanders.
* Yü Juan of Ch'enliu: one of the "Seven Masters of Peace Making" served Ts'ao Ts'ao (A.D. 155 – A.D. 220) in his military headquarters. Juan here stands for Shi Kao, who had served at Fengchiu near Ch'enliu, who was then a secretary in Han Koshu's headquarters.
* Tien of Long Peace: Feng Tien from Long Peace, a high official in the Eastern Han dynasty.

投赠哥舒开府翰二十韵

今代麒麟阁,
何人第一功。
君王自神武,
驾驭必英雄。
开府当朝杰,
论兵迈古风。
先锋百战在,
略地两隅空。
青海无传箭,
天山早挂弓。
廉颇仍走敌,
魏绛已和戎。
每惜河湟弃,
新兼节制通。
智谋垂睿想,
出入冠诸公。
日月低秦树,
乾坤绕汉宫。
胡人愁逐北,
宛马又从东。
受命边沙远,
归来御席同。
轩墀曾宠鹤,
畋猎旧非熊。
茅土加名数,
山河誓始终。
策行遗战伐,

契合动昭融。
勋业青冥上,
交亲气概中。
未为珠履客,
已见白头翁。
壮节初题柱,
生涯独转蓬。
几年春草歇,
今日暮途穷。
军事留孙楚,
行间识吕蒙。
防身一长剑,
将欲倚崆峒。

Presented to General Han Koshu

In the Unicorn Hall of this age,
Who's the first person to there stand?
Our Lord is so divinely blessed,
His heroes to safeguard the land.
The general stands out in this reign,
His art of war outstrips those past.
Our vanguard has fought countless wars,
And conquered territories vast.
In Kokonor no arrows shot,
And in Mt. Heaven bows laid by.
P'o Lien can still deter the foes;
With fierce tribes Chiang Wei can now tie.
All sighed Northern Land had been lost.
In new post, you regained the place,

Sagacious, you win the throne's trust,
Surpassing all colleagues in grace.
Sun and moon linger on Ch'in's trees,
Gen and Kueen girt the House of Han.
The Huns grieve at their defeat,
Ferghana steeds come east again.
You get your mandate far on sands,
Back, the imperial mat you share.
On the red steps he stroked his crane,
What he once shot was not a bear.
To the reed soil he added names;
For China's great land he did swear.
Plan made, warfare you'll leave aside,
Great accord stirs his lasting glare.
Your merit is above the blue,
You make close friends while you can.
I am not your client in pearled shoes;
You see me a white-haired old man.
My boldness is at first inscribed;
Life's like thistledown upward tossed.
How many years have grasses dried?
Now at an end, I'm old and lost.
For warfare you can keep Chu Sun,
Among the ranks Meng Lü's the best.
To guard myself I've a long sword;
Against Mt. Hollow I would rest.

* Unicorn Hall: a memorial hall for worthies who have sacrificed their lives for the country. Emperor Hsuan of Han had martyrs painted and hung in Unicorn Hall in memory of their merits.
* Kokonor: also known as West Sea and Blue Sea (Ch'inghai), the great salt lake more

than 3,300 meters above sea-level in today's Ch'inghai Province.
* Mt. Heaven: also named Mt. Sky, one of the seven mountain chains in the world, 2,500 kilometers long, 250 to 350 kilometers wide on average. Mt. Sky in this poem probably refers to the Khangai Mountains in today's Mongolia, namely Mongolian People's Republic.
* P'o Lien: a renowned commander of Chao. Lien was a meritorious general but he envied Hsiangju Lin for he thought Lin was only good at gabbing. Lin remained polite in spite of Lien's disrespect because he had to put personal dispute aside to keep their state secured. Knowing that, Lien felt ashamed and carried thorns on his back to ask for forgiveness.
* Chiang Wei: Chiang Wei (? -552 B.C.), Sir Lush Wei, a minister of Chin, a strict and just judge and a great commander in the Warring States period.
* new post: In A.D. 754 Han Koshu was made Military Commissioner of Hohsi and Duke of Liang; in that same year he defeated the Tibetans.
* Gen and Kueen: two representations of opposite forces like Shade and Shine in the universe, for example, if Gen is man, then Kween woman, if Gen is Sky, the Kueen Earth, and so on.
* Hun: war-like nomadic peoples occupying vast regions from Mongolia to Central Asia in Chinese history, especially during the Han dynasty. They were a headache and a constant menace on China's western and northern borders.
* Ferghana: Ferghana was an ancient state existing in Ferghana Basin. According to historical records, the horses from Ferghana are a precious kind. As it sprints, its shoulders swell and it sweats like bleeding.
* Northern Land: the area between the Huang River and the Yellow River which had been ceded to the Tibetans in Sagciousire (Juichung)'s reign as provision for the Jincheng Princess, who had been married to the Tibetan king.
* stroked crane: referring to Duke E of Watch's pet crane, which rode with him in his carriage. This usage here suggests the favor that Han Koshu enjoyed.
* first inscribed: When Hsiangju Ssuma left Ch'engtu for Long Peace he inscribed a pillar with the words: "I will never pass over this bridge again unless driving a four-horse cart (the mark of a governor)."
* Chu Sun: Chun Sun (A.D. 220 - A.D. 293), employed by a general; Fu Tu seems to be referring to his friends in Han Koshu's service.
* Meng Lü: Meng Lü was raised to become a Wu general during the Three Kingdoms period.
* Mt. Hollow: a mountain in present-day Kansu Province, famous for martial arts. As is said, people here are brave and skillful at fighting battles. And it is a Wordist

sanctuary, where Lord Yellow learned the Word from Sir Goodharvest. Sir Lush keeps a record of this inquiry, as reads: Lord Yellow had reigned nineteen years and his orders were carried out all over the land. Having heard that Sir Goodharvest lived on Mt. Hollow, he went to pay him a visit, saying: "I hear that you know the very Word. May I inquire of you about the quintessence of the very Word? I would acquire the essence of Heaven and Earth to help five grains and sustain my people. And I also want to govern Shade and Shine so that all things may grow well." Because of this event, Mt. Hollow is esteemed as the first Wordist mountain in China.

寄高三十五书记

叹惜高生老，
新诗日又多。
美名人不及，
佳句法如何。
主将收才子，
崆峒足凯歌。
闻君已朱绂，
且得慰蹉跎。

To Secretary Kao Thirty-Five

Master Kao is old, I give a sigh;
He writes more with each passing day.
No other can match his good fame;
What is the knack, what is the way?
The general's gained a talent true;
With triumph song Mt. Hollow rings.
I hear you've received the red gown;
Which to my life some comfort brings.

* triumph song: according to *Rites of Chough*, a triumph song is played when a battle is won.
* Mt. Hollow: a mountain in present-day Kansu Province, famous for martial arts.
* red gown: a symbol of being an official.

送张十二参军赴蜀州因呈杨五侍御

好去张公子，
通家别恨添。
两行秦树直，
万点蜀山尖。
御史新骢马，
参军旧紫髯。
皇华吾善处，
于汝定无嫌。

Seeing Off Adjutant Chang on His Way to Shu, Presented to Censor Yang

Fare thee well, young Lord Chang, farewell;
Parting grief's intense for friends old.
In two rows, Ch'in's trees are so straight;
Ten thousand, Shu hills sharp look bold.
The censor's a new dappled steed,
The adjutant wears beards as e'er.
He, glorious, has treated me well,
No grudge of you will he e'er bear.

* Ch'in: the Ch'in State or the State of Ch'in (905 B.C - 206 B.C.), enfeoffed as a dependency of Chough by King Piety of Chough in 905 B.C and enfeoffed as a vassal state by King Peace of Chough in 770 B.C. In the ten years from 230 B.C. to 221 B.C., Ch'in wiped out the other six powers and became the first unified regime of China, i.e., the Ch'in Empire.
* Shu: one of the earliest kingdoms in China, founded by Silkworm according to legend.

In the Three Kingdoms period, a new Shu was established by Pei Liu, hence one of the three kingdoms in that period.

* a dappled steed: Because the Eastern Han censor Tien Huan rode a dappled steed, it became metonymy for a censor. This refers to Yang.

赠陈二补阙

世儒多汩没，
夫子独声名。
献纳开东观，
君王问长卿。
皂雕寒始急，
天马老能行。
自到青冥里，
休看白发生。

Presented to Chen Two, Remonstrant

So many scholars are unknown;
You enjoy a good name alone.
For advice opened is East Shrine;
Our Lord asks of Hsiangju's verse fine.
The black hawk grows keen in the cold;
The sky horse still travels though old.
In due course you will reach the blue,
So cease to watch your white hairs new.

* East Shrine: a Wordist temple in Loshine.
* Hsiangju Ssuma: Hsiangju Ssuma (179 B.C.- 118 B.C.), a famous litterateur and poet, Wenchün's husband. His *Sir Nothing* is a masterpiece, a literary genre between verse and prose, which can be termed as euph (a coinage based on euphuism and euphemism).
* hawk: a diurnal bird of prey, notable for keen sight and strong flight, usually used as a metaphor for one who takes military means in contrast with a dove, one who tries to

find peaceful solutions.
* sky horse: According to historical records, the sky horse from Kusana is a precious kind. As it sprints, its shoulders swell and it sweats as if bleeding.

病后过王倚饮赠歌

麟角凤觜世莫识,
煎胶续弦奇自见。
尚看王生抱此怀,
在于甫也何由羡。
且遇王生慰畴昔,
素知贱子甘贫贱。
酷见冻馁不足耻,
多病沈年苦无健。
王生怪我颜色恶,
答云伏枕艰难遍。
疟疠三秋孰可忍,
寒热百日相交战。
头白眼暗坐有胝,
肉黄皮皱命如线。
惟生哀我未平复,
为我力致美肴膳。
遣人向市赊香粳,
唤妇出房亲自馔。
长安冬菹酸且绿,
金城土酥净如练。
兼求畜豪且割鲜,
密沽斗酒谐终宴。
故人情义晚谁似,
令我手脚轻欲旋。
老马为驹信不虚,
当时得意况深眷。
但使残年饱吃饭,

只愿无事常相见。

After Being Sick, I Visited E Wang for a Drink and Presented Him This Song

Unicorn horn and phoenix beak are unknown;
Boiled to be string glue, their wonder is shown.
One sees such a craft Master Wang does boast,
Which I admire and I admire the most.
Coming to Wang soothes my feelings and woes;
I, though poor, well stand poverty he knows.
Hunger and cold cannot reduce my will;
For the whole year I have been weak and ill.
How morbid I looked Wang was so surprised;
I'd been bedridden, so hard, I replied.
Autumn long, the malaria who could bear?
For five score days burns and chills did me wear.
With scab and boils, my hair white, my eyes dim;
My flesh jaundiced, my skin wrinkled, no vim.
You sighed and my poor health you understood,
You took pains to send me delicate food.
You sent someone to buy scented best rice,
And for me called your wife to cook it nice.
In Long Peace green winter pickles sour taste;
The Goldton yogurt looks like white silk chaste.
And you went to get a pig for meat fine
And for a feast you bought a pot of wine.
For friendship, who can do like this, who can?
I feel air-borne, hand and foot, a drunk man.
"An old horse thinks itself a colt"—Yes, true;

I feel obliged, and feel your love accrue.
In my years left o'er, may I eat my fill,
And to meet with you often is my will.

* unicorn: a fabulous deer-like animal with one horn, a symbol of saintliness and divinity in Chinese culture. Confucius lamented the death of a unicorn captured and hence stopped compiling *The Spring and Autumn Annals* and died before long.
* phoenix: the king of all birds, an auspicious sign in Chinese civilization. In Egyptian mythology, it is a legendary bird of great beauty, unique of its kind, which was supposed to live five or six hundred years before consuming itself by fire, rising again from its ashes to live through another cycle, a symbol of immortality. In Chinese mythology, the phoenix is the most beautiful bird that only perches on phoenix trees, i. e., firmiana, only eats firmiana fruit, and only drinks sweet spring water, and this mythic bird appears only in times of peace and sagacious rule.
* Long Peace: referring to Ch'ang'an if transliterated, the capital of the T'ang Empire, at which time it boasted a population of one million, the largest walled city ever built by man, and a cosmopolis of world religions, Buddhism, Confucianism, Wordism, Nestorianism, Zoroastrianism, and even Islamism represented by Saracens. It was the wonder of the age that reached the pinnacle of brilliance in Emperor Deepsire's reign: The main castle with its nine-fold gates, the thirty-six imperial palaces, pillars of gold, innumerable mansions and villas of noblemen, the broad avenues thronged with motley crowds of townsfolk, gallants on horseback, and mandarin cars drawn by yokes of black oxen, countless houses of pleasure, which opened their doors by night all made this city a kaleidoscope of miracles.
* Goldton: an ancient county under the Capital Region.

送裴二虬作尉永嘉

孤屿亭何处，
天涯水气中。
故人官就此，
绝境兴谁同。
隐吏逢梅福，
游山忆谢公。
扁舟吾已僦，
把钓待秋风。

Seeing Off Chiu P'ei Two to His Post as Sheriff in E'erfair

Where's Kiosk of Solitary Isle?
Far off, in the mist o'er the brine.
My old friend goes to his post there;
With his altitude who'll combine?
Among hermits you'll meet Plum Foo,
In the hills, you'll recall Lord Glee.
I have already hired a tiny boat
To fish in autumn breeze at sea.

* E'erfair: what is today's Wenchow, Chechiang Province.
* Solitary Isle: in the E'erfair (Yungchia) River, having two peaks which have pavilions.
* Plum Foo: a constable of Southboom (Nanch'ang) in the Han dynasty, who was said to have become immortal.
* Lord Glee: the poet Lingyün Hsieh (A.D. 385 – A.D. 433), who held a post at E'erfair and wrote a famous poem on this site.

赠献纳使起居田舍人澄

献纳司存雨露边，
地分清切任才贤。
舍人退食收封事，
宫女开函近御筵。
晓漏追趋青琐闼，
晴窗点检白云篇。
扬雄更有河东赋，
唯待吹嘘送上天。

Presented to Ch'eng Tien, Petition Commissioner and Imperial Servant

You do your duty beside rain and dew,
A post pure and clean for talented few.
You decline meals and receive letters sealed;
The palace maid opes the case as appealed.
With dawn hourglass, you rush to the blue gate;
Window sunlit, white-cloud writings you rate.
To praise, a Male Yang will his brush ply
To raise you on my behalf to the sky.

* Male Yang: Hsiung Yang (53 B.C.- 18 B.C.), a thinker and euphuist in the Western Han dynasty.

崔驸马山亭宴集

萧史幽栖地，
林间蹋凤毛。
洑流何处入，
乱石闭门高。
客醉挥金碗，
诗成得绣袍。
清秋多宴会，
终日困香醪。

A Banquet at Adjunct Groom Ts'ui's Mountain Pavilion

Where Flute Man lives in solitude,
One treads Phoenix down in the wood.
From where does the fountain flow by?
Rock riprap hides your gate on high.
The guests drunk, wave cups up and down,
Poem written, one gets a silk gown.
Autumn banquets there're quite a few;
All day I'm raised with fragrant brew.

* Flute Man: Shi Hsiao if transliterated, a legendary immortal in the Spring and Autumn period, who is said to be able to play the flute like the singing of a phoenix.
* Phoenix: In Chinese myths, phoenixes, auspicious birds, unlike ordinary ones, only perch on parasol trees, and only eat bamboo shoots and pearly stone.

示 从 孙 济

平明跨驴出，
未知适谁门。
权门多噂沓，
且复寻诸孙。
诸孙贫无事，
宅舍如荒村。
堂前自生竹，
堂后自生萱。
萱草秋已死，
竹枝霜不蕃。
淘米少汲水，
汲多井水浑。
刈葵莫放手，
放手伤葵根。
阿翁懒惰久，
觉儿行步奔。
所来为宗族，
亦不为盘飧。
小人利口实，
薄俗难可论。
勿受外嫌猜，
同姓古所敦。

Shown to My Grandnephew Chi

At dawn I rode my donkey out,

Not knowing to whose gate I'd go.
The mighty ones back-bite a lot,
So I went to my grandnephew.
My nephew, poor, you are now free,
And your abode's rank with grass tall.
Before your hall there grows bamboo;
Day lilies grow behind your hall.
In autumn the day lilies die;
The bamboo twigs languish in frost.
Draw less from the well to wash rice,
If much is drawn, mud will be caused.
When cutting mallows do take care;
Or, the mallows' roots you will break.
This old fellow has long been lax;
A scurry the boy seems to make.
I have come because of our clan,
Not for the sake of a good meal.
What flunkies care is only food;
Such vain customs we should repeal.
Don't be influenced by those outside;
In the same surname we confide.

* Chi: Chi Tu, Fu Tu's grandnephew, who was once a court advisor-inspector and mayor of Long Peace.
* day lily: any of several lilyworts, with lanceolate leaves, and large flowers on a round thick scape, usually lasting one day. Two species *H. fulva*, tawny red, and *H. flava*, bright yellow, are commonly cultivated.
* bamboo: a tall, tree-like or shrubby grass in tropical and semi-tropical regions, a symbol of integrity and altitude, one of the four most important images in Chinese literature, which are wintersweet, orchid, bamboo and chrysanthemum.
* mallow: a plant of the genus *Malva* with edible leaves, which was one of the five most popular vegetables in ancient China.

* Not for the sake of a good meal: Seeking out wealthy and remote relatives to visit and be treated to a free meal seems to have been common practice. Here it seems that Chi Tu (or someone in his family) has suggested to Fu Tu that he has visited only because he wants to be fed. In the closing Fu Tu protests—perhaps too much—that this was not his purpose.

九日寄岑参

出门复入门，
雨脚但如旧。
所向泥活活，
思君令人瘦。
沈吟坐西轩，
饮食错昏昼。
寸步曲江头，
难为一相就。
吁嗟乎苍生，
稼穑不可救。
安得诛云师，
畴能补天漏。
大明韬日月，
旷野号禽兽。
君子强逶迤，
小人困驰骤。
维南有崇山，
恐与川浸溜。
是节东篱菊，
纷披为谁秀。
岑生多新诗，
性亦嗜醇酎。
采采黄金花，
何由满衣袖。

On the Double Ninth: to Shen Ts'en

Out the gate, in the gate again,
There are but raindrops, as before.
Wherever I turn, I slosh in the mud,
Thinking of you, I'm gaunt and sore.
I sit on west porch brooding there,
Confused in my meals, a bored soul.
The Bent River's a step away,
I've no mind to go for a stroll.
Alas, all humans in the world,
Your harvest can't be saved, oh, no.
How can I the cloud-master kill;
I'd have fixed heavens long ago.
The lights, sun and moon, have been veiled;
In the wilds birds and beasts cry out.
Gentlemen are forced to wind on,
The folk in pains, hurry about.
Due south a high mountain does stand,
It'll be by the Bent soaked I fear.
This festival, mums by East Hedge
Spread in brilliance, brilliant with cheer.
Master Ts'en has many new poems,
And in liquor he seems to drown.
With those golden flowers blooming so,
Can we fill the sleeves of our gown?

* Shen Ts'en (cir. A.D. 718 – A.D. 769): a frontier fortress poet in the T'ang dynasty.
* the Bent River: Ch'uchiang if transliterated, a river and a royal river park of T'ang,

located in the southeast of Long Peace, the capital.
* cloud-master: God of Clouds.
* East Hedge: When Poolbright T'ao (A.D. 365 - A.D. 427) lived in seclusion, he used to plant chrysanthemums by his east hedge.
* golden flower: chrysanthemum, which can be used as stuff for the brewing of chrysanthemum wine.

叹庭前甘菊花

檐前甘菊移时晚，
青蕊重阳不堪摘。
明日萧条醉尽醒，
残花烂熳开何益。
篱边野外多众芳，
采撷细琐升中堂。
念兹空长大枝叶，
结根失所缠风霜。

Sighing over Sweet Chrysanthemums in the Yard

Sweet mums before my eaves, transplanted late,
At Double Ninth I couldn't pick their sprays.
The next day I sober up in the chill;
What is the use of the last flowers ablaze?
By the hedge in the wilds many flowers bloom;
They are gathered and into the hall brought.
These plants grew into lush foliage in vain,
Rooted amiss, with wind and frost distraught.

* mum: chrysanthemum, any of a genus of perennials of the composite family, some cultivated varieties of which have large heads of showy flowers of various colors, a symbol of elegance and integrity in Chinese culture, one of the four most important floral images in Chinese literature, which are wintersweet, orchid, bamboo and chrysanthemum.
* Double Ninth: referring to the Ninth of the Ninth moon, a day for the aged in Chinese

tradition. There is a long tradition that people go climbing on this day, carrying chrysanthemums for their deceased dear ones and sprigs of cornel to exorcize evil spirits.

承沈八丈东美除膳部员外，阻雨未遂驰贺，奉寄此诗

今日西京掾，
多除南省郎。
通家惟沈氏，
谒帝似冯唐。
诗律群公问，
儒门旧史长。
清秋便寓直，
列宿顿辉光。
未暇申宴慰，
含情空激扬。
司存何所比，
膳部默凄伤。
贫贱人事略，
经过霖潦妨。
礼同诸父长，
恩岂布衣忘。
天路牵骐骥，
云台引栋梁。
徒怀贡公喜，
飒飒鬓毛苍。

Sir Tungmei Shen Great Eight Has Been Made Vice-Director of the Catering Department; I Am Not Able to Gallop Off to Congratulate Him Due to the Rain. So Respectfully I Send Him This Poem

Many aides are appointed now
In the Privy Council alone;
But Shen is my family friend,
Who like T'ang Feng calls on the throne.
All ask him about rules of verse;
A scholar, annals he does know.
In clear autumn, he's on night shift;
The constellation casts its glow.
I've no time to give compliments,
I am restrained, enhanced in vain.
What can be compared to your charge?
Catering Post leaves me in pain.
For one debased, rites are abridged;
I'm hindered by rain from your place.
Courtesy should be paid to seniors,
How could I forget your kind grace?
A fine steed's led to Heaven's roads,
To Cloud Terrace a beam is brought.
In vain I embrace Lord Kung's delight,
But wind-ruffled, my hair distraught.

* the Privy Council: one of Triune Dais, the official system in the T'ang dynasty, which includes Privy Council (Central Secretariat Department), Censorate (Undergate

Department) and Executive (Administration Department).
* T'ang Feng, a descendant of a famous general, a petty official renowned for his filial piety. He was outspoken and unselfish, hence elbowed out.
* Catering Post: a logistics department in charge of sacrificial utensils, foods, drinks, fruits, hoarded ice and so on.
* Lord Kung: Yü Kung (127 B.C.- 44 B.C.), known for his rectitude and chasteness, advancing employing the able and sage, punishing evil officials and proposing thriftiness.

苦雨奉寄陇西公兼呈王征士

今秋乃淫雨，
仲月来寒风。
群木水光下，
万象云气中。
所思碍行潦，
九里信不通。
悄悄素浐路，
迢迢天汉东。
愿腾六尺马，
背若孤征鸿。
划见公子面，
超然欢笑同。
奋飞既胡越，
局促伤樊笼。
一饭四五起，
凭轩心力穷。
嘉蔬没混浊，
时菊碎榛丛。
鹰隼亦屈猛，
乌鸢何所蒙。
式瞻北邻居，
取适南巷翁。
挂席钓川涨，
焉知清兴终。

The Pain of the Rain: Respectfully Sent to Lord West Bulge and Presented to Recruit Wang

This autumn's one of flooding rains,
In mid-autumn, cold wind comes on.
Those trees are in a watery light,
Images of all things mist don.
The man I miss is blocked by flood;
Nine Leagues I cannot reach, it's true.
So silent, the road by the pale Ch'an,
Rolls east of the Milky Way blue.
I would make my six-foot horse bound,
Its back like a lone-faring swan.
And I'd meet my prince face to face,
And share his joys, a happy man.
Flying off so far in my dream,
"Cramped up in a cage" I lament.
I rise a few times at a meal,
I lean on the door, heart's strength spent.
Vegetables smeared in the muck;
Seasonal mums choked in the brush.
E'en hawks and falcons curb their force,
In vain the ravens and kites rush?
To my north neighbor I long gaze,
And like the old man of South Lane.
We will hoist sail to fish in flood;
How can I image my blessed gain?

- Lord West Bulge: Yü Li, Emperor Hand-over's sixth son, conferred Count of West Bulge and later Prince of Mid-Han.
- Recruit Wang: a recruit from Ivory Mound of today's Shantung Province.
- Nine Leagues: where Count of West Bulge lived.
- the Milky Way: the Milky Way is a figure for the Wei River. Both the Wei and Ch'an seem to have flooded so that Fu Tu cannot reach Yü Li's residence. The Milky Way, known as the Silver River in Chinese mythology, is a luminous band circling the heavens composed of stars and nebulae; the Galaxy. As legend goes, the Milky Way maid, the granddaughter of Emperor of Heaven fell in love with a worldly cowherd and they gave birth to a son and a daughter. When their love was disclosed to Emperor of Heaven, he sent Queen Mother to take the fairy back to Heaven. While Cowherd was trying to catch up in a boat the cow had made with its horn broken, Queen Mother rived the air with her hairpin, so there appeared the Silver River, i.e., the Milky Way to keep them apart, and the fairy and the cowherd became two stars called Vega and Altair.
- mum: chrysanthemum, any of a genus of perennials of the composite family, some cultivated varieties of which have large heads of showy flowers of various colors, a symbol of elegance and integrity in Chinese culture, one of the four most important floral images in Chinese literature, which are wintersweet, orchid, bamboo and chrysanthemum.
- hawk: a diurnal bird of prey, notable for keen sight and strong flight, usually used as a metaphor for one who takes military means in contrast with a dove, one who tries to find peaceful solutions.

秋雨叹三首
Sighing over Autumn Rain, Three Poems

其 一

雨中百草秋烂死，
阶下决明颜色鲜。
着叶满枝翠羽盖，
开花无数黄金钱。
凉风萧萧吹汝急，
恐汝后时难独立。
堂上书生空白头，
临风三嗅馨香泣。

No. 1

All have rotted and died in autumn rain,
But fresh cassias beside the steps, behold.
They put forth lush leaves like kingfisher plumes,
Their flowers bloom resembling coins of gold.
The chill winds are howling, and blow on you;
I fear hereafter, you can't yourself keep.
The scholar in the hall, his hair turns white;
In the wind he sniffs the fragrance to weep.

* cassia: any of a genus of herbs or shrubs, and trees of the caesalpinia family, common in tropical countries.
* kingfisher: a beautiful bird looking like a halcyon pileata.

其 二

阑风伏雨秋纷纷,
四海八荒同一云。
去马来牛不复辨,
浊泾清渭何当分。
禾头生耳黍穗黑,
农夫田父无消息。
城中斗米换衾裯,
相许宁论两相直。

No. 2

Winds and rains in autumn all come in gusts;
Four seas and eight wilds lie neath the same sky.
How can one tell the Ching clear from the Wei?
E'en horses and oxen can't it descry!
Fungus grows on grains, millet ears are black;
Of farmers' hardship no one dare complain.
In the town rice is exchanged for bedding fine;
The bargain's struck, each having had his gain.

* the Ching: the Ching River—the largest branch of the Yellow River, originating from Kansu and flowing into the Yellow River in Sha'anhsi, and also a branch of the Wei River originating from Ninghsia.
* the Wei: the Wei River: the largest branch of the Yellow River, originating from today's Mt. Birdmouse in Kansu Province, flowing through Precious Rooster, Allshine, Long Peace, and meeting the Yellow River at T'ung Pass.
* E'en horses and oxen can't it descry: an allusion to a scene in *Sir Lush*—When autumn water comes, all rivers and brooklets are filled, and they surge and swell. Between banks and shoals is something even cows and horses cannot discern.

* fungus: any of a large division of thallophytes, including molds, mildews, mushrooms, rusts, and smuts, which are parasites on living organisms or feed upon dead organic material, lack chlorophyll, true roots, stems, and leaves, and reproduce by means of spores.
* millet: a member of the foxtail grass family, or its seeds, cultivated as a cereal, used as a stable food in ancient times, having been cultivated in China for more than 7,300 years, one of the earliest crops in the world.
* Of farmers' hardship no one dare complain: Kuochung Yang, Right Minister, cheated Emperor Deepsire, saying that the rain did not cause flood, did no harm to the crops, so no one dared talk about the disaster.
* bedding fine: probably suggesting the bedding that is part of a bride's trousseau, finely embroidered by the bride herself and used on the wedding night.

其 三

长安布衣谁比数，
反锁衡门守环堵。
老夫不出长蓬蒿，
稚子无忧走风雨。
雨声飕飕催早寒，
胡雁翅湿高飞雁。
秋来未曾见白日，
泥污后土何时干？

No. 3

Who can compare with commons in Long Peace?
I lock my barred gate and keep to my walls.
The young boy free of care, runs in the storm;
The old man stays in, and wormwood grows tall;
The sound of rain whooshes, the cold sets in,
The Hun wild geese are wet, hard to fly high.
Since autumn came I have never seen the bright sun;
Mud befouls the great Earth—when will it dry?

* Long Peace: Ch'ang'an if transliterated, the metropolis of gold, the capital of the T'ang Empire, with 1,000,000 inhabitants, the largest walled city ever built by man, and now the capital of today's Sha'anhsi Province. Long Peace saw the wonder of Chinese civilization that reached the pinnacle of brilliance in Emperor Deepsire's reign.
* wormwood: any of a genus (*Artemisia*) of herbs or small shrubs related to the sagebrush, especially a common species, aromatic, tonic, bitter, and used in making absinthe.
* Hun: war-like nomadic peoples occupying vast regions from Mongolia to Central Asia in Chinese history, especially during the Han dynasty. They were a headache and a constant menace on China's western and northern borders.

奉赠太常张卿二十韵

方丈三韩外,
昆仑万国西。
建标天地阔,
诣绝古今迷。
气得神仙迥,
恩承雨露低。
相门清议众,
儒术大名齐。
轩冕罗天阙,
琳琅识介珪。
伶官诗必诵,
夔乐典犹稽。
健笔凌鹦鹉,
铦锋莹鷞鹈。
友于皆挺拔,
公望各端倪。
通籍逾青琐,
亨衢照紫泥。
灵虬传夕箭,
归马散霜蹄。
能事闻重译,
嘉谟及远黎。
弼谐方一展,
班序更何跻。
适越空颠踬,
游梁竟惨凄。
谬知终画虎,

微分是醯鸡。
萍泛无休日,
桃阴想旧蹊。
吹嘘人所羡,
腾跃事仍睽。
碧海真难涉,
青云不可梯。
顾深惭锻炼,
才小辱提携。
槛束哀猿叫,
枝惊夜鹊栖。
几时陪羽猎,
应指钓璜溪。

Respectfully Presented to Chang, Chamberlain for Ceremonials

Square Isle lies beyond three Koreas,
Mt. Queen's west of myriad domains;
Markers set for Heaven and Earth,
Far off, a mystery it remains.
Your air resembles that of gods;
You win the rain and dew in bliss.
Your minister's family's praised;
Your Confucian arts can match his.
By palace gates carts are arrayed,
From trinkets, a disc you discern.
The musicians chant your fine verse,
Kui's musical art you still learn.
Your brush surpasses "the Parrot";

The sharp points glisten to grebe fat.
Your friends are all talents great,
Each is in high esteem like that.
Registered, you pass the blue gate;
In Broad Way, you shine purple paste.
Eve mark sent by Dragon Divine,
Your horse its frosty hooves does haste.
Your merit known, translated wide,
E'en remote folk your ideas prize.
Once your conciliation is shown,
To what place or rank will you rise?
I went to Yüeh and fell down there,
And toured Liang, sad and mad like that.
I, painting tigers, what a fool,
Unimportant like a small gnat.
A duckweed adrift, I ne'er rest,
Fancying the shade of peach tree.
Thank you for your commendation,
But the chance to climb high shuns me.
There is no ladder to the sky.
And it is hard to cross the blue.
Your love's deep, but I'm unrefined,
Abased, I'm not worth your love true.
Caged so tight, the gibbon cries out;
Twigs startled magpies perched to shriek.
When will you escort the crown's hunt?
You'll find one fishing in Jade Creek.

* The recipient is Chi Chang, the son of the former minister Yüeh Chang and the husband of Princess of Ningch'in.
* Square Isle: one of the isles of the immortals in the Eastern Ocean. In the T'ang

Empire, the Korea peninsula was divided into three kingdoms, hence called Three Koreas.
* Mt. Queen: in the northwest, supposed to be the dwelling of immortals.
* Kui: a music officer of Shun's day. This alludes to Chi Chang's position in the Court of Ceremonials.
* grebe fat: used to oil the finest swords; the "point" of this sword probably refers to the sharpness of Chi Chang's writings.
* registered: To have one's name on the palace registers permitted access to the palace.
* Dragon Divine: the dripper of the water-clock, whose marker indicates evening.
* Yüeh: referring to south part of China, particularly present-day Shaohsing, Chechiang.
* Liang: present-day Kaifeng.
* A duckweed adrift, I ne'er rest: This refers to Fu Tu's wandering after his first examination failure.
* gibbon: any of a family of small, slender, long armed, tree-dwelling, anthropoid of apes of India, South China, and the East Indies.
* magpie: a jaylike passerine corvine bird, having a long and graduated tail and featured with black-and-white coloring, which often makes loud chirps to report good news, as is believed by many Chinese.
* Jade Creek: referring to Pan Stream, where once a jade trinket was gained which Great Grand was fishing there, hence also known as Jade Creek. This is an allusion to the story of Great Grand, an influential strategist and statesman. He was once a slaughterer at his early age and remained diligent in hardship, expecting to display his ability for the country one day, but did not make any achievements until he was 70 years old. He went west at the age of 72. While fishing, he waited for King Civil so that he could sell his strategies, which finally won the king's appreciation. After Great Grand helped King Civil win his reign, Yingknoll was given him as his fief owing to his contribution.

上韦左相二十韵（见素）

凤历轩辕纪，
龙飞四十春。
八荒开寿域，
一气转洪钧。
霖雨思贤佐，
丹青忆老臣。
应图求骏马，
惊代得麒麟。
沙汰江河浊，
调和鼎鼐新。
韦贤初相汉，
范叔已归秦。
盛业今如此，
传经固绝伦。
豫樟深出地，
沧海阔无津。
北斗司喉舌，
东方领搢绅。
持衡留藻鉴，
听履上星辰。
独步才超古，
馀波德照邻。
聪明过管辂，
尺牍倒陈遵。
岂是池中物，
由来席上珍。
庙堂知至理，

风俗尽还淳。
才杰俱登用，
愚蒙但隐沦。
长卿多病久，
子夏索居频。
回首驱流俗，
生涯似众人。
巫咸不可问，
邹鲁莫容身。
感激时将晚，
苍茫兴有神。
为公歌此曲，
涕泪在衣巾。

Presented to Chiensu Wei, Premier of the Left

By the end of this years, as known,
The dragon's flown two score years' course.
The wilds ope a realm of long life,
Potter's Wheel is turned by One Force.
He longs for a rain-like good aide;
His old official's in his mind.
As is drawn, he seeks a fine steed;
Great, a unicorn he does find!
The Long, the Yellow scoured of mud,
All renewed and raised out and in.
Like Hsien Wei, who served Court of Han,
Or Shu Fan who came back to Ch'in.
Such is now your glorious success

In spreading Classics deep and broad.
Camphor trees are rooted down ground;
The gray sea's vast, without a ford.
The Dipper governs throat and tongue;
East you lead those who wear a badge.
Your shoes are heard when climbing high.
Holding the scale, you sort and gauge.
Unique, your talent outshines all,
Your virtue lights up all around.
Your wisdom surpasses Lu Kuan,
Your letters o'erwhelm Ts'un's, profound.
How could you be fish in the pool,
Which are treasured dainties at feast?
In shrines you know rituals and rites
To make folks pure, not vain the least.
All talents have now been employed,
But I, benighted, sink obscure.
Hsiangju has long been very sick,
Tsuhsia often lives alone, poor.
How I have dashed through the dust world,
All my life I've been like most men.
There's no place for me in Ts'ou or Lu,
I need not ask of my fate then.
There must be God in the vast wild:
I'm stirred as I'm in my last years.
For you, sir, I sing out this song,
My gown and kerchief wet with tears.

* this year: This years according to "phoenix calendar". When Young Sky (Shaohao), Cartshaft or Yellow Emperor's son, became a ruler, the arrival of a phoenix led him to call the calendar the "phoenix calendar."

* The dragon's flown two score years' course: This line means that Emperor Deepsire has been on the throne for forty years.
* Potter's Wheel: Heaven, the sky or the universe.
* One Force: the unitary vim of Heaven and Earth. The "Potter's Wheel" is Heaven that produces the myriad things.
* unicorn: a fabulous deer-like animal with one horn, a symbol of saintliness and divinity in Chinese culture. Confucius lamented the death of a unicorn captured and hence stopped compiling *The Spring and Autumn Annals* and died before long.
* the Long: the Long River, the longest river in China, regarded as Mother of Chinese culture, originating from the T'angkula Mountains on Tibet Plateau, flowing through 11 provincial areas, more than 6300 kilometers long.
* the Yellow: the Yellow River, the second longest river in China, flowing across Loess Plateau, hence yellow water all the way. It is 5,464 kilometers long, with a drainage area of 752,443 square kilometers. It has nurtured the Chinese nation, hence regarded as the cradle of Chinese civilization. As legend goes, the river derived from a yellow dragon that, couchant on Midland Plain, ate yellow soil, flooded crops, devoured people and stock, and was finally tamed by Great Worm, the First King of Hsia (21 B.C.– 16 B.C.).
* Hsien Wei: Hsien Wei (149 B.C.– 60 B.C.), Prime Minister and a great Confucian scholar of the Western Han dynasty.
* Shu Fan: alias Sui Fan (? – 255 B.C.), a politician, military strategist, and Prime Minister of Ch'in.
* the Dipper: the Big Dipper, a constellation composed of seven bright stars, which looks like a spoon in the sky. The Dipper has an important position in Chinese literature, likened to an emperor or a personage of noble character and high prestige, or likened to a beacon for the guidance of one's career or pursuit.
* Lu Kuan: Lu Kuan (A.D. 209 – A.D. 256), a wizard of Weigh in the Three Kingdoms period.
* Ts'un: Ts'un Ch'en, a man of letters and Prefect of Honan.
* Hsiangju: Hsiangju Ssuma, a famous litterateur and poet living between 179 B.C. and 118 B.C., Wenchün's husband. His *Sir Nothing* is a masterpiece, a literary genre between verse and prose, which can be termed as euph (a coinage based on euphuism and euphemism); it has exerted great influence upon later generations of scholars.
* Tsuhsia: Sir Summer (507 B.C.– 400 B.C.) Confucius's student, one of Ten Wisest Under Confucius and One of the Seventy-two Sages Under Confucius.

沙 苑 行

君不见
左辅白沙如白水,
缭以周墙百馀里。
龙媒昔是渥洼生,
汗血今称献于此。
苑中騋牝三千匹,
丰草青青寒不死。
食之豪健西域无,
每岁攻驹冠边鄙。
王有虎臣司苑门,
入门天厩皆云屯。
骕骦一骨独当御,
春秋二时归至尊。
至尊内外马盈亿,
伏枥在坰空大存。
逸群绝足信殊杰,
倜傥权奇难具论。
累累塯阜藏奔突,
往往坡陀纵超越。
角壮翻腾麋鹿游,
浮深簸荡鼋鼍窟。
泉出巨鱼长比人,
丹砂作尾黄金鳞。
岂知异物同精气,
虽未成龙亦有神。

Sand Park: A Ballad

Don't you espy
White sands of Left Bulwark like waters white,
Which the buttress for thirty miles does brace?
The dragon-steeds born in Wowa before
With sweat-blood praised, are given to this place.
The park boasts three thousand stallions and mares,
Which survive coldness in green rolling wide.
They grow strong and tough, no such in the West;
Each year they bear colts, the borderland's pride.
A strong soldier's in charge of the park gate,
Where one sees studs all like clouds in the sky.
But Cool Frost steeds are fit for the court's use,
Each spring and autumn, sent to the Most High.
Within, without, the crown's a million steeds,
Those at the trough or out, all live in vain.
The peerless, supreme of hoof, are so rare,
So powerful, hard to find in this domain.
Rolling hummocks and dunes their gallop hide;
O'er slopes and hills they bounce ahead and leap.
Vying in vim, they prance, roaming with deer,
To turtle lairs the waves surge up to sweep.
The abyss brings forth fish as long as men;
The tails were cinnabar, gold were their scales.
Who knows different things the same essence share;
Though not dragons yet, their spirit prevails.

* Left Bulwark: the region to the east of Long Peace (presuming the imperial orientation

facing south) that supports the capital region.
* dragon-steed: Emperor Martial of Han's song about the "horses of Heaven," describes such horses as "dragon-steeds"; i.e., they bring true dragons. The Han history "*Annals of Emperor Martial*" describe the horses of Heaven as actually being born in the Wowa's waters, further strengthening their link to dragons. The Wowa is a river in the Dunhuang region.
* Cool Frost: the name of an exceptional horse, hence the type.
* turtle: referring to a tortoise-like beast in mythology. In China, tablets of great importance were usually carried on the back of a turtle-like creature, which is said to be a figure of the sixth son of the dragon, who is strong and keen on carrying a heavy load.
* dragon: Though variously understood as a large reptile, a marine monster, a jackal and so on in Western culture, it has been esteemed as a fabulous serpent-like giant winged animal, a totem of the Chinese nation and a symbol of benevolence and sovereignty in Chinese culture.

桥陵诗三十韵因呈县内诸官

先帝昔晏驾,
兹山朝百灵。
崇冈拥象设,
沃野开天庭。
即事壮重险,
论功超五丁。
坡陀因厚地,
却略罗峻屏。
云阙虚冉冉,
风松肃泠泠。
石门霜露白,
玉殿莓苔青。
宫女晚知曙,
祠官朝见星。
空梁簇画戟,
阴井敲铜瓶。
中使日夜继,
惟王心不宁。
岂徒恤备享,
尚谓求无形。
孝理敦国政,
神凝推道经。
瑞芝产庙柱,
好鸟鸣岩扃。
高岳前嵂崒,
洪河左滢溁。
金城蓄峻趾,

沙苑交回汀。
永与奥区固,
川原纷眇冥。
居然赤县立,
台榭争岧亭。
官属果称是,
声华真可听。
王刘美竹润,
裴李春兰馨。
郑氏才振古,
啖侯笔不停。
遣辞必中律,
利物常发硎。
绮绣相辗转,
琳琅愈青荧。
侧闻鲁恭化,
秉德崔瑗铭。
太史候凫影,
王乔随鹤翎。
朝仪限霄汉,
客思回林坰。
轗轲辞下杜,
飘飖陵浊泾。
诸生旧短褐,
旅泛一浮萍。
荒岁儿女瘦,
暮途涕泗零。
主人念老马,
廨署容秋萤。
流寓理岂惬,
穷愁醉未醒。

何当摆俗累，
浩荡乘沧溟。

Poem on Bridge Hill, to Be Shown to the Officials of the County

When the Most High made his last tour,
A hundred hill gods did Him call.
The lofty hill enfolds his tomb;
The fertile wilds ope as his hall.
One man did more than five stout men.
Now the layered rocks protrude ahead,
With their slopes along the thick earth,
And drawn back, a high screen is spread.
The towers scraping clouds seem air borne,
The pine wind blows solemn instead.
Moss and lichens green the jade hall;
Frost and dew white on the stone gate.
Shrine officers at dawn see stars;
Till dawn harem ladies sit late.
By the beams cluster painted spears;
At the well there clinks a bronze pot.
Messengers come day and night,
Our king's not at peace, he is not.
He's concerned with all offerings,
And he still seeks what is called void.
With filial rules he rules the state,
In the Word his mind is employed.
Ganoderma on columns grow;
Good birds sang out by the cliff door.

The high mountain looms ahead;
The river surges left to pour.
There spread the relics of Gold Wall;
Sand Park crosses the sandbar mound.
Firm for ever with the core land,
The great plains are dim all around.
Safely established is Red Town;
Terraces and kiosks for height vie.
All officers suit their office,
As they have done so well, praised high.
Wang and Liu, like handsome bamboo,
Pei and Li, like orchids so lush.
Cheng's talent can surpass all past,
Without stop runs on Count Tan's brush.
Their words and phrases match in rhyme,
Fresh like sharpened knifes off the hone.
Silk and damask, turned o'er and o'er,
Rare jade glimmers, of a good tone.
I've heard of Kung Lu's gracefulness;
Yüan Ts'ui's inscriptions best remain.
Grand Historian learns from wild ducks;
Prince of Front goes astride a crane.
Court rites reach to the Milky Way;
To wild woods travelers' thoughts go.
In all hardships I leave Hsiatu,
And 'cross the muddy Ching I row.
A scholar, in short homespun robe,
Like duckweed I drift to and fro.
A famine year, my kids grow thin;
On the dusk road my sad tears flow.
My host cares about his old horse;

> The stable autumn fire-worms fly.
> How can I feel happy adrift?
> Ne'er sober, with worries I lie.
> When shall I shake off the dust world
> And cruise the sea with blue waves whirled?

* The famine in Long Peace and Fu Tu's failure to find patronage finally led him to take his family north to Fenghsien County. Here Fu Tu is essentially begging for food and lodging for himself and his family.
* Bridge Hill: fifteen miles northwest of Fenghsien.
* moss: a tiny, delicate green bryophytic plant growing on damp decaying wood, wet ground, humid rocks or trees, producing capsules which open by an operculum and contain spores. Under a poet's writing brush, it may arouse a poetic feeling or imagination.
* lichen: any of various small plants composed of a particular fungus and a particular alga growing in an intimate symbiotic association and forming a dual plant, commonly adhering to rock, wood, soil, etc.
* the Word: referring to Tao if transliterated, the most significant and profoundest concept in Chinese philosophy. According to Laocius's *The Word and the World*: "The Word is void, but its use is infinite. O deep! It seems to be the root of all things."
* ganoderma: *Ganoderma Lucidum Karst* in Latin, a grass with an umbrella top, a pore fungus, used as medicine and tonic in China.
* the high mountain: referring to Mt. Flora, one of the Five Mountains in China, located in Sha'anhsi Province, along with Mt. Ever in Shanhsi, Mt. Arch in Shantung, Mt. Scale in Hunan, and Mt. Tower in Honan.
* Gold Wall: Sand Park Wall built in the first year of Lord Piety of Ch'in's reign.
* Red Town: an alias of Old China.
* bamboo: a tall, tree-like or shrubby grass in tropical and semi-tropical regions, a symbol of integrity and altitude, one of the four most important images in Chinese literature, which are wintersweet, orchid, bamboo and chrysanthemum.
* orchid: any of a widely distributed family of terrestrial or epiphytic monocotyledonous plants having thickened bulbous roots and often very showy distinctive flowers, one of the four most important floral images in Chinese literature, which are wintersweet, orchid, bamboo, and chrysanthemum.
* Prince of Front: Prince of Front (567 B.C.- 547 B.C.), the first son of King Spirit of Chough. He was an intelligent and courageous young man. Though high as a prince, he

had few desires and was keen on the Word. As legend goes, he met Master Floating Knoll at the Lo River, followed him to deep mountains, and after he died young, he rose to the sky, riding a white crane, and became immortal.
* the Milky Way: the Silver River that Queen Mother made with her hair pin in Chinese mythology; a luminous band circling the heavens composed of stars and nebulae; the Galaxy.
* Hsiatu: 7.5 kilometers south of Long Peace County.
* Ching: the Ching River, the largest branch of the Yellow River, originating from Kansu and flowing into the Yellow River in Sha'anhsi, and also a branch of the Wei River originating from Ninghsia.
* duckweed: any of several small, disk-shaped, floating aquatic plants common in streams and ponds.
* famine year: the thirteenth year of Heaven-Blessed (A.D. 742 - A.D. 756), great famine occurred in Mid China.

送蔡希鲁都尉还陇右因寄高三十五书记

蔡子勇成癖，
弯弓西射胡。
健儿宁斗死，
壮士耻为儒。
官是先锋得，
材缘挑战须。
身轻一鸟过，
枪急万人呼。
云幕随开府，
春城赴上都。
马头金匼匝，
驼背锦模糊。
咫尺雪山路，
归飞青海隅。
上公犹宠锡，
突将且前驱。
汉使黄河远，
凉州白麦枯。
因君问消息，
好在阮元瑜。

Seeing Commander Hsilu Ts'ai Off on His Return to Bulge Right, Thereby I Write to Secretary Kao Thirty-Five

Master Ts'ai's courage's a mad one;

He shoots Huns from west, bent his bow.
A soldier would die in combat;
Scholar-like? A bold man says: "No."
Your rank depends on how you fight;
Your ability warfare tries.
Your fleet is as swift as a bird;
Your spearing the world does surprise.
Tents like clouds follow the leader,
Setting out for spring's Upper Town.
The horse's head wrapped with gold works,
The camel's back like a silk gown.
The road to Mt. Snow's a short way;
You fly back to Blue Sea instead.
Your superior's granted favor,
As a general you charge ahead.
Like the Han envoy you trek far,
While wheat in Coolton is ripe now.
May I ask of his condition:
How is he in the army, how?

* Bulge Right: one of the aliases of today's Kansu Province.
* Hun: war-like nomadic peoples occupying vast regions from Mongolia to Central Asia in Chinese history, especially during the Han dynasty. They were a headache and a constant menace on China's western and northern borders.
* tent: as a camp or a military office.
* Upper Town: alias Capital Region, a prefecture consisting of twenty-three counties, including today's Central Sha'anhsi, Southeastern Kansu and some areas of Ninghsia and Ch'inghai.
* Mt. Snow: a mountain where Manjusri used to teach Buddhism, 30 kilometers from Chinch'ang County, Melon Prefecture, bordering T'uyühun in the south.
* Blue Sea: also known as West Sea and Kokonor, Ch'inghai if transliterated, the great salt lake more than 3,300 meters above sea-level in today's Ch'inghai Province.
* Coolton: Martial Might, Wuwei if transliterated, a prefectural city located in present-

day Kansu Province, built by Emperor Martial of Han (156 B.C.- 87 B.C.) to garrison the border, so named because Swift Huo defeated Huns and thus showed the martial might of the great Han Empire. It has been prosperous as the hub of the Silk Road and famous for wine brewage, hence styled Grape Wine Town.

醉 歌 行

陆机二十作文赋,
汝更少年能缀文。
总角草书又神速,
世上儿子徒纷纷。
骅骝作驹已汗血,
鸷鸟举翮连青云。
词源倒流三峡水,
笔阵独扫千人军。
只今年才十六七,
射策君门期第一。
旧穿杨叶真自知,
暂蹶霜蹄未为失。
偶然擢秀非难取,
会是排风有毛质。
汝身已见唾成珠,
汝伯何由发如漆。
春光澹沱秦东亭,
渚蒲牙白水荇青。
风吹客衣日杲杲,
树搅离思花冥冥。
酒尽沙头双玉瓶,
众宾皆醉我独醒。
乃知贫贱别更苦,
吞声踯躅涕泪零。

A Drunken Song

Hair in tufts, your cursive script shows great speed,
While other boys running around, all those.
Chi Lu at twenty wrote euphs, prose lyric;
E'en younger, you could articles compose.
When Brownie is but a colt that sweats blood,
The bird of prey flutters and flies to the blue.
Your eloquence pours and flows to Three Gorges,
And your brush sweeps away an army true.
But now you're just sixteen or seventeen;
In Grand Test you've aimed to be number one.
He who shoots a poplar leaf knows himself;
If his horse kicks up frosted hooves, he's won.
The chance to be select you can well get,
A time will come when you take wings to fly.
In your case, you have turned spittle to pearls;
How can your uncle have hair like black dye?
Spring light wafts around the kiosk east of Ch'in,
Young reeds by isles white, and water-grass green.
The breeze blows my clothes, and the sun shines bright,
The trees stir my nostalgia, the flowers keen.
The wine's gone on the sands, there two jade pots;
All the guests are drunk, I'm sober alone.
I know when debased parting is more pain;
My voice choked back, I linger, with tears strewn.

* hair in tufts: indicating a child before adolescence.
* cursive script: a peculiar traditional art of calligraphy characterized by brief flowing

strokes, as came into being based on the clerical script in the Han dynasty, and with the incorporation of regular script by Right General Wang, his son and others in the Way and Chin dynasties and the development of Hold Plain in the T'ang dynasty it has evolved to what it is now.

* Chi Lu: Plain Land (A.D. 261 – A.D. 303), a young brilliant general in Wu and then a renowned litterateur and calligrapher in the Western Chin dynasty.
* euph: a high-brow flowery prose lyric, a genre having features of both poetry and prose.
* Brownie: a legendary fine horse with red-brown body and a red mane and tail.
* Three Gorges: referring to the three gorges of the Long River, including Big Pond Gorge, Witch Gorge, and Westridge Gorge, a set of spectacular gorges formed where the Long River cuts its way through the formidable Witch Mountains, forming a three-hundred-kilometer stretch of very narrow canyons.
* Grand Test: also called Court Test or Court Examination, the highest level of the civil-service examinations aiming at selecting qualified officials, instituted by Emperor Highsire of T'ang (A.D. 628 – A.D. 683), held every three years and the final decision of ranking was made by an emperor himself.

陪李金吾花下饮

胜地初相引，
徐行得自娱。
见轻吹鸟毳，
随意数花须。
细草偏称坐，
香醪懒再酤。
醉归应犯夜，
可怕李金吾。

Accompanying Li Drinking Amid Flowers

First led here to this blooming scene,
Walking slowly, I feel at ease.
As bird-down's light, I blow it off,
And I count stamens as I please.
Fine grass, well-suited as a seat,
Good brew, too lazy to buy more.
If back drunk, the curfew we'll breach;
Of Court Guard Li we are in awe.

* Court Guard: Gold Crow Guard, to which Li belongs were in charge of enforcing curfew at the palace.

官 定 后 戏 赠

不作河西尉，
凄凉为折腰。
老夫怕趋走，
率府且逍遥。
耽酒须微禄，
狂歌托圣朝。
故山归兴尽，
回首向风飙。

Playfully Presented After My Post Was Decided

I won't serve as Hohsi's sheriff,
Not to bow down to the other.
I've fears having to run about;
A post in Right Guard is better.
For wine, I need a modest pay,
To sing like mad rests on Sage Lord.
My will to withdraw is now gone,
I turn my head while wind is roared.

* Hohsi's sheriff: a civil-military governor of Hohsi (West of the River literally), an area comprising today's Northwest Kansu and West Inner Mongolia, generally the area west of the Yellow River.
* Right Guard: usually the guard in defense of East Palace where a crown prince lives. Fu Tu held a minor position probably in charge of the management of armors.
* Sage Lord: a sagacious, liberal emperor.

去 矣 行

君不见韝上鹰,
一饱则飞掣。
焉能作堂上燕,
衔泥附炎热。
野人旷荡无腼颜,
岂可久在王侯间。
未试囊中餐玉法,
明朝且入蓝田山。

Gone

Don't you espy the hawk on the gauntlet?
Having eaten, it flies away.
How could it be a swallow in the hall,
By the heat, its beak holding clay?
A man of the wilds, broad and free of shame,
How can I with lords and princes long stay?
Not having tried the knack of eating jade,
At dawn, to Mt. Blue Field I'll make my way.

* hawk: a diurnal bird of prey, notable for keen sight and strong flight, usually used as a metaphor for one who takes military means in contrast with a dove, one who tries to find peaceful solutions.
* swallow: a passerine black bird, with short broad, depressed bill, long pointed wings, and forked tail, noted for fleeting flight and migratory habits. In Chinese culture, swallows are welcome to live with a family with their nest on a beam.
* Mt. Blue Field: a mountain 15 kilometers away from Blue Field County under today's Hsi-an, Sha'anhsi Province, famous for jade mined there, called Blue Field Jade.

夜听许十诵诗爱而有作

许生五台宾，
业白出石壁。
余亦师粲可，
身犹缚禅寂。
何阶子方便，
谬引为匹敌。
离索晚相逢，
包蒙欣有击。
诵诗浑游衍，
四座皆辟易。
应手看捶钩，
清心听鸣镝。
精微穿溟涬，
飞动摧霹雳。
陶谢不枝梧，
风骚共推激。
紫燕自超诣，
翠驳谁剪剔。
君意人莫知，
人间夜寥阒。

Listening to Hsu Ten Chanting a Poem at Night and Writing Mine as I'm Perturbed

A sojourner on Mt. Five Heights,
Hsu left Stone Cliff, finished, profound.

From my teachers I also learned,
But to the still Zen I'm still bound.
How can I command things like you?
By mistake, I've become your peer.
Secluded, I have met you late,
With you my haze will disappear.
In chanting verse you are so free,
All there present with you comply.
We watch you deftly play your sword,
And listen to your arrow fly.
Delicate, you pierce prime chaos;
Your flight's propelled, the thunder chased.
T'ao and Hsieh can't obstruct your course;
For *Airs* and *Woebegone* you're praised.
Purple Swallow does surpass all;
Azure Dapple, well trimmed, takes flight;
Your mind no one can understand;
The human world's still under night.

* Mt. Five Heights: one of the four most famous Buddhist mountains in China, located in Shanhsi Province, the other three being Mt. P'ut'uo in Chechiang, Mt. Nine Flower in Anhui, and Mt. Brow in Ssuch'uan.
* Zen: a kind of performance of quietude in a form of meditation or contemplation. When Sanskrit jana was introduced to China, it was translated as Zan or Zen for this kind of practice. In the T'ang dynasty, educated Chinese were imbued with Zen, and many of them were associated with zen monks and spent much time in Zen monasteries.
* T'ao: Poolbright T'ao (A.D. 352 – A.D. 427), Yüanming T'ao if transliterated, a complex figure and a poet of complex poems—a verse writer, poet, and litterateur in the Chin dynasty, and the founder of Chinese idyllism, who was once the magistrate of P'engtse.
* Hsieh: referring to Lingyün Hsieh (A.D 385 – A.D 433), a Buddhist and traveler in the Northern and Southern dynasties, and a representative topographical poet in Chinese

history.
* *Airs:* referring to *Airs of the States*. *The Book of Songs*, the first collection of Chinese poetry compiled by Confucius in Seventh Century B.C., which consists of *Airs of the States*, *Psalms*, and *Odes*.
* *Woebegone*: *Lisao* if transliterated, a long poem by Yüan Ch'ü (340 B.C.- 278 B.C.), a great patriotic poet and official of Ch'u.
* Purple Swallow: name of a fine horse in ancient China and a metonymy for fine horses.
* Azure Dapple: name of a fine horse in ancient China and a metonymy for fine horses.

戏简郑广文虔兼呈苏司业源明

广文到官舍,
系马堂阶下。
醉则骑马归,
颇遭官长骂。
才名四十年,
坐客寒无毡。
赖有苏司业,
时时与酒钱。

A Playful Message to Dr. Chien Cheng, Delivered to Yüanming Su, Director of Studies, as Well

When Doctor Cheng reaches his post,
He ties his horse to the hall stairs.
When drunk, he rides back on his horse;
His superior's scolding he bears.
His talent known for forty years,
Cold, there's no felt as his guests dine.
Luckily, there's Director Su,
Who oft gives him money for wine.

* Dr. Chien Cheng: Chien Cheng (A.D. 691 - A.D. 759), who held a professorship at Liberal Arts College, one of the seven colleges under Imperial Academy. He was a versatile scholar, a litterateur, poet, painter, calligrapher, versed in astronomy, geography, natural sciences, military art, and medicine.

* Yüanming Su: Yüanming Su (? – A.D. 764), a Mid-T'ang poet, who starved in Long Peace.
* Director of Studies: name of a post under the National Academy, aiding the president in teaching.

夏日李公见访

远林暑气薄，
公子过我游。
贫居类村坞，
僻近城南楼。
旁舍颇淳朴，
所愿亦易求。
隔屋唤西家，
借问有酒不。
墙头过浊醪，
展席俯长流。
清风左右至，
客意已惊秋。
巢多众鸟斗，
叶密鸣蝉稠。
苦道此物聒，
孰谓吾庐幽。
水花晚色静，
庶足充淹留。
预恐尊中尽，
更起为君谋。

Visited by Lord Li on a Summer Day

The far wood's the sultry but mild;
To me a touring childe comes down.
My poor dwelling's a rural one,

Beside the tower south of the town.
My neighbors are simple and pure;
What I wish for can be well got.
I call my next door to the west,
Asking if they have wine or not.
Thick brew spreads balm over the wall;
By the long stream I spread my mat.
Cool breezes come from left and right,
Autumn's come suddenly like that.
Nests are many, flocks of birds caw;
Leaves are so dense, cicadas shrill.
By such creatures I'm much annoyed;
Who would say my cottage is still.
The dusk veils the calm lotus flowers,
Which I hope can make you remain.
I'm afraid we'll run out of wine,
To buy you more, I rise again.

* Lord Li: Yan Li (A.D. 814 – A.D. 846), Emperor Martial of T'ang, who reigned for seven years. When Fu Tu wrote this poem, Yan Li was a chamberlain of the crown prince.
* cicada: a homopterous insect that sings its song of summer and shrills in autumn, a symbol of death and resurrection in Chinese culture because of its metamorphosis and recycle. Therefore, in ancient China, a jade cicada figure was put in the mouth of a dead body with such an intention of eternal life.
* lotus: one of the various plants of the waterlily family, noted for their large floating leaves and showy flowers, a symbol of purity and elegance in Chinese culture, unsoiled though out of soil, so clean with all leaves green.

天育骠骑歌

吾闻天子之马走千里,
今之画图无乃是。
是何意态雄且杰,
骏尾萧梢朔风起。
毛为绿缥两耳黄,
眼有紫焰双瞳方。
矫矫龙性合变化,
卓立天骨森开张。
伊昔太仆张景顺,
监牧攻驹阅清峻。
遂令大奴守天育,
别养骥子怜神俊。
当时四十万匹马,
张公叹其材尽下。
故独写真传世人,
见之座右久更新。
年多物化空形影,
呜呼健步无由骋。
如今岂无騕褭与骅骝,
王良伯乐死即休。

A Song for the Mount of the Imperial Stables

I hear Son of Heaven's steed can three hundred miles run,
What I see pictured here is one of these, lo.

How brave and proud, the temper of this one!
When its mettlesome tail sweeps, north winds blow.
Its hair is pale green, its two ears are gold;
Its eyes blaze purple, and its pupils square.
Prone to change, its dragon vim, tough and bold,
Its bones extend, mysterious, and so rare.
Chingshun Chang, Stable Keeper, in those days,
Tended pasture, reared colts, choosing the best.
And left Stabled Steeds to Chief Slave to raise,
Who gave special care to those horses blessed.
There were four hundred thousand steeds back then;
Chang sighed, with their talents unsatisfied.
But he had this painted for today's men;
Hung right of my seat, it looks vivified.
The outline's left, the picture hung in vain;
For all its strong stride, it's no chance to run.
Don't we have thoroughbreds or unicorns with us remain?
No, Liang Wang has died and Lord Glee has gone.

* Son of Heaven: a metaphor for a king or emperor to suggest divine kingship.
* dragon vim: the best horses were born by dragon in ancient times according to legend.
* Chingshun Chang: royal Stable Keeper, a deputy minister in charge of carts and horses.
* Liang Wang: a horse trainer from the State of Chao in the Spring and Autumn period.
* Lord Glee: Glee, a horse connoisseur from the State of Ch'in in the Spring and Autumn period.

骢 马 行

邓公马癖人共知,
初得花骢大宛种。
夙昔传闻思一见,
牵来左右神皆竦。
雄姿逸态何崷崒,
顾影骄嘶自矜宠。
隅目青荧夹镜悬,
肉鬃碨礧连钱动。
朝来久试华轩下,
未觉千金满高价。
赤汗微生白雪毛,
银鞍却覆香罗帕。
卿家旧赐公能取,
天厩真龙此其亚。
昼洗须腾泾渭深,
朝趋可刷幽并夜。
吾闻良骥老始成,
此马数年人更惊。
岂有四蹄疾于鸟,
不与八骏俱先鸣。
时俗造次那得致,
云雾晦冥方降精。
近闻下诏喧都邑,
肯使骐驎地上行。

The Dappled Gray

Sir Teng's passion for horses, was well-known;
He did a Ferghana dapple gray own.
He'd see it as he's heard of it before;
They led it in, and all were stirred with awe.
Aloof, so high it looks, a virile way;
It looks at its shadow, gives a proud neigh.
So like mirrors are its sparkling green eyes;
Its flesh and mane the linked dapples surprise.
At dawn they test him with a cart so nice;
E'en a thousand gold cannot be its price.
Some red sweat appears in its hair snow-white;
O'er scent-silk shines a silver saddle bright.
What the Chamberlain once gave he could gain;
This steed's second but to Imperial Strain.
For a bath in the Ching and Wei it leaps;
For dawn the night of Yu-and-Ping it sweeps.
Only when old will the steed perfect grow;
And it'll be a more surprise as years go.
With four hooves it runs like a bird that flies;
When going with Eight Chargers it first cries.
What makes the horse unique is time and space,
With essences sent down from clouds and haze.
A decree's proclaimed in the town I hear;
How could a unicorn walk aground mere?

* Ferghana: Ferghana was an ancient state existing in Ferghana Basin. According to historical records, the horses from Ferghana are a precious kind. As it sprints, its

shoulders swell and it sweats like bleeding.
* its flesh and mane: the flesh and mane of the horse Yung Li presented to the emperor in 741 looked like those of a unicorn.
* the Ching: the Ching River the largest branch of the Yellow River, originating from Kansu and flowing into the Yellow River in Sha'anhsi, and also a branch of the Wei River originating from Ninghsia.
* the Wei: the Wei River: one of the largest branch of the Yellow River, originating from today's Mt. Birdmouse in Kansu Province, flowing through Precious Rooster, Allshine, Long Peace, and meeting the Yellow River at T'ung Pass.
* Yu-and-Ping: Yuchow in today's Hopei Province, and Pingchow in today's Shanhsi Province, the two places famous for their brave young men in history.
* Eight Chargers: eight famous horses of King Solemn of Chough.
* unicorn: a divine deer-like animal with one horn, a symbol of saintliness in Chinese culture; a very good horse is also called a unicorn.

魏 将 军 歌

将军昔着从事衫,
铁马驰突重两衔。
披坚执锐略西极,
昆仑月窟东崭岩。
君门羽林万猛士,
恶若哮虎子所监。
五年起家列霜戟,
一日过海收风帆。
平生流辈徒蠢蠢,
长安少年气欲尽。
魏侯骨耸精爽紧,
华岳峰尖见秋隼。
星躔宝校金盘陀,
夜骑天驷超天河。
檿枪荧惑不敢动,
翠蕤云旄相荡摩。
吾为子起歌都护,
酒阑插剑肝胆露,
钩陈苍苍玄武暮。
万岁千秋奉明主,
临江节士安足数。

Song for General Wei

In helpers' clothes the general was dressed;
His horse biting two bits charged on, so brave.

Fully armed, he ran and seized the far west,
To his east towering Mt. Queen and Moon Cave.
The Lord's Gate Guard are ten thousand men fierce,
Fierce like tigers roaring out of a dale.
In five years there aligned are frosty spears,
One day you cross the sea and furl your sail.
Your peers are scuttling around for naught,
The vim of Long Peace youths melting away.
Count Wei's bones jut up, his temper is taut,
As o'er Mt.Flower one sees a hawk of prey.
Jeweled stars and gold trappings on its fur;
By night it gallops 'cross the Milky Way.
Comets and fire stars do not dare to stir;
Purple tassels and cloud pennons there sway.
I rise and sing "Governor-General" for you;
The wine drunk now, so bold, you sheathe your sword.
Black Stars gone, Kouchen Stars are in the blue;
For ten thousand years, you'd serve your wise Lord.
How can Linchiang's warriors compare with you?

* Mt. Queen: Mt. Kunlun if transliterated, the most sacred mountain in China. It starts from the Eastern Pamir Plateau, stretches across New Land (Hsinchiang) and Tibet, and extends to Ch'inghai, with an average altitude of 5,500 – 6,000 meters. In Chinese myths, Mt. Queen is where Mother West dwells.
* Moon Cave: the moon's home in Chinese mythology.
* Long Peace: Ch'ang'an if transliterated, the capital of the T'ang Empire, with 1,000,000 inhabitants, the largest walled city ever built by man, and a cosmopolis of world religions, Buddhism, Confucianism, Wordism, Nestorianism, Zoroastrianism, and even Islamism represented by Saracens. It was the wonder of the age that reached the pinnacle of brilliance in Emperor Deepsire's reign: The main castle with its ninefold gates, the thirty-six imperial palaces, pillars of gold, innumerable mansions and villas of noblemen, the broad avenues thronged with motley crowds of townsfolk, gallants on horseback, and mandarin cars drawn by yokes of black oxen, countless

houses of pleasure, which opened their doors by night all made this city a kaleidoscope of miracles.

* Mt. Flower: also known as Mt. Flower, one of the Five Sacred Mountains in China, representing the west, regarded as the steepest and saintly mountain in China as it is one of the progenitors of Chinese culture, the shrine of Wordism and the abode of God of Mt. Flora, located in today's Flowershade, Sha'anhsi Province.
* the Milky Way: the Silver River in Chinese mythology, a luminous band circling the heavens composed of stars and nebulae; the Galaxy. As legend goes, the Milky Way maid, the granddaughter of Emperor of Heaven fell in love with a worldly cowherd and they gave birth to a son and a daughter. When their love was disclosed to Emperor of Heaven, he sent Queen Mother to take the fairy back to Heaven. While Cowherd was trying to catch up in a boat the cow had made with its horn broken, Queen Mother rived the air with her hairpin, so there appeared the Silver River, i.e., the Milky Way to keep them apart, and the fairy and the cowherd became two stars called Vega and Altair.
* Linchiang: the only resource available is that Emperor Scene of Han demoted the Crown Prince to be Prince of Linchiang.

白水明府舅宅喜雨(得过字)

吾舅政如此,
古人谁复过。
碧山晴又湿,
白水雨偏多。
精祷既不昧,
欢娱将谓何。
汤年旱颇甚,
今日醉弦歌。

Happy with the Rain at the House of My Uncle, Magistrate of Whitewater

My uncle's governance is such;
Of ancients who could surpass it?
At Whitewater the rain is much.
The hills are wet, by the sun lit.
His prayers bring good results about;
How in great delight we now play!
Hotspring's reign saw a bad drought;
We get drunk with music today.

* Whitewater: a county located in Northeast Sha'anhsi, in the transitional zone between Mid-Pass Plain and North Shanhsi Plateau.
* Hotspring: Hotspring of Shang (cir. 1670 B.C.- 1587 B.C.), the founding king of Shang, who annihilated Hsia with the help of two talents Yin Ee and Chunghui as his two prime ministers.

九日杨奉先会白水崔明府

今日潘怀县，
同时陆浚仪。
坐开桑落酒，
来把菊花枝。
天宇清霜净，
公堂宿雾披。
晚酣留客舞，
凫舄共差池。

On the Double Ninth Yang, Magistrate of Fenghsien County, Meets with Ts'ui, Magistrate of Whitewater County

Yüeh Pan, magistrate of Huai and,
Chün Lu, major of Chün-e today.
The host sets out mulberry wine,
Holding a chrysanthemum spray.
The sky purified by clear frost,
O'er Town Hall night fog spreads out.
Tipsy late, the guest stays to dance,
Wild duck sandals scattered about.

* Yüeh Pan: Yüeh Pan (A.D. 247 – A.D. 300), referring to An Pan, a renowned litterateur in the Western Chin dynasty.
* Huai: Huai County established in 221 B.C. at the end f the Ch'in dynasty in today's Chiaots'o, Honan Province.

* Chün Lu: a scholar in the Chin dynasty, Chi Lu's younger brother, and the brothers are known as "Two Lus".
* Chün-e: a county established in the Western Han dynasty, in today's Kaifeng, Honan Province.
* mulberry: the edible, berry-like fruit of a tree (genus *Morus*) whose leaves are valued for silkworm culture, and the tree itself, first cultivated in the drainage area of the Yellow River in China about five thousand years ago, concurrent with the time when silkworms were raised.
* chrysanthemum: any of a genus of perennials of the composite family, some cultivated varieties of which have large heads of showy flowers of various colors, a symbol of elegance and integrity in Chinese culture, one of the four most important floral images in Chinese literature, which are wintersweet, orchid, bamboo and chrysanthemum.

自京赴奉先县咏怀五百字

杜陵有布衣，
老大意转拙。
许身一何愚，
窃比稷与契。
居然成濩落，
白首甘契阔。
盖棺事则已，
此志常觊豁。
穷年忧黎元，
叹息肠内热。
取笑同学翁，
浩歌弥激烈。
非无江海志，
萧洒送日月。
生逢尧舜君，
不忍便永诀。
当今廊庙具，
构厦岂云缺。
葵藿倾太阳，
物性固莫夺。
顾惟蝼蚁辈，
但自求其穴。
胡为慕大鲸，
辄拟偃溟渤。
以兹悟生理，
独耻事干谒。
兀兀遂至今，

忍为尘埃没。
终愧巢与由,
未能易其节。
沈饮聊自遣,
放歌颇愁绝。
岁暮百草零,
疾风高冈裂。
天衢阴峥嵘,
客子中夜发。
霜严衣带断,
指直不得结。
凌晨过骊山,
御榻在嵽嵲。
蚩尤塞寒空,
蹴蹋崖谷滑。
瑶池气郁律,
羽林相摩戛。
君臣留欢娱,
乐动殷胶葛。
赐浴皆长缨,
与宴非短褐。
彤庭所分帛,
本自寒女出。
鞭挞其夫家,
聚敛贡城阙。
圣人筐篚恩,
实欲邦国活。
臣如忽至理,
君岂弃此物。
多士盈朝廷,
仁者宜战栗。

况闻内金盘，
尽在卫霍室。
中堂舞神仙，
烟雾散玉质。
暖客貂鼠裘，
悲管逐清瑟。
劝客驼蹄羹，
霜橙压香橘。
朱门酒肉臭，
路有冻死骨。
荣枯咫尺异，
惆怅难再述。
北辕就泾渭，
官渡又改辙。
群冰从西下，
极目高崒兀。
疑是崆峒来，
恐触天柱折。
河梁幸未坼，
枝撑声窸窣。
行旅相攀援，
川广不可越。
老妻寄异县，
十口隔风雪。
谁能久不顾，
庶往共饥渴。
入门闻号咷，
幼子饥已卒。
吾宁舍一哀，
里巷亦呜咽。
所愧为人父，

　　　　　无食致夭折。
　　　　　岂知秋未登，
　　　　　贫窭有仓卒。
　　　　　生常免租税，
　　　　　名不隶征伐。
　　　　　抚迹犹酸辛，
　　　　　平人固骚屑。
　　　　　默思失业徒，
　　　　　因念远戍卒。
　　　　　忧端齐终南，
　　　　　澒洞不可掇。

My Trip from the Capital to Fenghsien County, a Hundred Lines

I'm the one from Mt. Birchleaf Pear,
More clumsy as more life I lead.
How foolish I've been to compare
Myself to King of Corn and Deed.
At last, too useless to live on,
I, white-haired, fall to suffer pain.
When the coffin's closed, all is gone
But I hope to come by a gain.
I care the folks as ends the year,
I heave long sighs, and my guts burn.
Mocked by my classmate, my old peer,
I sing aloud and highly yearn.
It's not that I'm not nature-bound
To see time elapse, free of care.
But that with Hibiscus and Mound,

I cannot bear to leave for e'er.
Now all halls and courts are well run;
In the structure nothing's amiss.
Like mallows, I bend to the sun;
None can change a thing as it is.
I turn to consider ants small;
In their small hole I'd like to be.
Why aspire to join whales at all
To leap across the surging sea?
Life I rethink, its what and how;
To beg for favor is a hurt.
I have gone on like this till now;
I can't bear to fall into dirt.
Nest and Freedom put me to shame;
They did remain staunch and upright.
I drink, and drink on all the same
Till bursting into song in plight.
All grasses die to end the year;
The wind bursts the mound, rends the height.
Broad Way lies sunk in shadows sheer;
I start in the dead of the night.
The severe frost has my sash worn;
My fingers so still can't it tie.
I pass Mt. Black Steed in the morn;
On its top Royal Couch does lie.
The great haze has stuffed the cold skies,
Trampling the slippery vale track.
Vapors from Jadeite Pool there rise,
Where Escort guards scramble and clack.
Lord and courtiers their play prolong;
The music stirs, quaking the hills.

No homespun clothes join in their song;
Those granted baths wear jewels and frills,
In red halls the silk bolts that shine
Come from women weavers weighed down.
Whips flogging their menfolk to whine,
For taxes to send to the town.
The Most High grants this to men ace.
So that the state they could sustain.
If courtiers disregard His grace,
Haven't this been given in vain?
Officers are filling the court,
Which conscientious courtiers awes.
And I've heard gold plates of the sort,
Are owned by imperial in-laws.
In the midst of the halls belles dance;
Perfumed mists disperse o'er their fair skin.
Sable cloaks do the guests enhance;
Notes of flutes from zithers flow in.
Hump soup the guests are urged to eat;
Tangerines dewed, oranges gold!
In great mansions stink wine and meat;
The roads there find bones frozen cold.
Wealth or want, just a foot apart,
So upsetting, it's a hard tale.
How queer, the horse behind the cart!
The ferry changed into a trail!
From the far west ice floes rush down,
Looming beyond the scope of eyes.
It seems that Mt. Hollow would crush
The Heaven's Pillars from the skies.
The bridge, not yet collapsed, still stands;

Yet its cross beams seem to collide.
Travelers each to each give their hands,
They can't cross the river so wide.
My wife's in a different town there,
The ten mouths suffer the snow worst.
Who could do, not showing them care?
I would share their hunger and thirst.
When I come in, I hear a whine,
My young son of hunger has died.
I can not suppress wailing mine,
As if the whole lane sobs to tide.
My role as a father shames me,
The lack of food has killed my boy.
Ere the harvest I can't foresee,
The disasters that all destroy.
All my life, from taxes I'm free,
And free of conscription as well.
Seeing what has happened to me,
The folk must have suffered like hell.
I brood on those deprived of all,
And think of our garrisons cold.
My care's like Mt. South prone to fall,
The chaos great I cannot hold.

* Mt. Birchleaf Pear: located in today's Hsi-an, Sha'anhsi Province, Fu Tu's ancestral home.
* King of Corn: also known as Magic Farmer, one of Three Sovereigns in remote ages, along with Hidden Spirit and Nüwa, regarded as the father of herb medicine and agriculture.
* Deed: the forefather of Shang (cir.1600 B.C.- cir.1046 B.C.), once a minister under Hibiscus and Worm, hence enfeoffed to govern what was later called Shang.
* Hibiscus: Hibiscus (cir. 2277 B.C.- 2178 B.C.), Shun if transliterated, the Double-

* pupiled One, Mound's son-in-law, an ancient sovereign, a descendant of Lord Yellow (2717 B.C.- 2599 B.C.), regarded as one of Five Lords in prehistoric China.
* Mound: Mound (2377 B.C.- 2259 B.C.), Yao if transliterated. Divine and noble, Mound has been regarded as one of Five Lords in ancient China.
* mallow: a plant of the genus *Malva* with edible leaves, which was one of the five most popular vegetables in ancient China.
* whale: a large sea mammal larger than, but distinguished from, dolphins and porpoises, often a sign of great ambition and fortitude, and sometimes a symbol of opposition from an enemy.
* Nest and Freedom: referring to Fu Ch'ao and Yu Hsu. They were both hermits of talent and declined to be king when Mound intended to abdicate the throne to them.
* Mt. Black Steed: the mountain south of Lintung, an important offset of Mt. Ch'in Ridge, 1,302 meters above sea level, the location of the royal palace of Ch'in and tomb of Emperor First.
* Jadeite Pool: also called Queen Mother's Pool and Jade Pool, a fairy pool on Mt. Queen, by which Mother West holds banquets. It's a metaphor for a hot spring on Mt. Black Steed.
* tangerine: a variety of Mandarin orange with a deep-reddish-yellow color and segments that are easily separated.
* orange: a reddish, yellow, round, edible citrus fruit, with a sweet, juicy pulp; any of various evergreen trees (genus *Citrus*) of the rue family bearing this fruit.
* Mt. Hollow: a mountain in present-day Kansu Province, famous for martial arts. As is said, people here are brave and skillful at fighting battles.
* Heaven's Pillars: According to Chinese mythology, there are pillars holding up the sky at its four corners, known as Heaven's Pillars.
* a different town: referring to Fenghsien County. Ten members of Fu Tu's family were separated by heavy snow.
* Mt. South: also known as Mt. South End and the South Hill and so on, the mountains south of Long Peace, a great stronghold of the capital, towering in the middle of Ch'in Ridge and rolling about 100 kilometers.

甘 园

春日清江岸，
千甘二顷园。
青云羞叶密，
白雪避花繁。
结子随边使，
开筒近至尊。
后于桃李熟，
终得献金门。

The Orange Orchard

The spring day does the river please,
A two-*qing* grove, one thousand trees.
The clouds roll thick, the leafs seem shy;
The snow dims clean, the flowers look spry.
Their fruit go far with an envoy;
Crates and crates ope to our Lord's joy.
Unlike peach and plum they ripe late;
At last they are sent to Gold Gate.

* orange: a reddish, yellow, round, edible citrus fruit, with a sweet, juicy pulp; any of various evergreen trees (genus *Citrus*) of the rue family bearing this fruit.
* *qing*: a Chinese area unit, 100 *mu* or 66666.67 square meters.

秦州杂诗二十首（其十六）

东柯好崖谷，
不与众峰群。
落日邀双鸟，
晴天卷片云。
野人矜绝险，
水竹会平分。
采药吾将老，
儿童未遣闻。

Miscellanies of Ch'inchow, Twenty Poems (No. 16)

Eastern Bough is a valley fine,
Not joining peaks to make a crowd.
The setting sun invites two birds;
The azure sky rolls up a cloud.
Water and bamboo half to half,
A rustic boasts how steep it is!
I will grow old there picking herbs;
I've not yet let my kids know this.

* Ch'inchow: what is a part of today's Sky Water, Kansu Province.
* Eastern Bough: the name of a valley.
* bamboo: a tall, tree-like or shrubby grass in tropical and semi-tropical regions, a symbol of integrity and altitude, one of the four most important images in Chinese literature, which are wintersweet, orchid, bamboo and chrysanthemum.

春 夜 喜 雨

好雨知时节，
当春乃发生。
随风潜入夜，
润物细无声。
野径云俱黑，
江船火独明。
晓看红湿处，
花重锦官城。

A Blessing Rain on a Spring Night

A good rain knows its time to come,
And brings things to life right in spring.
It steals into the night with wind
And mutely moistens everything.
Over wild paths, clouds are all black,
A boat afloat, its lone fire bright.
At daybreak one sees wet and red;
Flowers in Brocade Town make a sight.

* Brocade Town: alias Silkton, Ch'engtu, a city once prosperous with fine silk, now the capital of Ssuch'uan Province.

咏怀古迹(其一)

支离东北风尘际，
飘泊西南天地间。
三峡楼台淹日月，
五溪衣服共云山。
羯胡事主终无赖，
词客哀时且未还。
庾信平生最萧瑟，
暮年诗赋动江关。

Chanting Historical Sites (No. 1)

Dispersed by wind and dust, we loaf around;
Between sky and earth, drifting here and there.
In Three-Gorge towers we just idle our time;
And with Five Streams folks hill and cloud we share.
The crafty Rams and Huns one can ne'er trust;
The poet has not come back for the times' sake.
For all Hsin Yü's sadness during his life,
His last years' verse did the river pass quake.

* Three-Gorge: of Three Gorges, that is, the three gorges of the Long River, including Big Pond Gorge, Witch Gorge, and Westridge Gorge, a set of spectacular gorges formed where the Long River cuts its way through the formidable Witch Mountains, forming a three-hundred-kilometer stretch of very narrow canyons.
* Five Streams: five streams called Yüan, Martial, You, Witch, and Ch'en, in today's West Hunan and East Kuichow.
* Ram: an ancient nationality in North China, who ate Han people in history.

* Hun: one of barbaric nomadic Asian peoples who frequently invaded China, a general term referring to all northern or western invaders.
* Hsin Yü: Hsin Yü (A.D. 513 – A.D. 581), a famous litterateur in the Northern and Southern Dynasties period.

寄从孙崇简

嵯峨白帝城东西,
南有龙湫北虎溪。
吾孙骑曹不记马,
业学尸乡多养鸡。
庞公隐时尽室去,
武陵春树他人迷。
与汝林居未相失,
近身药裹酒长携。
牧竖樵童亦无赖,
莫令斩断青云梯。

Sent to My Grandnephew Ch'ungchien Tu

Whitegod on high, its walls stretch east and west,
South is Dragon Tarn, and north Tiger Crest.
My nephew serves his post, steeds he knows not;
He keeps hens and in Corpse Town learns a lot.
When Pang retired, his kin joined him to stay;
Spring trees in Martial Ridge all lose their way.
I'll live uphill and with you I'll combine,
My herb bag's close to me, and I have wine.
E'en herdboys, wood-gatherers are not true;
Don't let them pave a path into clouds blue.

* Whitegod: a city founded in A.D. 25 at the end of the Western Han dynasty (202 B.C.- A.D. 8), located at Mt. Whitegod, near present-day Double Gain (Ch'ungch'ing). Shu

Lordson heard that there was a well called White Crane in the town, wherefrom white mist in the shape of a dragon often rose to the sky, and he regarded it as a symbol of his ascension to the throne, so he crowned himself as White God or White Emperor. And it is famous in history as the place where Pei Liu, the Emperor of Shu, died in the Three Kingdoms Period (A.D. 220 – A.D. 280).

* Corpse Town: the name of an ancient town, which is today's New Ts'ai of Honan Province.
* Martial Ridge: an ancient town, which is today's Constant Virtue (Ch'angte) of Hunan Province.

闻斛斯六官未归

故人南郡去，
去索作碑钱。
本卖文为活，
翻令室倒悬。
荆扉深蔓草，
土锉冷疏烟。
老罢休无赖，
归来省醉眠。

Hearing That the Official Hussu Has Not Returned

My old friend has gone off to south,
To ask pay of his inscription.
Selling his writings to live on,
He's set his home in confusion.
His brushwood gate is deep in vines;
So cold, there lies his earthen pot.
Old and retired, a knave you are!
When back at home, you sleep, a sot.

* brushwood: a low thicket; underwood.
* brushwood gate: a symbol of country life or hermitage.

送路六侍御入朝

童稚情亲四十年，
中间消息两茫然。
更为后会知何地，
忽漫相逢是别筵。
不分桃花红胜锦，
生憎柳絮白于绵。
剑南春色还无赖，
触忤愁人到酒边。

Seeing Off Attendant Censor Lu Six to Court

Our childhood friendship's lasted forty years;
Neither has the other's news, not the least.
I wonder where once again we will meet.
That encounter turned out our parting feast!
The peach blossoms burst, redder than brocade!
That catkin is whiter than cotton fluff.
The spring wind in Sword South is such a knave,
Who stirs my rue, and shakes my wine so rough.

* Lu Six: a censor, Fu Tu's friend, life unknown.
* peach blossoms: flowers of a peach tree, which beautiful ladies are often compared with.
* catkin: a deciduous scaly spike of flowers, as in the willow, an image of helpless drifting or wandering in Chinese literature.
* Sword South: a protectorate south of Mt. Sword Gate, covering most parts of modern Ssuch'uan Province, some part of Yünnan Province, the northern part of Kuichow Province and a small part of Kansu Province.

江上值水如海势聊短述

为人性僻耽佳句,
语不惊人死不休。
老去诗篇浑漫与,
春来花鸟莫深愁。
新添水槛供垂钓,
故着浮槎替入舟。
焉得思如陶谢手,
令渠述作与同游。

By the River I Come on Water Looking Like a Sea: A Short Account

Eccentric, I dote on words and lines best;
If not breath-taking, I will never rest.
As I'm old, my verse gets easy for all;
In spring, I see flowers smile and hear birds call.
To fish, I have set a rail by the blue,
And I have used a raft as a canoe.
How could I find lords like Poolbright and Glee
So that we can compose poems and roam free?

* Poolbright: Ch'ien T'ao(A.D. 352 – A.D. 427), Poolbright T'ao or Yüanming T'ao if transliterated, a verse writer, poet, and litterateur in the Chin dynasty, and the founder of Chinese idyllism, who was once the magistrate of P'engtse.
* Glee: Lord Glee, the court title of Lingyün Hsieh (A.D. 385 – A.D. 433), a highborn poet, Buddhist, traveler, famous for landscape poems, and a famous mountain climber, who invented special mountain shoes.

中　宵

西阁百寻馀，
中宵步绮疏。
飞星过水白，
落月动沙虚。
择木知幽鸟，
潜波想巨鱼。
亲朋满天地，
兵甲少来书。

Midnight

West Tower towers a hundred yards high;
At night I pace its shade nearby.
The star shoots over water white;
The moon falls, stirring eaves with light.
The birds choose branches to perch on;
The whales chase waves on the run.
Friends and kin fill the world and more.
Yet few letters come from the war.

* whale: a cetaceous mammal of fish-like form, especially one of the larger pelagic species, as distinguished from dolphins and porpoises. Whales have the fore limbs developed as broad flattened paddles, hind limbs absent, and a thick layer of fat or blubber immediately beneath the skin. A whale is a symbol of great ambition, fortitude and uniqueness.

晓　　望

白帝更声尽，
阳台曙色分。
高峰寒上日，
迭岭宿霾云。
地坼江帆隐，
天清木叶闻。
荆扉对麋鹿，
应共尔为群。

A Dawn View

At Whitegod the watch sounds stop;
Sun Mound o'erlooks twilight atop.
High peaks send up the chilly sun;
Layered ridges merge one after one.
The earth cracks, vanishing the sails;
The sky clears, showcasing green dales.
My brushwood gate sees elks and deer;
I should join in your flock to cheer.

* Whitegod: an ancient city built by Shu Lordson (? - A.D. 36) in the Western Han dynasty, located near present-day Double Gain (Ch'ungch'ing). It is famous in history as the place where Pei Liu, the Emperor of Shu, died in the Three Kingdoms Period (220 - 280 AD).
* Sun Mound: the place where Goddess of Mt. Witch stays, implying a place where lovers may date.
* brushwood: a low thicket; underwood.

* brushwood gate: a symbol of country life or hermitage.
* elk: a large deer originally of Asia (genus *Alces*), with palmated antlers and the upper lip forming a proboscis for browsing upon trees.
* deer: a ruminant, the prototype of a unicorn in Chinese culture and white deer being a Wordist symbol often seen in Chinese paintings: the mild animal ridden by an immortal.

奉酬李都督表丈早春作

力疾坐清晓,
来诗悲早春。
转添愁伴客,
更觉老随人。
红入桃花嫩,
青归柳叶新。
望乡应未已,
四海尚风尘。

Respectfully to My Uncle, Governor Li's Written in Early Spring

I force myself to sit at dawn,
In my poem the early spring I mourn.
The increasing sorrow frets me,
And old age follows up to be.
Red tints peach blossoms soft and light;
Green shines willow leafs fresh and bright.
Homeward you gaze and you gaze more;
In this sea-girt world there's still war.

* peach blossoms: flowers of a peach tree, which beautiful ladies are compared with. As a section of a poem in *The Book of Songs* reads: The peach twigs sway, / Ablaze the flower; / Now she's married away, / Befitting her new bower.
* willow: any of a large genus (*Salix*) of shrubs and trees related to the poplars, having generally smooth branches, and often long, slender, pliant, and pendent branchlets, a symbol of farewell or nostalgia in Chinese culture.

译 者 简 介

赵彦春教授致力于中华经典典籍的翻译和传播。他持表征之神杖,舞锐利之弧矢,启翻译范式之革命,将诗歌之"不可译"变为"可译";将"译之所失"变为"译之所得";将中华五千年的语言、哲学、诗学和美学的智慧融为一体,进行大胆尝试而细腻创新;他坚持译诗如诗,译经如经,从音韵形式、思想内容和文化意蕴上完美诠释了音美、形美和意美的统一;他相信语言与宇宙同构,将翻译的"诗学空间"不断延伸和拓展。

为了讲好"中国故事",引领中国文化"走出去",他带领一批志同道合的专业人士兢兢业业,孜孜不倦,锐意进取。从编辑、出版经典译著到举办国学外译研修班,从召开经典外译与国际传播学术研讨会、举办中华文化国际翻译大赛到创办 Translating China(《翻译中国》)国际期刊,他和同仁将忙碌的身影融入到了中华文化复兴的背景之中。

他带着"赵彦春国学经典英译系列"等一大批优秀的翻译成果走向世界,向世界展示中华文明的无尽魅力。

他无愧为中华典籍传统文化的传承者和传播者。

About the Translator

Professor Yanchun Chao devotes himself to the translation and transmission of Chinese classics. To inherit the traditional Chinese culture, he holds the divine scepter of Representation and sways the sharpness of bow and arrow to initiate a paradigm revolution out of fallacies, turning "untranslatability" of poetry into "translatability", "losses of translation" into "gains of translation", integrating the wisdom of five thousand years of Chinese language, philosophy, poetics and aesthetics to make bold attempts and exquisite innovations; he insists on translating Poesie into Poesie and Classic into Classic, perfectly interpreting the beauty of sound, form and sense from prosodic features, ideological contents and cultural implications; he also believes that language is isomorphic to the universe and constantly expands the "Poetic Space" of translation.

To tell good "Chinese stories" and lead them to "go global", he guides a group of like-minded specialists to work with diligence and fortitude, editing and publishing classic translations, convening seminars on English translation of Chinese culture, holding conferences on Classic Translation and International Communication, organizing "CC CUP" International Chinese Culture Translation Contest and editing an international journal *Translating China*, their busy figures silhouetted against the background of the revival of traditional Chinese culture.

With "Yanchun Chao's English Translation Series of Chinese Classics" going global, he shows to the world the endless appeal of the Chinese civilization.

He is a true inheritor and promoter of Chinese classics and traditional Chinese culture.